Conner Hall throttled back his 'Mech and prepared to turn back to the base.

As he checked the rearview image in his HUD before turning, he saw Jorgen's 'Mech, following at the end of the formation, disappear as the ground gave way beneath it.

The 'Mech dropped into a deep pit, until only the cockpit and superstructure could be seen aboveground. A large cloud of dust fountained up from the hole, momentarily clouding his visuals. As the dust cleared, Conner could see the 'Mech slumped unmoving against the side of the pit. Even with the 'Mech's suspension and a cockpit crash couch to cushion the fall, fifteen meters was still fifteen meters.

"Jorgen! Can you hear me? Jorgen."

There was no answer. If the man was still alive, he was unconscious.

Conner's mind raced as he threw the safeties off all his weapon systems.

It could be an accident. The city was centuries old and the veteran of many wars; it was riddled with unmarked tunnels, pipes and underground structures.

It could be an accident, but he didn't think so. "Formation! Spread out! Be ready for—"

There was a shout of alarm on the command circuit. Duncan Huntsig, third in the formation, yelled, "ConstructionMechs! They were playing possum!"

MechWarrior
Dark Age

TRIAL
BY CHAOS

A BATTLETECH™ NOVEL

J. Steven York

A ROC BOOK

ROC
Published by New American Library, a division of
Penguin Group (USA) Inc., 375 Hudson Street,
New York, New York 10014, USA
Penguin Group (Canada), 90 Eglinton Avenue East, Suite 700, Toronto,
Ontario M4P 2Y3, Canada (a division of Pearson Penguin Canada Inc.)
Penguin Books Ltd., 80 Strand, London WC2R 0RL, England
Penguin Ireland, 25 St. Stephen's Green, Dublin 2,
Ireland (a division of Penguin Books Ltd.)
Penguin Group (Australia), 250 Camberwell Road, Camberwell, Victoria 3124,
Australia (a division of Pearson Australia Group Pty. Ltd.)
Penguin Books India Pvt. Ltd., 11 Community Centre, Panchsheel Park,
New Delhi - 110 017, India
Penguin Group (NZ), cnr Airborne and Rosedale Roads, Albany,
Auckland 1310, New Zealand (a division of Pearson New Zealand Ltd.)
Penguin Books (South Africa) (Pty.) Ltd., 24 Sturdee Avenue,
Rosebank, Johannesburg 2196, South Africa

Penguin Books Ltd., Registered Offices:
80 Strand, London WC2R 0RL, England

First published by Roc, an imprint of New American Library,
a division of Penguin Group (USA) Inc.

First Printing, June 2006
10 9 8 7 6 5 4 3 2 1

Dedicated to my uncle, Gary Jones,
for being a fan when it wasn't a familial requirement.

Acknowledgments

With special thanks to my editor, Sharon Turner Mulvi-hill, for her patience as I finished the last leg of a long marathon.

1

*From the Great Work of
Galaxy Commander Isis Bekker*

That day is like a dream to me now: distant and surreal, yet vividly clear. I can see the dark clouds, as much smoke as water, hanging low in the sky, turning day into night. I can see lightning streaking down, turning the landscape into snapshots of chaos and destruction, punctuating a darkness full of small fires burning like stars fallen from the sky. Quilting it all together were stitches of death: lasers flashing through the smoke, the burning trails of missiles, jagged lines of tracers like incendiary swarms of hornets.

In this darkness things stirred like maggots in rotting flesh; soldiers in armor, tanks and, striding above it all, the gigantic forms of BattleMechs, unstoppable titans by whose force planets trembled, and wars were won and lost.

The place was Vega, a world of considerable strategic importance, once a center of commerce and political power for all of Prefecture I. We, the Omega Galaxy of Clan Ghost Bear, had been dispatched here with the mission to restore order and stability. That was our mission.

As for the real reason we were sent, I suspect it was a good deal more byzantine. But at that time I only suspected the complexity of our situation, and I had no time to ruminate on politics and hidden motives.

We knew our duty, my Galaxy and I, and we did not hesitate. We found a broken world, hanging on the ragged edge of a precipice, at the bottom of which waited only savagery. We waded into the chaos, identified the cancer that seemed to be the cause of it, and set about cutting out that cancer.

Never have I seen such a terrible thing, and I swear on my dying breath, I will never see it again. I am a soldier, first and foremost, and I think myself hardened to war and battle. War is one thing. War is terrible, and the Inner Sphere is no stranger to war.

Again and again, after the fighting is done, civilized men and women crawl from the rubble and rebuild. It was always so. Or so I had believed.

But this, this was the end of civilization, the end of the thing I had always imagined to be universal and invincible. Factions might battle, ideologies might clash, but always, no matter its color, no matter its flag, civilization would rise from the ashes. And where there was civilization, even if it was the home of the enemy, there was hope of redemption, of revolution, of reconciliation.

This was a world that, in a single year, fell into chaos and civil war. In a single night, an insane act of terror wiped out its government and unleashed the festering conflicts of a dozen internal factions. Great buildings were blown to rubble. The factories ceased to run. Water stopped flowing from the taps and power stopped coming through the wires. Medicine ran short and sickness spread through the squalid cities.

The only order, if you could call it that, came from bandits and warlords. They battled each other through the bones of the cities, costing countless innocents their lives, until only a few remained and they all deferred to one man: Jedra Kean, self-styled Lord of Vega.

We came to make war in a place that looked as though it had already lost the war. And in a way it had.

We came because no one else would.

We came, I believe, because civilization needs its champions, and that has ever been the purpose of the Clans, to restore civilization. Not merely to make it whole, but to restore it to a state of purity and enlightenment not seen since the fall of the fabled Star League. And that is part of what made this so terrible in my mind, that caused me to reexamine everything I am, and everything I believe. Just more than five centuries earlier, Vega was where the Star League had been born. If Vega fell, in my mind, there was no hope for any of us. Our dream would be shattered, our Clan history a joke. It could not be. I could not let it be. Yet in those grim, early days on Vega, I stood at the edge of the abyss and saw only blackness below.

I can tell you now, to stand on the edge of oblivion is a kind of gift. In a universe of uncertainty, you at least know where you are, and you know the way you must go. Faced with the abyss, you achieve a kind of certainty.

If you ask now, why have the Raging Bears gone the way they have gone? If you ask how our path strayed so far from the ancient ways of the Clans, or even of our own Clan, I tell you this: we went the only way we could.

Around us, The Republic had crumbled, the prefecture government had withdrawn, and the rest of the Inner Sphere had turned its back on Vega. It was hardly alone in the growing chaos; only the worst example. Around it, other worlds were falling to fragmentation and old rivalries long held in check by The Republic. Each world held tightly to what it had, and left its poorer neighbors to fend for themselves.

To restore the glory that was the Star League is our very reason for existing. In the Great Father Kerensky's hand, we are a message from the past, sent forward to some unknown but hopefully deserving future. We arrive in great ships descending from the sky on fusion fire. But now as then, we do not fight for Vega.

We fight for tomorrow.

Nasew (provisional capital), North Central District
North Nanturo continent, Vega
21 November 3136

The sixty-five-ton 'Mech called the *Karhu* walked through the narrow streets of the city like thunder, like a storm funneled into a narrow canyon, black clouds boiling in frustration against unyielding cliffs. In the 'Mech's tiny cockpit, Star Colonel Conner Hall felt more acutely confined by those streets and buildings than by the alloy-steel cockpit bulkheads that were only slightly farther apart than the width of his broad shoulders.

He clutched the 'Mech's throttle in his hand, wishing more than anything to slam it against the stops and simply cut loose his mechanical beast. It wasn't to be.

It had been ten minutes since they'd received the scramble from their improvised base near the spaceport. The water-pumping station at the near end of the Lincoln Pass was under attack by insurgent forces.

Labor Separatists, remnants of the old warlord gangs, anti-Clan rioters—it didn't matter, really. His forces should have been there by now, instead of tiptoeing through the streets dodging traffic. On any other world, in any other situation, they *would* have been there. But nothing on Vega was war as usual. In fact, they said it wasn't a war at all.

Conner Hall knew better.

With a grunt of frustration, he toggled his radio to the city control channel. "City Control, this is Star Colonel Hall. We are responding to an attack at the Lincoln pumping complex. My 'Mechs are tripping over buses here—literally. Get this traffic clear!"

The hated voice responded immediately. Despite many requests, Hall had never met any of the handful of controllers who manned this channel, or even learned their names. His warriors had given the voices names, so they could identify one or another as they traded horror stories between missions. They called this one "Fred."

Fred's voice was high and slightly nasal, always tinged with a kind of bored, bureaucratic annoyance. He never got excited, never seemed to care that his city was under siege by terrorists and revolutionaries, that his fellow Vegans were in danger. To Fred, it all seemed to be business as usual.

Traffic jams, terrorists bombs, or the MechWarriors of the Rasalhague Dominion rushing to respond—it was all the same to Fred. They were all sources of annoyance to one degree or another, and little more.

"It's a weekday rush hour. You have to expect traffic."

"You have control of every traffic signal and police officer in the city. Open a route for us."

"This is a city of almost a million people, Star Colonel. It can't just spin on its heel like one of your 'Mechs."

"To be technical, nothing spins on its heel, man or 'Mech. You turn on the ball of the foot, or you fall over."

"Then, Star Colonel, you understand that *some things* have to be done a certain way. I'm doing all I can to clear the expressway for you, but all lanes are jammed."

Hall grimaced. Their formation consisted of three *Karhu*s and three modified AgroMechs. The bigger 'Mechs had jump jets, plasma rockets that would have let them speed to their target in 150-meter leaps, but that would have left the slower AgroMechs far behind. In any case, use of jump jets within the city was also forbidden except in the most dire of emergencies, because of the damage they would cause.

Another transmission cut in on his command channel. It was the voice of Jorgen, a green warrior seeing his first combat here on Vega. Jorgen was assigned as his wingman, the sort of adaptation of Inner Sphere tactics for which the Omega Galaxy, the Raging Bears, were famous among the other Galaxies.

Or perhaps more properly, infamous.

In combat, Jorgen's job was to watch Hall's back while Hall acted as the aggressor on attacks. It was a very un-Clannish approach to combat. Clan MechWarriors were supposed to crawl all over each other to get the first kill and the most kills. To wait passively while another warrior took the kills should have been unthinkable. But the tactic had cut the Raging Bears' combat losses by fifteen percent without affecting their overall kill rate.

The key to making this tactic palatable was to frequently rotate each MechWarrior from leader to wing, in order to give everyone ample opportunity for action. But there were other ways to use the wing position. In this case, it let Hall work closely with his new man, simultaneously keeping an eye on him and showing him how things worked in the unusual theater of operations that was occupied Vega.

Trouble was, at the moment, Jorgen was not watching his back, he was watching *everyone's* back. Jorgen was bringing up the rear of their formation, since Mech-Warrior Duncan Huntsig had balked at taking the trailing position.

Huntsig's continued challenges to his authority were becoming an issue. Hall had considered making the positioning of the formation a direct order, just to see what would come of it, but Huntsig was a good warrior and he didn't want to lose him to an unnecessary trial. The Clan had ways of settling such minor disputes quickly and efficiently, but given the urgency of their mission it had been faster to flip the formation than force the issue with Huntsig.

Now, his decision seemed to be working to their advantage. Huntsig didn't care much for the locals or even the First Vega Regulars MechWarriors who were their comrades in arms, and he paid little attention to how things worked in their society. Conner doubted that Huntsig would have spotted the skyway access, had he been in the position to see it.

Jorgen continued. "Star Colonel. There's an overturned truck on the skyway. Northbound traffic is stopped, and southbound has been detoured off the road somewhere back up the line. It's wide open. We could be through town in no time."

"Good eye, Jorgen. I will check on it." He switched channels again. "City Control, what about the skyway?"

"The skyway is closed. We've got an overturned—"

"I know what you have got! 'Mechs can just jump over the accident, or step over it. Permission to divert."

There was a pause. "Negative! No! The road deck isn't reinforced to handle your 'Mechs."

"I am willing to chance it."

"Star Colonel! This is vital city infrastructure we're talking about here!"

Hall cringed. Infrastructure was a word he was coming to hate more with each passing day. "I remind you that the pumping station is vital infrastructure too. That pipeline supplies water for the entire Northgate Plateau industrial region."

"And if I let you use that road, it will be closed six months for repairs, instead of just long enough to clear a wrecked truck. We lost half our major roads in the Warlord Massacres, and the Median Interway is still closed because of those bridge bombings last month. If you people had stopped those—"

Conner slapped the mute button and slammed his stick hard right, swerving his 'Mech to avoid a construction vehicle stuck halfway across a gridlocked intersection. Startled commuters gawked as three Clan OmniMechs and three local AgroMechs filed past them like a parade of giants, moving rapidly north.

The AgroMechs looked out of place in the city, but they had never actually seen farm duty. They'd been built just across the pass in Northgate, shipped here factory-new, and modified for combat duty. Though Vega was a major producer of IndustrialMechs, or had been before the planet's recent troubles, there were no BattleMechs available with which to outfit the volunteer First Vega Regulars. When the decision had been made to incorporate the local militia into the Ghost Bear security forces, they'd been equipped with the best the planet had to offer: modified AgroMechs.

Using AgroMechs had been a controversial decision; one about which Hall still had mixed feelings. Shortly after the fall of the HPG network and during the early troubles in The Republic, IndustrialMechs had seen much use on the battlefields of the Inner Sphere. But they'd always been a desperate compromise while nations rearmed, and now 'Mechs and heavy conventional arms had largely supplanted their use on most worlds.

But Vega, of course, was not "most worlds."

"Star Colonel, this is Captain Tupolov."

As though he wouldn't instantly recognize her voice. Captain Karen Tupolov was the commander of the local FVR 'Mech forces and a MechWarrior of exceptional talent for a freeborn. She was his good right hand, and he often considered her as something more than that. "Go ahead, Captain."

"If the 'Mechs can't use the skyway, why not send your elementals?"

Of course! In consideration of the needs of urban combat, the Raging Bears now deviated from the long-standing Clan practice of elemental infantry riding into combat perched on the backs of 'Mechs. Instead, special cargo trucks had been modified to accommodate a full Star of the genetically engineered giants in their powered armor. In many circumstances, the trucks could get to trouble spots in the city faster and with less difficulty than a 'Mech, or at least close enough that the elementals could then close in using their armor's built-in jump jets.

"Star Captain Vong. Where are you? Can you divert your truck onto the skyway?"

"Let me check the map." A pause. "We can backtrack up the Sixth Street off-ramp three blocks ahead. With"— the tone dripped sarcasm—"permission of City Control, of course."

Again Conner switched channels. "City Control, we're diverting the truck with our elementals up the Sixth Street off-ramp and north onto the skyway."

Fred was uncharacteristically slow to respond. Hall imagined him searching for some reason to object. "The vehicle is—barely—within the weight limits, but that ramp is just this side of the accident. They won't be able to get past."

Conner couldn't help but grin. "City Control, this is a full Star of men in Rogue Bear battle armor, collectively as strong as a bulldozer and each equipped with missiles, machine guns and claws that can rip through 'Mech armor like it was wet paper. Your accident is about to be cleared in record time."

It was small satisfaction that the elementals would arrive on scene in a timely fashion. "This is no way to fight a war," he muttered.

"This is no war, Star Colonel," Tupolov's voice replied, and he realized to his embarrassment that he'd left the command circuit open. "Or," she continued, "so they tell us."

"A discussion for later," he said firmly, stepping his 'Mech over a wire safety fence and leading his 'Mechs on a three-block shortcut across a construction site.

"This is Vong. We have cleared the truck and we're en route."

"Good hunting, Star Captain. We'll be there to back you up as soon as we can." His eye twitched as he caught himself using a contraction. It was all too common in the Raging Bear Galaxy these days, a by-product of decades of living among the non-Clan population of the Rasalhague Dominion, fighting alongside their forces, adopting their tactics and, in some cases, picking up their vulgar habits.

He knew Vong would notice, and that he wouldn't approve, though he'd never say it to Conner's face.

Common occurrence or not, as a Bloodnamed officer of the Ghost Bear Clan Conner had always tried to hold himself to higher standards. *Maybe,* he thought bitterly, *that too is a losing battle.*

He shook his head, focusing on the flickering green and blue lights of his 'Mech's heads-up display, trying to drive the unwanted negative thoughts from his head. *I am a warrior of the Ghost Bear Clan, Star Colonel of the Omega Galaxy, the Raging Bears. I am the product of three hundred years of genetic selection.*

We will prevail!

But his optimism was hollow. He and his troops were indeed fierce warriors, the equals or betters, in his opinion, of any troops in the Inner Sphere. But this was no true war, no true test of their abilities. It was a holding action against an underground army that wore no uniform, respected no rules of combat or engagement.

Compared to their OmniMechs and combat armor, the enemy's weapons were weak, but they made up for it by stealth, surprise and cleverness. He'd developed a grudging respect for the abilities of his unseen enemy, if not for their sense of honor.

They diverted across another construction zone. Half the city was in some stage of construction or repair, and progress was slow. They passed a line of dump trucks and construction IndustrialMechs sitting idle for lack of pilots, drivers and construction workers.

"This is Vong. We are within sight of the pumping station. I believe this is a false alarm. There is a small fire in one outbuilding, some minor blast damage. I pick up two unidentified hostiles in battle armor rapidly jumping away into the forested slopes above the station."

"Any chance of catching them?"

"Doubtful. They've got a good head start, and a million places up there to hide. It was only by using maximum magnification on my optics that I spotted them at all."

Conner sighed. The insurgents liked to keep them running, but he had a sense that that was not all that was happening here. "Secure the area and search for planted explosives. Check for armor tracks and try to identify what equipment they were using, especially if it looks like Draconis Combine gear. I will expect a full report."

"Aye, Star Colonel."

He throttled back his 'Mech and prepared to turn back to the base.

As he checked the rearview image in his HUD before turning, he saw Jorgen's 'Mech, following at the end of the formation, disappear as the ground gave way beneath it.

The 'Mech dropped into a deep pit, until only the cockpit and superstructure could be seen aboveground. A large cloud of dust fountained up from the hole, momentarily clouding his visuals. As the dust cleared, Conner could see the 'Mech slumped unmoving against the side of the pit. Even with the 'Mech's suspension and a cockpit crash couch to cushion the fall, fifteen meters was still fifteen meters.

"Jorgen! Can you hear me? Jorgen."

There was no answer. If the man was still alive, he was unconscious.

Conner's mind raced as he threw the safeties off all his weapons systems.

It *could* be an accident. The city was centuries old and the veteran of many wars; it was riddled with unmarked tunnels, pipes and underground structures.

It could be an accident, but he didn't think so. "Formation! Spread out! Be ready for—"

There was a shout of alarm on the command circuit. Duncan Huntsig, third in the formation, yelled, "ConstructionMechs! They were playing possum!"

He checked his rear camera in time to see the entire

row of ConstructionMechs stir into motion. They headed directly for the FVR AgroMechs, placing themselves behind the friendly units so that Conner and Huntsig couldn't open fire. IndustrialMechs were fierce melee fighters, but a true OmniMech could take them apart easily with distance weapons.

"Flank them," he ordered Huntsig, "so at least one of us will be able to get a clear shot."

"Star Colonel," Tupolov called, "dump truck inbound."

Though occupied holding off two of the ConstructionMechs, she'd caught movement from one of the trucks in the line parked to their west. It was now lumbering towards them, accelerating rapidly. It could not be ignored as a potential threat.

The truck was a monster, probably weighing more than his 'Mech. But it wasn't as agile and it wasn't armored, and if he couldn't shoot at the IndustrialMechs, the truck was a satisfying alternative.

He swung his extended-range lasers around and fired off a quick volley at the truck's huge radiator. Metal seemed to splash like water as the lasers hit, and greenish clouds of escaping coolant began to spew forth. There seemed to be little point in destroying the truck. He could easily dodge its charge and wait for the engine to seize up or stall, thus preserving an expensive and valuable piece of equipment. *One for you, City Control.*

The truck began to slow, and he turned his attention back to the ConstructionMechs. Huntsig was now on the far side of the melee, and the hostiles were trying, unsuccessfully, to stay out of both their weapon arcs.

Conner saw his opening as one of the 'Mechs attacking Tupolov gave him a clear shot at its back. He opened fire with his lasers. Armor glowed and melted like butter along one shoulder joint. He hit something critical and there was an explosion, the unit's excavator arm falling away to hang loosely, connected by only a few cables and strands of synthetic myomer muscle.

Thrown off balance, the unit staggered in a turn, trying to slip behind Tupolov again. He targeted its wounded flank, now broadside to him, and opened fire with his autocannon. The shot narrowly missed the weapon arm on Tupolov's 'Mech and found its intended target.

The damaged 'Mech lurched backward. There was a puff of smoke and a flash of the canopy spinning through the air as the pilot ejected. Then, to Conner's surprise, the other ConstructionMech pilots ejected from their relatively undamaged machines.

They think they're getting away!

But even as his brain demanded that he run down the nearest insurgent pilot, still descending on his parachute, his gut knew something was wrong. "Ignore the pilots," he shouted into the command circuit. "Scatter and watch for other threats!" He glanced at the damaged dump truck, nearly invisible in a cloud of its own smoke and steam, barely moving towards them. That wasn't the threat.

Then mortars started exploding around them. "Scatter! Scatter! Scatter!"

It was too late for one of the FVR IndustrialMechs, which took a critical hit on the power plant and slumped over, a sitting duck as more rounds exploded around it, preventing the pilot from ejecting.

He swiveled his Mech's torso, looking for the source of the barrage, but there were dozens of potential hiding places around the site and among the surrounding buildings. They couldn't just start firing at random without risking hundreds of civilian casualties.

Couldn't they? His finger twitched over his trigger, and he fought the impulse.

Then the truck exploded.

Later, they would estimate that several tons of high explosives had been packed inside the truck's endosteel frame, passed through a one-meter inspection hatch and painstakingly placed by hand deep inside the frame members. Jagged hunks of the hardened metal flew in all directions. Conner watched in horror as the truck's cab flew straight at him and disintegrated against his cockpit's ferroglass, just inches from his face.

Red lights appeared all over his status display, but he was still moving. There was a lurch and a grinding noise with each movement of his 'Mech's right leg, but he could still maneuver, and he could still fight.

Two of the FVR IndustrialMechs were crippled. Huntsig's 'Mech was immobilized as well, but still able to stand and fight. He saw that Karen was still on the move, circling the edge of the site, unhealthy blue smoke belching from her 'Mech's exhaust stacks. "I've already called in helicopters to extract our pilots," she reported. "Let's get these bastards!"

His lasers and missiles were out, but he still had his autocannon. Careful to keep his shots inside the construction site, he started hammering anything that might conceal an insurgent. Then he spotted a ground car fleeing the construction site. It probably had come through and picked up the surviving insurgent pilots in the confusion.

He slammed his 'Mech to a stop. It would make him an easy target, but he couldn't make an accurate shot at this distance with his damaged leg shaking things around. He locked the car in his crosshairs just as it crashed through a fence and careened into the street. He squeezed off a short burst, and the unarmored car exploded into a satisfying cloud of fragments.

"Good shooting, Star Colonel!" Karen's voice quickly sobered. "We've got to stay on the bubble. Whoever pulled this off is devious as hell, and they pile the surprises on like layers in a cake. That might not be the last one." Conner agreed with Karen's advice, but the mortar fire had stopped. No more traps had sprung, and there was no sign of incoming hostiles.

"Star Colonel." It was Star Captain Durant from the command center. "Star Colonel, Point Commander Davis at the MechWarrior barracks demands to speak with you. Should I patch him through?"

Still scanning for threats, Conner answered almost without thinking. "Patch him through."

"Star Colonel." Davis' voice sounded tense and angry. "There is something unusual going on here. I think—" There was a roar of static, and then the circuit went dead.

Conner waited for the link to be restored. When nothing happened after several seconds, he rekeyed the command center link. "Durant! Report."

"One moment."

"Durant!"

"One moment."

He looked at the horizon in the direction of the base, and saw a rising ball of black smoke.

Now fully focused on what was surely the third volley in the insurgents' attack, he opened another channel. "City Control, we are returning to base. Clear us a path. Clear us a path if you have to drive every car in the city through a storefront to do it! Get those cars out of the way or at least get them empty, because we will crush them if necessary to pass. *Now!*"

Still nothing from the command center. He slammed his throttle to the stop, and with a lurching stagger, his 'Mech started running. Karen fell in with him.

"Durant!"

"Star Colonel." Durant's voice was like ice. "The barracks have been destroyed. Some kind of truck bomb, we think. It's still unclear—"

They walked their wounded 'Mechs through the perimeter defenses surrounding their makeshift base, dodging modular blast walls, earth berms and gun emplacements, all useless against what had probably been an inside job.

Conner could not tear his eyes away from the roaring flames. Already, an armada of fire trucks and spaceport crash trucks were swarming in, dousing the flames with water and foam. But it was obvious there was nothing to save.

"Durant," he spoke into his comm. "How many?"

"Sir?"

"Losses! Report!"

There was a long pause. "Fifteen we think. Maybe sixteen, including Davis."

Fifteen warriors dead. Not with honor. Not in battle. No glory to their codex. Good men. Good women.

Wasted.

He tore his eyes away from the flames. Karen's 'Mech stood next to his, and he looked over at her cockpit. He could not see her past the dust and glare on the ferroglass, but he could imagine her looking his way with something like pity. Though he was likely as invisible to her as she was to him, he couldn't bear the thought, and turned away.

He found himself looking at the flat concrete wall of a nearby 'Mech hangar.

There was something written in crude letters on the wall, in paint as red as blood. He realized he'd seen that splash of red a hundred times before. The graffiti had been there for months, probably created at great personal risk by some Clan laborer hanging from the roof above, the lettering carefully positioned so as to be at eye level for a 'Mech pilot.

He'd seen it a hundred times, and seen graffiti like it all over the city. Seen it, but never really read it. Never parsed it. Never let it slip through the armored layers of pride and discipline that came with being a Bloodnamed Clan warrior.

But he read it now: THINK THE UNTHINKABLE.

And he did.

2

So this was the Vega on which we found ourselves. To us, it was just "the battlefield." There was no time to think of history or politics. Our Clan had sent us to do a job—to restore order and stability to this tortured world—and to do that, the warlords must be destroyed. We were outmanned, if not outarmed, fighting on unfamiliar soil, with little logistic support.

It did not matter. We were Clan, bred for three centuries to be the finest warriors in the universe. We were Ghost Bears, Omega Galaxy, the Raging Bears. We would not be stopped. I led my troops into battle again and again, each time driving back the warlords' forces, first establishing firm beachheads upon the planet, then taking control of key cities, and finally closing in on the stronghold of the devil himself.

The last warlord, Jedra Kean—I still refuse to call him "Lord Kean"—put up a surprisingly fierce resistance. Even taking into account that he controlled nearly all of the planet's surviving military might, one still had to wonder at the source of all his firepower, especially the

'Mechs. We speculated at the time that Vega, like many worlds, had maintained hidden caches of 'Mechs, hidden rather than destroyed during the disarmament that was the watchword of Devlin Stone's rule. That may have been true. Certainly I suspect it was a factor.

But now we know there was more to the story.

Hall of the Provisional Planetary Congress
Nasew, North Nanturo continent, Vega
21 November 3136

Galaxy Commander Isis Bekker stood at her podium in the congressional hall, formerly the corporate headquarters for MyoMaxx Corporation, her face purposefully calm, but her knuckles white where they gripped the smooth wooden edge of the lectern. At another podium, slightly smaller and lower than her own, Acting Provisional Governor Vincent Florala stared up at her defiantly, feet apart, one hand resting on the latest draft of the planetary Articles of Reunification, a determined frown on his handsome features.

Rather than meet his eyes, she looked up and let her gaze sweep around the octagonal room. The raised stage on which she and the other senior members of the provisional government stood was surrounded by armored-glass walls. Beyond that, the floor sloped up, lined with rows of desks where the individual delegates sat, all seventy-eight of them. Many of them stared at her too, with expressions that ranged from polite interest to outright hostility.

Other than the tunnel stairway behind her, there were only two doors into the chamber, each guarded by a contingent of a dozen heavily armed Clan paramilitary policemen, plus four more wearing "Constable" battle armor, a lighter and more agile, though vastly less capable, version of the feared Rogue Bear armor.

She considered the situation. If not for the glass, and despite the metal detectors, someone would probably have tried to shoot her already. If not for the guards, somebody would probably be shooting at the glass anyway just out of frustration.

Part of her wished the glass was not there, and that she could fall back on her formidable martial skills. The weight of the sidearm and ceremonial short sword hanging from her belt gave her some comfort, if little satisfaction at this point. She imagined wading into the delegates, pistol in one hand, sword in the other, eliminating the "loyal opposition" in one bloody stroke. They would try to fight back, of course, but if they bested her, then they deserved to take her place.

But that was not how things were done here among the mongrel freeborn of the Inner Sphere. She could not allow herself to think of them in Clan terms, where disputes were settled by honorable trials and combat. No, here it was all debate, pontification, negotiation, treaties, contracts and lawyers, with the bloodshed planned in secret and carried out with no honor.

She forced herself to strengthen her mask of freeborn civility, an expression hard-won through long practice, and turned back to Vincent. "I find it outrageous, Governor, that you could hold our warriors at fault for this morning's violence. They were deployed in defense of important Vegan assets, and responded with live fire only after being viciously attacked by insurgents."

"Destroying or damaging several million Vega dollars worth of construction equipment and materials in the process."

"To be fair, most of the damage was caused by the truck bomb and by fire directed against ConstructionMechs commandeered by the insurgents."

"I would gladly be fair, Galaxy Commander, but the people I represent won't see it that way at all, and that is what you fail to appreciate. At this point, perception is everything. They see only the fresh damage you've caused to their already war-ravaged city, and that a defenseless civilian vehicle full of Vegan citizens was destroyed by 'Mech fire on a public street well inside the city."

"A vehicle full of insurgent combatants fleeing the scene of an attack."

"So you say. We are conducting our own investigation, independent of your paramilitary police and the Vegan Police Militia, whom most Vegan citizens view as willing collaborators."

"You know as well as I do, Governor—"

"Perception, Galaxy Commander. It is not what *I* know, it is what the *people* believe."

"The people will believe the facts."

Vincent laughed derisively. "You don't understand the situation at all. You fight on our streets every day, and yet this war can never be won by force of arms. You must win the hearts of the Vegan people, or military victory is impossible."

Isis scowled. "With all due respect, Governor, your people are ungrateful for the stability the Rasalhague Dominion has provided to Vega. When our forces arrived, all of your senior officials had been killed by a terrorist attack, your capital was in ruins and civil war had left your people under the domination of ruthless warlords. We've given you order, helped you to begin rebuilding, and we stand here at the dawn of a new and better government. Where would you be without us right now?"

"We would be without you, and for most of the people outside this building, and a few within, that's all that really matters. They want you gone. Our problems, terrible though they were, were *our* problems. We did not ask for your assistance. It was thrust upon us."

"For your own good."

"The slogan of tyrants throughout human history."

"I must have said it a hundred times before, but I will state it again for the record. We come not as invaders or occupiers. Our intent is to help Vega and other key planets in the prefecture to restore stability, order and prosperity. When that job is done, we will leave. That is all we want here."

"Galaxy Commander, do you know what the people of Vega are talking about today, in every neighborhood, refugee camp and marketplace? They are talking about the day. Do you know what this day is?"

"November the twenty-first."

"But it is also a Clan holiday, is it not? A holiday known as 'Invasion Day,' celebrating the day the Clans voted to invade the Inner Sphere in what later became known as the 'Great Refusal.' "

"That is ancient history. That holiday, where it is still observed at all, is celebrated by Crusader Clans. We are a Warden Clan. Their ways are not our ways."

"So you say. But actions speak louder than words." Vincent smiled slightly. "What of the constant flow of ships that arrive, bringing more Clan oppressors, and leave loaded with shipments of myomer, refined armor alloys, IndustrialMechs and heavy machinery—"

"Those so-called oppressors are specialists sent to aid in rebuilding your cities, factories and mines. As production resumes, a percentage of production is being diverted to the Ghost Bears as in-kind payment for the resources expended on our mission here. Nothing more. We would not insult your people with charity. We're here to restore your dignity, not take it away."

He laughed again. "Galaxy Commander, do you have any idea how that sounds?"

It sounds logical and reasonable. But she said nothing.

"And what of the continued harassment attacks by the Draconis Combine? Are we to be grateful for them as well?"

"Surely you can't blame us for their military aggression: their interest in Vega long predates our arrival in this part of the Inner Sphere."

"Again, it is not what *I* think. It's entirely possible that they would be attacking us anyway, given that you believe their fear of your forces is all that is holding off a full-blown invasion. But the Vegan people know well that there is old and bad blood between the Ghost Bears and the Draconis Combine. They don't wish to be pawns in your ongoing conflict. The more you make them feel abused and powerless, the more they are susceptible to—other influences."

A high, reedy voice echoed through the chamber. "Will you yield the floor to the Speaker of Labor?"

"Speak of the devil," Isis muttered under her breath, looking out to see the cadaverous figure of Speaker of Labor Chance Elba standing behind his desk. He was a thin man, his skin wrinkled and transparent, his scowling face marked with age spots, his nearly bald head covered by a thin crown of white hair that crossed his shiny skull in wispy ballistic arcs.

Elba raised a shaggy eyebrow. "Excuse me?"

"Nothing. I yield the floor for one minute."

He opened with his usual ramble praising the outstanding qualities of the Vegan workers, then moved on to what Isis hoped was his point. "Galaxy Commander, the people of Vega are not taken in by your fairy tales explaining away your criminal occupation of our fair world. It is clear that you desire only our resources, our surviving production capabilities and, of course, the famed skill and industriousness of our glorious, underappreciated and always exploited workers! We know well that is the Clan way. We know how you treat your own labor caste. They're fifth-class citizens, little more than slaves, and you hold even them in higher regard than the most celebrated Vegan worker!"

Isis sighed. As far as she was concerned, Elba was only one step removed from the insurgent terrorists, if that. Most of the known insurgents were members of radical labor-separatist groups with close ties to the Labor Party. Though he made a great show of distancing himself and his party from those groups, Elba was careful never to denounce them, and often obliquely argued their cause in congress.

Elba continued, "This oppression must—"

"Your minute," she announced, "is up."

"Galaxy Commander, I must protest! This is an outrageous—"

There were mutterings and shouts of derision from the quadrants of the hall reserved for the rival Centralist and Freedom Vega parties. The Planetary Nationalists, more in sympathy with the Labor Party, sat quietly. Reaction in the small section reserved for the ten minority party delegates was mixed.

"Your minute," she repeated firmly, "is up. Please do not force me to ask the nice men in the armor to remove you from the hall."

Elba glared at her, but said nothing. He leaned down, grabbed a piece of paper and a pen and wrote one word in large letters, then held it up to her, then so the rest of the hall could read it, and then, most dramatically, for the ever-present cameras. It read, TYRANNY.

Isis descended the stairs below the stage toward what had once been a group of executive office suites, now turned into apartments and private offices for her and other senior Clan officials in the occupation government. As she reached the bottom of the stairs, a tall, blond man in a knee-length blue-and-white coat fell in next to her, ignored by the police escorts that appeared from behind the stairway.

The thin man combed the fingers of his right hand through his hair, matching her pace as she strode down the carpeted corridor. He brandished a computer access pad in front of her with his left. "I have the latest security and logistical reports, if you'd care to see them. Crime statistics: stable, though not declining as we'd hoped. Public outrage over Invasion Day has resulted in rioting in Nasew, Halo and Jalonjin, all controlled without military intervention. There are progress reports on water, sewer projects, food distribution, repairs to the power grid, shipments of construction materials over the pass to Northgate, reopening the westside hospital."

She pushed the pad away. "Only if there's something in there of immediate military importance, which there isn't, Trenton, or you would have passed me a message while I was still on the floor."

"You are correct, Galaxy Commander. I'll take care of it all." He paused, his eyes narrowing. "And you know well that I prefer to be called Dr. Tuskegee."

She grimaced. The scientist caste had been handing out "labnames" to their most honored members for quite some time now, but until recently they were never used outside the scientist caste. The warrior caste continued to hold them in open contempt. Now some scientists not only insisted that they be addressed by their labnames, but also by relevant Inner Sphere titles such as "doctor" and "professor," as well.

"Trenton, you are an arrogant and vain man who does not know his place. Why do I tolerate your eccentricities?"

He looked at her out of the corner of his eye, but did not answer.

"Doctor," she finally said, to break the silence. She still could not bring herself to use the hated labname. She would not. Not even for him.

"You tolerate me because I am immensely useful, and I relieve you of countless logistical tasks that otherwise would distract you from the larger task of trying to bring order to this hopeless planet. I tolerate *you* because, frankly, completing this mission is likely the only way I'll ever get back in a proper research lab again."

"Do your job, Trent—*Doctor.* Do your job and get out of my hair."

He laughed and peeled off down a side corridor, headed to his small apartment jammed with computers and books.

It was obvious why Trenton was here, and it had nothing to do with his brilliance or his abilities as a scientist, which were celebrated. It was his personal eccentricities, the labname, the title, his prideful use of contractions

("It's more efficient," he had once told her, "and efficiency, it's the Clan way!"), the ridiculous-looking lab coat he always wore to remind everyone that he was a scientist. But he *was* useful, and Isis Bekker firmly believed in delegating as many secondary tasks as possible to talented people, then taking a hands-off approach to managing those people. Despite his quirks, she trusted the man, and over time, had even come to like him.

Isis dismissed her paramilitary police escorts at the door of her small apartment, a converted office located on the tenth floor of the provisional capital building's tower. It was, as befitted a warrior of the Clans, a spartan place.

A row of metal shelves and repurposed horizontal filing cabinets held her clothing and most of her belongings. A modular kitchenette took up one corner, next to a small dining table with two folding chairs. Two more comfortable chairs, each with a reading lamp, sat near a trio of tri-vid screens, each silently presenting a different news and information network.

On two walls simulated windows, large tri-vid screens connected in real time to cameras outside the building, showed the bloodred of the late afternoon sky. The windows were a luxury left over from the original office, and she could have lived without them. But, as a security precaution, the tower had been built almost completely without windows, and it was nice to at least be able to know at a glance if it were day or night.

Through a door to her right, an adjoining room held a bed, and beyond that, a small bathroom. In the center of the room, several desks were covered with neat piles of papers, publications, and a dozen tablet computers, each dedicated to a different aspect of managing her forces, the government and the planet itself.

She walked past each computer, pausing at each long enough to tap a button that would wake the device, and taking a few moments to study the updated screen before moving to the next.

The MechWarrior whose 'Mech had fallen into the pit had a severely fractured spine and neck injuries, and likely would not return to duty in less than six months. Strikes by plumbers and concrete truck drivers had halted work on the Public Sanitary Market. There was a letter from the adjunct general of the Clan, just off the JumpShip. She tagged that for later attention. The speaker of the Centralists wanted to meet and discuss recapitalization of the major banks. A worker slowdown had cut myomer production at the MyoMaxx plants to fifteen percent below projections. And Field Security Chief Ricco wanted to discuss the Freeminders situation.

She flinched at the last one. *Freeminders. As if I do not have enough problems without our own people going rogue.* A few taps on the screen set the meeting for early the next morning.

"Freeminders?" Vincent's voice came from right behind her, making her jump. She hadn't heard him enter through the apartment's private side door.

She turned and glared at him. "Your insistence on discretion in our relationship does not mean you have to sneak up on me like an assassin. I could snap your neck by accident one of these days."

He smiled slightly, making a river delta of wrinkles form at the corner of each eye. He was about her age, late forties, which meant that he looked old to her eyes. Clan warriors just weren't supposed to live this long.

But then, Vincent wasn't Clan. But that also meant that she shouldn't be thinking of him, a freeborn, not of the Clans, as an equal. Even if he *was* a former Mech-Warrior. How things had changed—

"I didn't sneak. I thought I made a polite amount of noise coming in. Either you were too distracted, or—" The smile faded, and he stopped himself short.

"Or what?"

He frowned and sighed. "Have you had your hearing checked?"

"What?"

"Your hearing. The cockpit of a 'Mech is a loud place. War is loud. Over time, some hearing damage is to be expected."

She blinked in confusion. What was he talking about?

He tilted his head in that way he did, like someone addressing a child. "You just don't get it, do you? I guess it's been a long time since the Clans, despite all your advanced medical technology, have had much experience with geriatrics."

The word was unfamiliar. "Geriatrics?"

"Medical treatment of the symptoms of aging."

She felt her face harden, her brow wrinkle with annoyance. "I am *not* old!"

He laughed and stepped closer. "Nobody said you were. I was just suggesting that you might consider getting tested for a hearing aid. One of Vega's lesser known, and less strategic, industries. We make some especially small and sensitive ones." He seemed to think of something new. "Or can your Clan medical technicians replace eardrums as well as limbs?"

She just scowled, blanking the screen with the Freeminder reference before he could ask about it again.

"Hearing aids are one of the few things on Vega of which there isn't a shortage. There's a glut, actually, as you fill all the outgoing cargo ships with myomer and IndustrialMechs. Every street vendor and stall at the market has a jar of them for sale cheap."

"I am not old," she repeated.

He sighed. "On Vega, and for that matter, on a lot of worlds, age is considered an accomplishment, something to be respected."

"Not in the Clans."

"I know. You should have had your head blown off by now. It's the warrior way."

She should have, but it didn't work out that way. "I cannot be weak."

"You're the strongest woman I've ever met." He swept his arm around her shoulders, pulled her close, and kissed her hard on the lips.

She considered pushing him away, compiling a short mental list of the bones she could break with minimal effort. She wasn't in the mood. But she let him linger, and after a time it wasn't so bad. Finally it was he who drew back.

She found him looking into her eyes. She remembered his speech in the congressional chamber, and felt a little flash of anger. She pulled his arm from around her. "Your speech, was that part of your attempt to hide our relationship?"

He smiled slightly. "You're calling it a relationship now?"

"Answer."

His smile faded. "It was honesty. I said what needed to be said. I gave voice to what the people of this world were saying already. If I hadn't said it, Chance Elba would have said it instead, and in much more hostile and provocative terms. I gave you ample opportunity to state your defense."

"I do not need what you refer to as help. I do not need you to protect me from Elba."

"To be brutally honest, which I gather is a virtue to your people, you do. You saw what happened when you engaged him directly. That business with the 'tyranny' sign, it was a priceless bit of showmanship. Much as I dislike Elba and what he stands for, I've got to give him a sliver of admiration for that one."

"It was childish."

He shook his head. "It was brilliant. Isis, for a Clansman, you're probably the best politician I've ever seen. But even you're in way over your head here, and you *need* me much more than you know."

He was right, of course. She did need him, a fact that made her brain itch. She was his genetic superior. She could kill him in a dozen ways. Still, he could do things she could not do. She needed him. "You have a very high opinion of yourself." She couldn't help a slight grin. "You could be Clan."

He grinned back. "Indeed I do. That's why you love me."

Rather than lie, or speak an uncomfortable truth, she said nothing.

He stared at her for a moment, his face unreadable, then turned away and feigned interest in one of the reports on her desk.

He does not understand. I am Clan.

Why then did she feel bad about using him? She cursed herself for her weakness. Perhaps years of living in the Rasalhague Dominion in close proximity to non-Clan freeborn really had made the Ghost Bears weak. It made her sick to think it, and to admit that many of her fellow Ghost Bears believed her Raging Bears were the weakest of the weak. If that were true, what did that make their leader?

Certainly the lower castes being sent to Vega to support their stability initiative were considered the dregs of Clan society. Every three months another of the huge military transports that were a signature of the Ghost Bears arrived with another load of technicians, scientists, merchants and, especially, laborers. Every time a transport arrived, the Freeminders problem got worse.

Vincent turned back to her. If he was upset about her lack of response, he was hiding it. "You're distracted. Maybe I should go."

She looked at him. "Don't," she said, not even sure where the word came from.

The fact that it came out as a contraction was even more ironic. There would have been a time he would have noticed, would have teased her. Now, there was only a tiny smile of satisfaction, as though she had used the vulgarism just for him.

Having said it, she felt required to justify it. "I was just trying to figure out how I got here, so far out on the edge of everything."

"Vega isn't the edge of anything. It's well into the Inner Sphere."

She picked up a combat readiness report, walked over, and slumped into one of the reading chairs. "You know very well that I am speaking figuratively, Vincent." She sighed. "I should not be talking to you about this."

He walked over and perched on the edge of the other chair, leaning towards her and propping his square jaw on his fist. "You should be talking to another Clansman?"

Her upper lip twitched. For this too, she needed him, and she did not like it. "I talk to you, Vincent, because you are the only one I *can* talk to. Any Clansman I shared my doubts and uncertainties with would certainly feel obliged to seek a trial against me. It might well have happened already, except that Galaxy commanders are rarely challenged except under special circumstances, and—"

He raised his left eyebrow questioningly. "Yes?"

Go ahead. Say it. She had wanted to say it for a long time.

"Nobody wants my job."

He leaned back in surprise. "Surely that's absurd. Advancement is everything to your people, isn't it?"

"Under normal circumstances. That's—that is—what I was mulling over. The circumstances I find myself in are extraordinary. Maybe unprecedented, in the Ghost Bears anyway."

"You sound— Forgive me. You sound—*afraid.*"

She flinched at the word. She was caught between the Clan imperative for honesty and her own contempt for the very concept of fear. "I am—gravely concerned."

He nodded sympathetically. "Call it what you will."

She looked up at him with a strange mixture of disgust and affection. *So this is what he has become these last* few months. My confessor. How far have we fallen that a Galaxy commander should need such a crutch?

But she did, and here he was, and here she was. And for some irrational reason, she trusted him with her most terrible secrets, any one of which he could use to destroy her.

He seemed to sense her hesitancy. "Whether or not you know it, this is good for you, opening up like this. You've literally got the weight of a world on your shoulders."

More than that. The future of the entire Omega Galaxy. Maybe the future of the entire Ghost Bear Clan. But she did not say so. To trivialize Vega's problems would likely anger him, but to her, the planet was only an objective that she wrestled to control, or even define.

Yet, for the present at least, their objectives, if not their preferred methods, were the same.

"Look," he said, "I know we have our differences on policy. Big differences. If you don't want to talk about those right now, there's always time to fight them out on the senate floor. This is person to person. Woman to man." He leaned closer and gently touched her forearm. "It's you I'm concerned about, not policy."

She took a deep breath, and let it out slowly. "I grew up in an experimental sibko, a wilderness camp designed to bring the modern warrior closer to his or her primal roots. Most of the Ghost Bears trained their warrior candidates in regular military facilities, but the Raging Bears were given a mandate to experiment in those days.

"This training facility had horses, and at a very young age we were all taught to ride. The idea was that many lessons from horsemanship carry over to mechanized combat, especially piloting a 'Mech." She realized she was still holding the status report in her hand, and tossed it on a nearby table. "In one of the first riding lessons, my horse was spooked by a snake and ran wild. I managed to stay on its back, no matter how it tried to buck or scrape me off, but for the life of me, I could not get it to stop." She sighed. "That is how I feel now. This situation cannot buck me off, but I cannot stop it, and"—she licked her dry lips—"I have no idea where it is going."

The room was little more than a closet with a single chair, illuminated only by the light of a dozen computer and tri-vid screens, and a holo panel positioned in front of the chair like a desktop. A man sat in the chair, watching half a dozen screens at once: a local news report that had somehow slipped past the censors on Freeminders graffiti, an intelligence report on the Dragon's Fury and Warlord Mitsura Sakamoto, and a vid of Chance Elba in the Congressional Hall holding up a sign that read TYRANNY.

The man considered each as it influenced his plans.

The first suggested that control of the local news media was far from complete, and that they might make useful pawns at some point.

The second presented a more pressing concern. Some elements in the Draconis Combine had long considered Vega a pilfered territory, rightfully theirs, and it was a lightning rod for Dragon's Fury aggression. He had to apply his intelligence assets to identifying their agents on Vega, and uncovering their intentions towards Vega.

The third was also both a concern and an opportunity. Speaker Chance Elba was an agitator and a potentially dangerous enemy, yet he was far less radical than some, and seemingly more open to reason and negotiation. It was better to turn an enemy to your side than simply to crush him. That was not the traditional Clan way, but— Well, he had never allowed Clan tradition to dictate his decisions.

The room was little more than a closet, yet the man sitting in that chair fancied himself the most dangerous person on Vega.

He smiled at the thought and enjoyed the irony of that thought on a planet recently dominated by warlords, and now by BattleMechs. *Pay no attention to the man behind the curtain. I should call myself* Oz.

Add it to the list. He had been called many things, many names.

One was pressed on him at birth. Another was given him by his peers. But one he had given himself. Of course, it was a title as much as a name, but when a title applies to one man, to one man in all of history, it was a kind of name. This title was the name by which he identified himself. All other names were a sham. Everything else was a disguise.

He had been raised Clan, brought up to conform, to obey tradition, to take gratefully what destiny had handed him. He had never been content with that, never at peace with a society that would require him to be less than he knew he could be.

But even as a child, he had known better than to express this discontent to others. He kept it secret, but he never forgot it, and never put it aside. He had taken his place in Ghost Bear society, rising, despite setbacks, through Clan society, watchful and patient, waiting for the day he could take one step sideways from the straight and narrow in search of his own destiny.

Then he had found it, quite by accident: an old, toothless and nearly forgotten underground movement on the brink of extinction. And in its principles, he saw the path for which he had been searching. In its meager resources he saw something he could leverage to true power.

He embraced it without hesitation. In a year he had reenergized the movement, selling his dreams to the Clan's restless and dissatisfied undercastes. In three years he had swept aside the old leaders and made the group his own. In five, he had built it into a growing secret empire.

Then another opportunity had come along from a most unexpected source: the crumbling of The Republic, with its countless opportunities for adventure and misadventure.

If he were to change Clan society, some part of Clan society itself would have to be thrown into a chaotic state.

He played his contacts, used all his resources, and found what he needed in the plans of the Council itself. They had not been idle during the relatively peaceful years of The Republic. That was not their way. The Ghost Bear does not only patiently wait, he plans.

The Council had played out thousands of scenarios, running war games and simulations for every contingency from the probable to the nearly impossible, from civil war to invasion by an imaginary alien species. They had predicted nothing, but they had planned for everything, even the failure of The Republic.

One plan called for a preemptive occupation of key planets in one prefecture to restore stability and order. These planets would in turn be used to leverage the restoration of that prefecture, and from there, the entire Inner Sphere, if necessary. But the projection was that it would not be necessary. They would bring order by example. If the other prefectures saw that order could be restored, that it *would* be restored, they would choose that path for themselves.

With minimal military resources they would restore a fallen Republic.

It would have been brilliant, if only it weren't doomed to failure. "Choose that path for themselves?" How logical. How naive. How *Clan*.

But if it was fundamentally flawed for its intended purposes, it suited his goals perfectly.

It wasn't a decision made lightly. He regretted sending the Ghost Bears into calamity, but this was not his plan, and given the circumstances it, or something like it, seemed likely to be on the table anyway. His intentions were ultimately good—a statement in which even he could see the irony. Though few in the warrior caste would agree, he saw himself as a patriot to Clan Ghost Bear, simply guiding it along a path that had been cho-

sen long before he was born, when their Clan had immigrated to the Inner Sphere. They *had* to continue to
evolve if they were not to stagnate and die.

And so he put someone else's plan into motion for his
own purposes. Strings were pulled. Favors were called in.
The right ears were whispered into. Evidence supporting
the plan was collected, massaged, spun and, where necessary, fabricated. It was not long before the Ghost Bears
were doing exactly what he wanted—and best of all, it
was their own idea.

Think unthinkable things, indeed.

In a society of conformists and traditionalists, he was
perhaps the only self-made man. He had earned his title.

He was the undisputed leader of the Freeminders in
the Rasalhague Dominion.

He was the *UnderKhan.*

3

From the Great Work of
Galaxy Commander Isis Bekker

We had battled for three days to breach Kean's stronghold in the planetary capital, three days without pause or sleep. But when we broke open the final bunker, he was not there. We had been deceived, and the devil had escaped through, appropriately enough, an abandoned sewer. So while we were digging through the rubble of his headquarters looking for a body that was not there, he was climbing into a fresh 'Mech that had been hidden in the hills outside the city, and rallying his remaining forces to attack our exhausted flank.

That was the black day of glory. That was when it ended.

That was when it began.

My warriors fought bravely, giving honor to their bloodlines, adding glory to their codex with each skirmish. But still they fell. I watched as three 'Mechs, three of my finest officers, were cut down around me in the space of five minutes. Still I fought on.

Then another 'Mech fell in on my left flank, and Conner Hall spoke to me over the command circuit. "We have to end this now," he said. "What are your orders?"

I cannot tell you with certainty how I identified Kean's 'Mech. It carried no special markings or identification. Yet there were signs that led me to my conclusion. That it should be so undamaged, mostly unmarked, this late in the fighting—that was suspicious. And it was a heavy 'Mech, an *Atlas,* one of the biggest and most fearsome of all 'Mechs, befitting the ego of a little man who would dare to call himself lord of an entire world.

There was also the matter of how it fought. The *Atlas* is a powerful 'Mech, but its ability to dissipate heat is poor. In battle, an *Atlas* is generally able to bring its full, formidable might to bear only in short bursts. Then it must hold back, venting excess energy through its meager complement of heat sinks, before it strikes again.

But this *Atlas* broke the rules, moving and fighting more aggressively than seemed possible, and in so doing, laying waste to my warriors.

I was not fooled.

This was no ordinary *Atlas*. Somehow it had been modified to improve its heat dissipation, and the great machine's most significant weakness had been minimized. It was the first field-modified 'Mech we would encounter on Vega. It would not be the last.

At the time, it did not occur to me to wonder about the source of this advanced tech, or who had installed it in Kean's *Atlas*. Instead, I was thinking about the man inside, and wondering what that modification had cost, how many smaller 'Mechs could have been upgraded with the same resources. But the self-proclaimed warlord's ego would allow him nothing less than the best.

I most surely faced Kean, and at that moment, the odds were not in my favor.

Nasew Spaceport, Southwest Industrial District
Nasew, North Nanturo continent, Vega
22 November 3136

Conner walked through the rubble of the MechWarrior barracks, stopping to tap the toe of his boot against a melted lump of metal. He barely recognized the object as an incomplete sculpture of an attacking bear rearing on its hind legs. Or at least, that was how he remembered it. Now the upper part was missing, the rest melted into a featureless mass. The legs, and the base, intended to resemble an outcropping of ice, were still identifiable if one knew what they were looking at.

Karen Tupolov stopped next to him and looked down at the object. "Something of yours?"

"It belonged to Shepard, one of the MechWarriors who was killed. It was his Great Work, a ceremonial object that each warrior of our Clan creates to symbolize his or her dedication and spirit. For those of us in Clan Ghost Bear, it is displayed at the warrior's funeral. Obviously, that will not happen this time."

She kneeled and looked at it closely. "It was a bear?"

"The Clan totem is always a popular subject for Great Works. This ghost bear was quite beautiful. The bear was roaring, and his front paws were slashing through the air, claws spread. You could almost see it moving."

"You have a Great Work as well?" She looked around. "I hope it wasn't—"

"Mine is a painting. Not a very good one. When I am not working on it, I keep it rolled up in a tube that I carry in my 'Mech. For what it is worth, it is safe."

She stood. "I'd like to see it sometime."

On the other side of the spaceport, he could see a small aerodyne DropShip coming in for a landing, its fusion engines throttled back to a low whistle. The air was heavy with smoke, and the slight breeze failed to move the pall, instead adding to it diesel exhaust, coal smoke from the refugee camps and slums, the stink of uncollected garbage and, from somewhere nearby, the stench of a broken sewer main. Smog hung over the city like a poisonous red blanket.

"I will share it with you," he finally answered.

"I'm sorry about your people."

"I appreciate your concern, but it is unnecessary. Warriors die. We accept that. I mourn that they died so poorly, through no effort of their own. No warrior wants to die in his bunk."

She grinned sadly. "Personally, I'd prefer it, but I don't have a genetic codex to worry about. No—actually, I'd prefer a four-poster bed, with silk pillows, a couple of cats and the sound of my grandchildren playing outside. That's a good warrior's death where I come from. Not that I'd lay long odds at the moment, mind you."

He was surprised by her answer, but only because the idea of *grandchildren* was so alien to him. A warrior of the Clans hoped only to die with honors enough that his or her genetic material would be incorporated into the eugenics program to create future warriors. But the concept of new warriors created from one's genetic material was a distant and abstract thing that could happen only after a warrior's death. To actually *see* the product of your genetic material. To *know* them—

But then, of course, they would be freeborns, and thus inferior . . . *only as inferior as my genes. And whoever's genes I blended them with.*

He shuddered, and tried to sweep the entire line of thinking out of his head. The very idea was forbidden, contrary to all Clan tradition and doctrine. *I sound like a Freeminder.*

But he realized that he was studying the line of Karen's back, the curve of her hips, and that some animal part of his brain was speculating about her genetic fitness. At least, that was the scientific way of putting it.

Stop it!

As though sensing his gaze, she glanced over her shoulder at him, then turned back to watch the activity at the far end of the ruined barracks. Behind lines of yellow tape, Clan paramilitary police and civilian technicians still searched for clues to the bombing.

She turned to him. "Where will you go?"

He didn't immediately answer. He hadn't thought that far ahead. They could double up with the elementals, but their barracks were located across the spaceport, inconveniently far from the 'Mech hangars. Civilian quarters would be even farther away. "We could set up tents."

She laughed. "I hope you brought your own. Between the homeless and the refugees, tents are in short supply."

Of course they didn't have tents. The Dominion had come prepared for an urban occupation, not a bivouac, and one simply didn't pack unnecessary gear on a long interstellar journey, even when you were traveling in the huge Ghost Bear transports. The assumption had always been that they would obtain most of their logistical needs locally.

Reasonably, then, they should simply go and *take* the tents they needed. The requirements of warriors always outweighed those of lesser castes, much less outsider freeborns. But they were under specific orders not to take materials without going through channels. Conner didn't understand it, but he was loyal to Galaxy Commander Bekker, and so he did as she said.

"We will continue sleeping in the hangars then, as we did last night."

"With operations ongoing there twenty-four hours a day? I don't see how you'll get any rest. I know you people pride yourselves on overcoming hardships, but it's going to cut into your combat readiness, sooner or later. Probably sooner."

"We will manage."

"Very tough of you, Star Colonel, but you know as well as I do that combat readiness is the critical difference between us and the enemy. I'm not prepared to get blown out of my cockpit because one of your MechWarriors is asleep at the stick. Come sleep at our barracks tonight."

He looked up at her, surprised. "Captain Tupolov, are you asking me to *couple?*"

She looked at him blankly for a moment, then, understanding, broke into laughter. "*Couple?* Is that what you call it? No, Star Colonel, I wasn't inviting you into my bunk. I was merely offering your warriors the hospitality of our barracks until other arrangements can be made, or your barracks rebuilt. It will be crowded, but I know our people will gladly make the sacrifice. Frankly, I think it will help morale on my side of things, and help cement the bond between your people and mine."

"That sounds like a good idea." The FVR hangars and barracks were half a klick away, close enough for a reasonably rapid scramble. By Clan tradition, he could have simply demanded that they surrender their barracks to his warriors, but the idea had not occurred to him.

She looked at him, an odd half smile on her oval face. "Couple." She chuckled. "You Clansmen crack me up. It's all about as romantic as animal husbandry for you, isn't it?"

"That," he said, "would imply that we were coupling for procreation, which we most certainly do not. Warriors are created through the eugenics program. Controlled breeding, procreation, is for lower castes."

Her smile faded and her eyes narrowed. "And people like us?"

"I meant no insult. I only mean to say that Clan warriors couple as a matter of friendship and bonding. It is hardly a mechanical matter. It is important to us."

Her smile grudgingly returned. "Well then, I'll take that as a compliment."

"I thought *you* were asking me to couple."

"So you don't want to?"

"I didn't say that. Are you asking me again?"

"I didn't ask the first time, so I'm certainly not asking now."

"Well then."

"Well."

He turned away from her, gazing off at the boxy red-block building that housed the FVR barracks. "I will see what sort of bedding, linens and cots we can requisition on short notice, then notify my warriors."

"That would be good."

Impulsively he turned and took a step closer to her. "You didn't ask, but would you?"

She blinked, her face seeming to stall just short of a laugh. "Would I what?"

"Would you like to couple?"

Then she did laugh. An incredulous laugh. That bothered him, and it shouldn't have.

She stopped laughing and shook her head. "No. You're amazing. I mean, not now." She self-consciously swept a lock of chestnut-colored hair behind her left ear. "Look, it isn't that I don't think you're an attractive man. You certainly are. But that isn't how we do things. That isn't how *I* do things. Maybe we could—" She seemed to be sidetracked by another thought. "You don't have rules against fraternization?"

He puzzled over the unfamiliar word for a moment. "If I understand you, no. Coupling among warriors aids bonding and teamwork." He tried to see the situation from her perspective, hoping to understand how such a simple and common question had gotten so complicated. "Do *you* have rules forbidding fraternization?"

She shrugged. "We did once—before this whole place fell apart. I guess that at this point, we're pretty much rewriting the book from scratch." She looked thoughtful, tapping the tip of her index finger on her chin. "I suppose we could do something socially. Go for a drink. See what happens. Would that be agreeable?"

His heart seemed to quicken just a little. In the Clan,

a request to couple was either declined or accepted, with few emotional consequences either way. Why did this nebulous and uncertain response intrigue him so? He felt like a MechWarrior crossing enemy lines, facing unknown territory and uncertain dangers, yet feeling confident and ready, even eager, to meet those dangers. "That would be very agreeable. The details—"

"We'll work it out later. I'm still figuring out how seriously to take this. It's been a while since I actually wore a dress. I need to get back to my barracks and start the preparations." She walked away, then hesitated, turned, walked back to him.

She reached up, gently put her hand behind his head, and pulled him close. Her lips found his, warm and soft. Her hair smelled like soap. It might as well have been exotic perfume.

She broke the kiss, and took half a step back, studying his face.

"That was—?"

She grinned. "Just a test." She tilted her head thoughtfully. "Not bad." She turned and walked briskly away.

He watched her go, enjoying the view, the animal part of his brain making genetic calculations.

Technician Reuben stood on the scaffolding near the hangar roof, looking at the stripped-down hulk of an *Ursus*. The scaffolding should have been buzzing with activity as the techs rushed the damaged unit back into service. But the hangar was nearly silent, nearly still. There were no chattering air tools, no welding sparks, no whirring hoists moving parts.

He could see the other techs and laborers below, standing in groups of two or three, talking quietly. They were all as shocked as he at the destruction of the MechWarrior barracks and the resulting deaths. Some of the people there had been their friends.

In truth, the techs felt more intimately connected to the dead MechWarriors than just as friends. They'd tended their 'Mechs, loaded their ammo stores, listened to their gripes, smelled their lingering sweat in the cockpits as they repaired a flickering display or lubricated a sticky foot pedal. And as those men and women had gone into battle, part of the support personnel went too. In some way, the warriors' victories belonged to all of them, and their failures as well.

For Reuben, it had been the only thing that had made his involuntary transfer from Policenigo to Vega bearable. He lived from victory to victory. Pride kept him going when his heart felt ready to break.

Now despair seemed to swallow him. His illusion of purpose, already fragile, had been shattered by the terrorist bomb. Shattered like glass.

Why were they here? The obvious military objectives were achieved. If the entire purpose of the techs' existence was to support the warriors, it was important for the warriors also to have a purpose. To die senseless deaths while politicians spent their time in endless bickering, and an invisible enemy seemed to build strength with each day—that was not a purpose.

No. It was pointless. They should never have come.

He thought of Policenigo, and the two families he'd left there; the meaningless one arranged by the Eugenics Board, a Clan wife he rarely saw and did not like and four children he had never lived with and hardly knew.

Then there was Doris. Not Clan. Not arranged. The woman he loved, the woman who had shown him there was so much more to life than the Clan way, and Kirse, the beautiful daughter born out of that love.

It was forbidden, of course, clandestine, and not recognized by the Clan, which had torn their family apart as though it did not exist. But at least he'd come here believing his sacrifice was for a *reason*.

Now he didn't know what to believe.

Without thinking, he put his hand into the pocket of his coveralls and felt the slip of paper. It had come from a printer slaved to the computer diagnostic system, used exclusively to print out 'Mech-system analysis reports and repair checklists. But this morning, every printer in the hangar had come alive simultaneously and printed out a single slip, identical to the one in his pocket.

He'd heard of this sort of thing happening before. The diagnostic equipment was all networked together, and somebody, somewhere, had hacked the system and used the printers to send a message. Most of the slips had been examined and tossed immediately into the trash bins, leading to nothing more than whispered speculation. But when Reuben had torn the slip from the printer nearest him, he'd somehow put the paper in his pocket rather than throwing it away.

Now he took the paper out again and examined it carefully.

There were two street names and a time. The streets he recognized as being not far beyond the edge of the spaceport. The time was late tonight.

It said one other thing. "Think the unthinkable."

He couldn't imagine the unthinkable, but he was willing to listen.

He began to plan how he would make the mysterious appointment.

Taylor Bane sat on the rough cushion of the open passenger tram and watched the aerodyne DropShip receding in the distance as they bounced over the cracked and occasionally bomb-cratered concrete toward the terminal. A light police 'Mech walked past them, headed out to join another one already guarding the DropShip. Taylor wasn't sure if they were protecting Vega from the DropShip, or the DropShip from Vega.

The sun beat down on them unmercifully, and the air was rank. He bent down to touch the metal briefcase resting on the floorboards and held tightly between his polished leather shoes, then leaned back to try to make the best of the ride.

The seat cushions seemed to consist largely of gray

hurricane tape, and as he lifted his arm, he discovered that a loose flap had adhered to the sleeve of his silk suit. He pulled his arm off in disgust. The tape pulled off with a ripping sound, leaving a sticky white residue on his sleeve. "Great."

Bruno Vic glanced over at him. "What?"

"Ruined a perfectly good suit is what."

Bruno looked down at him, lifting his dark glasses for a better look. Even sitting, Bruno was a head taller than he was. "That will come out.

"Yeah," he continued, nodding. "They got a special fluid, will get it out clean. My uncle was in the laundry business. Find a good cleaners, they'll fix you up."

Bane looked off at the city skyline, bombed and burned buildings making it look like a mouthful of broken teeth. "Forgive me, Bruno, if I'm a little cynical of my chances of finding one here. No wonder there are so few commercial ships headed here. What a hellhole. Hard to believe that it was, until recently, capital of a prefecture. I guess technically maybe it still is, but it's hard to have a capital when the government has moved off-world."

Bruno didn't seem interested in the skyline. He looked straight ahead. Behind those dark glasses, he could have been asleep. Bruno gave that impression, which was part of why he was so good at his job. Bruno wasn't asleep. Taylor wasn't even sure the big man *did* sleep. Finally, he spoke. "I guess the boss has his reasons for sending us. I ain't asking, mind you."

Bruno didn't ask questions, another good trait.

"The boss says that in adversity, there's opportunity," Bane said.

Bruno seemed to be sleeping again. Then, after a while, he said, "That doesn't sound like something the boss would say."

"I'm paraphrasing, mind you." He nodded at a family sitting at the other end of the tram. "There are children present."

The corner of Bruno's mouth twitched slightly. For Bruno, it was a big smile. Taylor had heard that Bruno Vic wasn't his real name. He'd heard once that it was actually Jean Tilden. It didn't matter. Bruno *looked* like a Bruno Vic. That was good enough.

Besides, that was the name on his travel papers, even though they were as forged as Taylor's own.

The tram bounced up to the terminal and drove through a door into the interior. There was an air curtain over the door to keep the air-conditioning inside. The air curtain was inoperative. Which was just as well; so was the air-conditioning.

They drove through the huge, dirty and nearly empty building, the air hot and stuffy, large walls of glass acting as efficient solar collectors. Finally they pulled up under a large sign that read, CUSTOMS—WELCOME TO VEGA.

A handful of customs officials waited, most of them wearing at least some part of a uniform mixed with worn and mended civilian clothing. They were a motley lot, and it made Taylor smile.

The passengers were lined up near a wall, then called up one by one and reunited with their luggage. Taylor watched the proceedings with interest. At this point, papers were produced, and a combination inspection and interview took place. Usually, after a while, the passengers and their luggage were allowed to continue on, but occasionally there was some irregularity, and the passenger was taken away to a row of small offices for further processing.

Taylor heard his name called. He picked up his briefcase and marched up to the waiting customs agent, a slender, middle-aged man with a thin moustache. He wore a uniform cap, a stained blue shirt, and a pair of dark blue slacks with a contrasting patch on one knee. Taylor presented his papers, which the official examined closely.

"These seem to be in order." He glanced down. "I'll need to look in the briefcase."

"Yes," said Taylor, "I understand. I'd like that very much. But not *here.*"

The official looked at him, puzzled. "Excuse me?"

"Perhaps," he said carefully, "there is some error in the papers you did not initially notice. He bobbed his head towards the offices. "Perhaps you will want to inspect them more closely."

The man blinked. Blinked again. Then looked down at the briefcase. It was a titanium shell. Brand-new. Very expensive. "Maybe I should call to verify certain matters. Please follow me."

They stepped into a small room with a table and two chairs, the kind of room sometimes used for interrogation. There were no two-way mirrors though, only an obvious camera mounted on an arm on the wall. As Taylor put his briefcase flat on the table, the man hung his hat over the camera.

Taylor keyed in the lock code, and the latches snapped open. He flipped open the briefcase, then spun it around so the inspector could see.

The man's eyes opened wide.

Taylor reached into the case and casually flicked a small gold ingot onto the table. Then after a moment, he flicked another. The man picked them up, inspecting the lettering embossed into the top of each ingot. A name: JACOB BANNSON. Then he looked up at Taylor, his eyes still wide.

Taylor spun the briefcase around and snapped it shut. "Everything is in order, then?"

The man hesitated. "Yes. Yes, of course."

"My baggage as well."

"I haven't even— Yes, of course."

"You have my gratitude, and that of my employer as well. You never know when that could come in handy."

Bruno was waiting outside the terminal in a battered black sedan. One front fender was crumpled, and the sunroof was sealed with hurricane tape. Bruno noticed him inspecting the car. "It was the best I could do. I won't tell you what I had to pay for it."

"As long as it drives." He climbed into the backseat.

Bruno glanced into the rearview mirror. "I was worried you'd found yourself an honest customs agent."

He snorted. "Everybody's for sale, Bruno, especially in a place like this. Only good thing I've seen about Vega so far. We can do business here."

"Let's hope so. Where to?"

"Let's see if there are any hotels left standing in this rat hole. Then we start spreading some of this gold around."

4

I have never favored a heavy 'Mech.

I am not a large person. I did not test out of my sibko as a warrior, fight my way up through the ranks to Galaxy commander, win my Bloodname and prevail though countless challenges by virtue of size and physical strength. In 'Mech battles, as in more personal ones, my fighting style calls for speed, agility, stealth and the ruthless application of surprise.

As such, the hundred-ton *Atlas* towered over my much-modified thirty-ton *Pack Hunter,* and I was heavily outgunned. Even if my 'Mech had been fresh and undamaged, which it was not, I would have been at a huge disadvantage. Of course, Conner Hall was there too, but his sixty-five-ton *Karhu* was even more damaged than my 'Mech—his missiles gone, his ammo depleted, only part of his suite of lasers operational. Mentally, I was prepared for this to be my last battle.

A Clan warrior does not fear death in battle. We welcome it. We embrace it, so long as it brings glory to our bloodline. To die in glorious battle is to ensure one's genetic legacy. It is to ensure that the iron wombs will one day bring forth our figurative sons and daughters as a new generation of warriors.

So I attacked Jedra Kean expecting to die, planning only that I would take the accursed freeborn with me, knowing the satisfaction that his legacy would die with him even as mine would live on.

Lightning flashed around us as I approached him, using natural cover to make myself a more difficult target. I fired my lasers, cutting a gash across the monstrous metal skull that forms the head of an *Atlas*. "Go for his vanity," I thought. "Make him angry."

It worked. The *Atlas* fired off a poorly targeted volley of missiles that tore up the trees and rock outcroppings around me, but did little damage to my 'Mech.

But the scar I scored onto his 'Mech served one other purpose as well. It provided a target, a place for my scattered forces to focus their fire. Conner Hall's lasers found my mark with flawless aim, and still more of the thick armor peeled and dripped away.

Blinded by exploding missiles and a nearby lightning strike, Kean hesitated before targeting me again, and I was able to slip closer. I traveled a serpentine course towards him, forcing him to swivel and turn to keep his weapons trained on me. Even though this machine boasted improved heat dissipation, the massive *Atlas* is still a slow and cumbersome 'Mech. Though I could not use my damaged jump jets, my *Pack Hunter* was maneuverable and at least twice as fast as the bigger 'Mech. I used that fully to my advantage.

He fired his lasers and Gauss rifles, near misses and glancing strikes that did minor damage to my already bleeding 'Mech. I watched the red lights growing in number on my heads-up display. Even if Kean did not score a direct hit, I could not take much more of this punishment, and the closer I came the easier a target I presented.

"Operation plink," I announced on the command circuit.

From a dozen points around the *Atlas* came weapons fire and the huge 'Mech paused, its torso swiveling as it tried to choose a target. Lasers played over its armor, and missiles exploded with little effect, but that was not my intent.

Conner Hall had not come alone. On his way, he had rallied what forces he could. No BattleMechs. But there were Elementals, the Clans' giant warriors in their fearsome battle armor; tanks crewed with aging warriors past their prime, desperate to die in glory; and a few other elements of light armor, far outclassed, but able to distract the big 'Mech for the precious seconds I needed.

Closer I came. Closer. I opened up with my microlasers, and the distracted *Atlas* again turned its attention to me.

I remember the flash.

At first I thought it was lightning, but my cockpit lurched violently, and I heard the screaming of metal as the lasers cut through something critical and the right arm of my 'Mech began to rip free at the shoulder. Hot oil scalded my face, and a haze of smoke filled the cockpit.

Still I advanced on the *Atlas* as he turned his missiles to bear on me. In a flash of lightning I saw the tips of the ready missiles, and the skull mask of the *Atlas* looking down at me.

I switched to an open radio channel and told as close to a lie as a Clan warrior is likely to tell. "What," I asked, "are your terms of surrender?"

Mind you, I never said that I was interested in agreeing to those terms, or that I would even consider them. I was just asking, you see.

Nasew Spaceport, Southwest Industrial District
Nasew, North Nanturo continent, Vega
22 November 3136

Despite the late hour, the FVR barracks were a buzz of activity: folding bunks being hustled down the corridors, lockers being pushed around, beds being made and room assignments being handed out by the FVR's executive officer. Conner Hall stood near a corridor junction, his back against the wall, powerful arms crossed over his broad chest, watching the proceedings with interest.

The Vega personnel seemed somewhat tentative around the Clan MechWarriors, even the FVR MechWarriors who worked with them on a regular basis. To work with the Clan warriors, to fight with them, was one thing. To live in intimate proximity to them was apparently quite another.

Conner had to admit he felt out of place himself. The layout of the barracks seemed strange. The building pre-dated the current conflict and was built to the standards of a time of peace and relative plenty. Originally, each MechWarrior, regardless of rank, had been given a pri-vate room with a very solid door. A door equipped with a lock. It bespoke a need for privacy and modesty that was alien to Conner. Their own barracks had been di-vided into only a few rooms, each MechWarrior assigned a bunk and a few items of functional furniture, each bunk separated from the rest only by a movable curtain.

Most of the time, the curtains had been left open. If they were drawn, it usually meant someone was inside coupling, but occasionally they weren't drawn even then. He had spent enough time around non-Clanners to know there would be incidents. A Clansman of either gender would think nothing of walking to and from the showers or latrines naked, or of changing clothes in a common area.

It had been his experience that while non-Clan warriors were less modest than the general populace—combat often made modesty a luxury—they still maintained their mod-esty where possible. Most especially, they made a habit of averting their eyes from their fellow soldiers' nudity, especially when dealing with the opposite sex.

To a Clan warrior, it was unnecessary nonsense. There was nothing unnatural, shameful or forbidden about the human body. It simply was. To surround it with elaborate social taboos was ridiculous.

But that was not the most pressing problem at the moment. Everyone needed to be situated, and there were countless minor logistical challenges; for example, most of their uniforms and personal kits had been destroyed in the fire. Replacements were in short supply. Some of his MechWarriors now wore borrowed FVR uniforms, with a few in mechanics' coveralls.

There was no sadness, no mourning for the day's losses among his warriors, only a cloud of anger and frustration that hung over them all. To die bravely in combat was a warrior's death, and something to be celebrated. Death by terrorist action—this was something they were less prepared to deal with.

Conner's mind flashed back to those first glorious days after their landing on Vega. He remembered the hot-metal-and-oil smell of his 'Mech's cockpit, the fusion flare of descending DropShips as they'd dug into the shattered spaceport and set about securing it to bring in the heavier aerodyne transports. They'd encountered a surprisingly heavy resistance: tanks, lots of light armor, armored infantry, artillery fire from emplacements far across the city and even a few 'Mechs.

It was then they'd first encountered the First Vega Regulars, though they hadn't given themselves that name yet. Then, they'd only been a ragtag resistance force loyal to The Republic, piloting whatever crudely modified IndustrialMechs they'd been able to lay their hands on. They took out the artillery batteries and helped Conner's warriors secure the spaceport. Given their inferior equipment, their losses had approached sixty percent by the time the fighting let up but, by then, they'd won Conner's respect. He'd personally advocated forming the survivors into a formal part of their defenses, to coordinate closely with Clan forces in restoring order to the war-torn planet.

As for Karen, she had been a junior officer when the fighting began. By the end of it, she was the most experienced and highest-ranking MechWarrior in the loyalist force.

Conner remembered the first time he'd become aware of her. Her MiningMech had been taking fierce fire from a damaged *Blade* that was defending the control tower. Though the BattleMech was damaged, it was in every way her superior, and its guns had been peeling the makeshift armor from her patched-together machine like a farmer shearing a sheep.

But still she'd waded forward, using the MiningMech's digging wheel to shield her cockpit until she could move inside his weapons' range and engage hand-to-hand. She squeezed every last erg of energy from her damaged machine, bleeding coolant and hydraulic fluid as she chewed into the *Blade*'s cockpit with her rock cutters. Her 'Mech had finally quit on her, slumped over from mechanical failure, but the *Blade* had fallen first, and its pilot would not live to fight another day.

That seemed an eternity ago. He treasured the memory of proper combat, as sweet as a lover's embrace.

"Are you all right, Conner? You seem a million klicks away."

He blinked, and looked down into Karen's eyes. She tilted her head and smiled ever so slightly, a look of concern on her face.

"Just thinking of better days."

"Well, there have been better ones than this, that's for sure. I'm just happy it's over."

"Let us hope that it does not happen again."

"They've doubled security around the base, and no vehicles are being allowed within fifty meters of any building until further notice." She watched two of her officers slide past them carrying a rolled mattress. "In any case, I think you'll be safer here. The insurgents are aggressive, but I think they're less likely to attack a barracks occupied by native Vega citizens."

"Perhaps you underestimate them. They seem as though they'll stop at nothing to drive us off this world."

She frowned. "I'm not counting on their mercy. I'm counting on their desire to court the goodwill of the common Vegan. Kill a Clansman in his bed, and you're a folk hero. Kill a Vegan in his bed, even one who opposes your philosophy, and you're a murderer. Our enemies are well versed in courting public opinion."

Then the frown turned into a sad smile. "That's the difference between this and so many other conflicts in human history. Vegans, despite all our differences, have a sense of ourselves as one people. Like the ancient Russians I gather you people so admire. Time and again our world has been invaded, fought over, occupied, and yet another government installed. Ultimately, we are all rats on the same leaking ship, cursing the raging sea, grimly awaiting our fate with little hope of controlling it."

His eyes narrowed. "Cursing, too, the pirates that have recently come over the rail?"

She shrugged. "I'm sure that's the way the insurgents see it."

He studied her, and could tell by the look in her eyes that she sometimes saw it that way too. "We are not pirates. We're the rescue party, come to reset the masts, mend the sails and help bail, if only you'll let us."

"Out of the goodness of your hearts." There was a trace of sarcasm in her voice.

"The Ghost Bears have their agenda, it's true, but ultimately we want what you want. A strong and stable Vega, that can once again take its rightful place as the capital of this prefecture."

She looked away and shook her head. "I'm sorry if I sound ungrateful. It's hard not to be cynical, after all we've been through these last few years." She again met his eyes, and there was something there that had been missing before. Something sad and desperate. She quickly looked away.

The frenzy of activity had finally slowed, and they were alone in the corridor, except for a few people sorting uniforms at the far end, out of easy earshot. She lowered her voice, so only he would hear. "I don't know that I'd be here if it wasn't for you, Conner. There have been so many times I've just wanted to give up the fighting, find someplace relatively out of harm's way, and try to live out my days with as much simplicity and peace as possible." She licked her dry lips. "Then I hear you talk about the lost glory of the old Star League, and how the Clans have devoted their entire existence to restoring that to the Inner Sphere. You don't talk about it often, but when you do, it isn't for show. It isn't a speech, or rhetoric, or a pep talk. You talk about it as naturally as you breathe."

She pursed her lips, and ran her fingers through her hair. It was dirty and tangled after their long, difficult day. It didn't bother him. He had a sudden desire to wash it for her, to run his fingers through her long, soapy locks. He shook off the image, and blinked himself back to reality.

She didn't seem to notice his distraction. "I never understood the Clans before. Probably I still don't. But when you talk like that, I understand *why* you exist and something deep in my heart wants—no—*demands*—that I help you. The Star League was born here on Vega, Star Colonel, and we hold it more dear, mourn its passing more deeply, than you can imagine. You remind me that we're fighting for something bigger than ourselves, something abstract, and grand and glorious. A fool fights for nothing. An idiot fights for trinkets or land. But a warrior—a true warrior—fights for the greater glory of all. If that's really what we're fighting for, then I'll fight on. I'll fight on with my last breath, and my last drop of blood."

His mouth opened, but nothing came out. Her words had snuck up on him, sliding past the distraction of his growing passion for her and crashing home like a storm wave breaking on rocks.

He inspired *her?* Yet to hear her repeating his own words and beliefs, it was as though he had never heard them before. He realized that after the Omega Galaxy's growing troubles, what many called their decline, and his time on Vega, it had made him cynical, dulled his sense of purpose.

What are we fighting for?

To restore the lost glory of the Star League.

He felt a clarity he had not felt in a long time. It was a good feeling, one he wanted to share. But there would be time enough for that.

She tilted her head slightly. "Have you been assigned quarters yet?"

He shook his head. "I did not want to complicate the process. I will take whatever bunk is left."

"You're the commander. I assumed you'd want your own room."

"Space is tight. I will share. It does not matter with whom." *Or did it?* He stumbled over the words, and it made him foolish and un-Clannish. "I could share yours."

She looked by turns surprised, bemused and then amused. She laughed softly, not as derisively as when he'd proposed coupling with her earlier. "You don't give up, I'll give you that." She grinned.

"I already have a roommate. Lieutenant Rodriquez, a new recruit from down south. You may not have met her yet, but I'm sure you will." She stepped back to allow an FVR MechWarrior, carrying a bathrobe and toothbrush, past her on his way to the showers. "It will be hard to avoid anyone from now on."

"Then I will not be able to avoid you."

She gave him a lopsided grin, a twinkle in her eye that made his heart pound a little faster. "No, I don't think you will."

Isis Bekker came awake suddenly, some instinct putting her mind in a state of instant alertness. Her training and experience allowed her to remain motionless, kept even her eyelids from fluttering. Though she could tell that the room was still dark, any movement she made might be detected by someone with night-vision goggles.

She lay still, forcing her body to remain relaxed, tried to keep her breathing slow and regular, listening intently for what had awakened her.

Long seconds glided past like dark, drifting clouds filled with the portent of a storm.

Then— *There!* A slight creak of the flooring. Not a step. Perhaps someone shifting their weight. She estimated that the sound came from somewhere in the direction of the bathroom door.

Vince? She listened closely, trying to hear breathing. There it was, barely discernible, but high in pitch, more like a child than a full-grown man. Certainly it wasn't Vincent Florala. The man had suffered some kind of congenital breathing difficulty as a child. Asthma? Allergies? Regardless, it was the sort of thing that had by now been bred and engineered out the warrior bloodlines, and she wasn't even familiar enough with such conditions to know what it was called. Whatever, it had left him with a slight but characteristic wheezing sound in his exhalation.

No, this was not Vincent.

She lay on her stomach, naked as she always slept, a cool sheet draped over her body, legs akimbo, left arm sprawled next to her body, right hand half tucked under her pillow. Slowly—ever so slowly—she uncurled the fingers of that hand, stretching out. Her pistol was out of her reach without obvious movement, but she just felt the smooth pearl handle of her dagger under her fingertips. Slowly, carefully she slid it closer, until she could wrap her fingers around it.

Again, the shifting of weight.

What are you waiting for? Why do you hesitate? I certainly wouldn't.

Then there was something else. A noise that was not the cocking of a gun, but something mechanical—things under tension.

She rolled, tossing the sheets to disguise her movement. There was a *thwip*, and something shot past her, so close that she felt the breeze from it against her ribs, and struck the mattress where her torso had been only a moment before.

She hit the floor in a crouch, knife at the ready. It was dark, but a slight glow came from the simulated window, and her dark-adjusted eyes could see well enough. A slight figure dressed in black, carrying a small crossbow.

Assassin!

Her instinct was to strike without mercy, end this decisively in blood.

Yet the dark silhouette she could see was small and unimposing, and there was an old saying that dead men tell no tales. Isis wanted to know who her assassin was, and more importantly, who had sent him or her. A corpse might not give her those answers.

She pounced, tackling the dark figure. She encountered little resistance. Her attacker was as small and thin as he or she had appeared to be, though wiry muscles flexed as they struggled.

Isis had jumped hard, just in case her attacker was more formidable than they had appeared. Now this worked against her as the attacker fell back, using her momentum against her, tossing her into a roll. She landed on her back, snap-rolling instantly into a crouch, blade still at the ready.

But the attacker was already swinging the stock of the crossbow at her. It connected painfully with her right cheek, slamming her head back, making her taste blood. She cursed herself for her sloppiness. She was old for a Clan MechWarrior, and right now she felt the weight of her age.

She shook off the momentary lapse like a dog shaking off water. Deep inside, she felt the bear spirit rising. She bared her teeth and snarled.

The attacker seemed to hesitate, crossbow held ready to swing again. Still he—or she—Isis thought she might have felt the curve of small breasts in their brief grappling—did not retreat.

You're not a coward. Good. That will make this easier.

Isis knew the location of every object in her room, the layout clearly defined in her mind's eye. Her left hand found the bathroom door frame, and instantly she was oriented. Just to her right was a floor lamp, a simple metal shade atop a long metal pole, all attached to a weighted base. It would make a good weapon, and with three times the reach of that crossbow stock.

She stepped quickly toward the lamp, the knife—she didn't want to drop it—clanging against the metal pole as her fingers wrapped around both. She lifted the lamp, grabbing it with her left hand as well, putting as much force as she could into an upward swing. The base swept the crossbow aside and slammed into the assassin's chest, throwing the intruder back.

In one continuous motion, Isis swung the lamp high, and brought it down hard between her attacker's shoulder blades, slamming her opponent facedown on the floor. Isis tossed aside the lamp and leaped onto the assassin's back. The attacker reached for something on his or her belt. A gun, a knife—it didn't matter. Isis grabbed the arm, twisted and with practiced skill pushed until there was as high cry of pain from the assassin (definitely female) and the crack of bone.

She leaned forward and put the point of her blade against the assassin's throat. "Move and you die," she hissed.

The door flew open, flooding the room with light from outside. The door guard stood there, a hulking elemental who had tested down, from the warrior caste to security, assault rifle quickly lining up on the intruder. Seeing that Isis had the situation under control, he felt for the light switch.

Isis squinted as the overhead lights came on. She made no move to cover her nakedness, and the door guard didn't seem to notice.

Isis glared at him. "How did she get past you?"

The guard blinked in surprise. "She did not, I swear, Galaxy Commander!"

Isis glanced at the side door, the one Vince used, but the locks were currently set so that they could only be opened from the inside, and they were still secure.

She looked down at the profile of her attacker, her face still pressed against the floor. She blinked in surprise. This was hardly more than a girl, with short blond hair, blood spattered over rosy cheeks, and an upturned nose, now bleeding. "Who sent you, child?"

The girl flinched in pain, but her expression was angry and defiant. "All of Vega! I strike for freedom!"

Isis sneered. "Spare me the rhetoric. Tell me what coward sends children to do their dirty work."

"Eat rocks!"

Isis still held the wrist of the girl's broken arm. She twisted it ever so slightly. The girl yelped, squirmed weakly and her eyes rolled back as though she might pass out. But still she was defiant. "I come in the name of freedom-loving Vegans. I'll never betray them!"

Isis thought about twisting the arm harder, but she had little stomach for torturing children. She didn't need to be told who her enemies were. Now she just wanted to know why. "You're just a girl. Why would they send you as an assassin?"

The girl hesitated, licked her bloodied lips. She seemed to consider the question. "I—I was the only one who would fit."

Isis frowned, then looked towards the bathroom. She glanced at the guard, then jerked her chin towards the door. He slipped past them into the bathroom, weapon held ready. He flicked on the light. "There is an open service panel here," he said, "under the sink. There is a space with pipes behind it. I can barely see how a rat could fit through there, much less a person, but that must be how she managed to get in."

Isis looked down at her prisoner. "You've got courage, child. It's a shame you chose to waste it on a lost cause." A contingent of guards appeared at the door, and she allowed them to take the girl prisoner. She showed the open panel to another of the guards. "Find out where that passage goes and secure it, so this will not happen again."

The guard looked apologetic. "There are no surviving blueprints to this building. You were warned it would be a security issue when we moved in."

She scowled at him. "I did not ask you to find the blueprints; I asked you to find where the tunnel goes. If that means you have to crawl though it yourself, then do it."

He looked nonplused. "I'll find a way, Galaxy Commander." He snapped a salute and strode briskly out the door. As she watched him go, she saw somebody step through behind him.

Vincent.

He looked at the blood on her, on the floor, and stared at her with open concern.

She reached up and, for the first time, touched the swelling where the butt of the crossbow had struck her cheek.

Vince grabbed up the sheet, noticing with alarm the shaft of the crossbow bolt projecting from the mattress, and threw it over her shoulders.

She shrugged off the sheet. "Vince, you're acting like a freeborn idiot. Make yourself useful and find me some real clothes."

He looked shocked, but walked over and started digging through the drawers of the filing cabinet-cum-dresser, pulling out the green sweat suit she used for her morning exercises.

She bent down to pick up the crossbow, admiring the clever way that it snapped apart into modular pieces.

It never would have fit through the narrow plumbing shaft assembled.

Vince handed her the clothes. The sweat on her skin was evaporating, and she suddenly felt chilly. She pulled on the pants and jacket, then reached to pull the crossbow bolt out of her mattress.

"Don't," Vincent said. "They'll want to investigate."

Her hand froze just short of the bolt.

"Leave it. You can stay in my apartment. This is a crime scene now."

She drew back, frowning. "This isn't crime, it's war."

Vincent remained silent.

"They're sending children against me, Vince." She met his gaze. "I am mistaken, and you are right. That is not war. That is a crime."

5

From the Great Work of
Galaxy Commander Isis Bekker

With my implied offer of surrender, the *Atlas* again hesitated. Despite his ego, despite his apparently huge advantage, I did not see my opponent as a man of excessive personal courage. If he could avoid battle, at least personal battle, he would.

That was his weakness.

A second passed as he considered. Another.

I was no longer advancing on his position, and the harassment fire had fallen off as the supporting units sought new positions. Per my orders, they were forming a defensive perimeter, leaving the *Atlas* to us. From their chatter on the command circuit, I knew more of Kean's forces were closing in on us from multiple vectors. Right now we were outgunned. In a few minutes more, we would be overwhelmed.

In battle, a few minutes can be an eternity.

But the distraction fire had done its job, giving Conner Hall time to move.

He found his ideal position behind Kean, and opened fire with everything he had on the *Atlas'* less-armored flank. It was an act of all-out desperation, but at last the *Atlas* showed some real damage. I smiled, thinking that behind that deadly skull, Jedra Kean might finally be seeing a few red lights of his own.

But the victory was short-lived. The *Atlas* turned. The missiles that moments before had been intended for me arced toward Conner Hall's 'Mech and struck with deadly force. The machine was enveloped in a ball of flame. It staggered a few steps, then slumped over, crippled and inert.

The *Atlas* swiveled back toward me, its pilot thinking to make another kill.

On the command circuit, I could hear our other forces facing the incoming 'Mechs and armor without hope, but without fear.

I heard Conner Hall's voice crackling in my headset, weak and gurgling, as though choking on his own blood. "Good hunting, Galaxy Commander."

The *Atlas* drew its sights on me, but I had been moving and, though my armaments were nearly spent, I had saved one volley of missiles. The range was ideal.

I targeted the already weakened armor on the skull, like a diamond cutter seeking out a flaw in the stone. I put my crosshairs on the target, waited for the moment, then fired.

Missiles flared across the darkened sky.

Flame enveloped the upper reaches of the big 'Mech, boiling into the air above it, then fading.

And as the flame cleared, I could see that the skull of the *Atlas* was cracked open like an egg. Inside, I could just make out the remains of the cockpit, and something still struggling.

Knowing that his gathering forces would be looking on, would be witness to what was about to happen, I targeted my remaining laser and thought to myself, "These are my terms for surrender!"

Brubaker Hotel, North Central District
Nasew, North Nanturo continent, Vega
23 November 3136

Taylor Bane sat slouched in a wicker chair in the middle
of the suite, his thick, manicured fingers wrapped around
the cool bentwood of the chair's arms, looking out the
window at the ragged city skyline. The glass sliding door
to the balcony was open, and the stained draperies rip-
pled inwards with a welcome breeze, heavily scented by
wood smoke. He was sweaty and uncomfortable. The
air-conditioning had failed within twenty minutes of
their checking in, and there was little indication when,
or if, it would be fixed.

He lifted the handset of the old corded phone on the
table and put it to his ear. There was a dial tone. At least
that was working—at the moment, anyway. He placed it
back in its cradle and stared out at the mountains beyond the city, their peaks shrouded in blue-gray haze.
He could see the bottom of the gap that the bellboy told
him was called Lincoln Pass, a gap in the mountain into
which snaked a wide highway, a parallel cargo-train
road, and a bank of pipelines, all beginning their long
journey to the industrial city of Northgate, which lay at
the far end of the pass.

It was the sort of thing that attracted Bane's attention.

Other people might have seen the pass as a lifeline
for resources or a corridor for commerce. Bane saw it
in much more fundamental terms. It was a path along
which wealth flowed, and where wealth flowed, he knew
his employer would covet a piece of the action.

But that would come later. His boss wasn't here yet,
wasn't welcome here yet. In fact, nobody even knew he
wanted to be welcome here.

That was Bane's mission. He had to find his employer
a welcome mat and figure a way to get it rolled out
for him.

He heard someone rattling the door lock and reached

for the pistol tucked neatly under his jacket, then relaxed as the door opened to reveal Bruno Vic, a leather-covered ice bucket under his arm. The big man entered and locked the door behind him.

"Bruno," he said. "You got ice?"

Bruno put the bucket on a side table and nodded. "I couldn't find any in the hotel. The desk guy sent me out into the alley behind the hotel, where some guy was selling it out of a cart. Then I get back and the elevators aren't working. Had to climb the twelve flights to our room."

"This planet is a rat hole. Did I mention that?"

"I think you did, maybe." Bruno pulled a bottle of scotch from one of their suitcases, put some ice in a glass and poured a drink. He carried the glass over and handed it to Bane, who accepted it gratefully. He took a sip, smiled and leaned back, closing his eyes. "Ah, the taste of civilization. Amazing how important the simple pleasures can be in a place like this."

"That ice," said Bruno, "it probably has all kinds of bugs in it. God knows where they got the water."

Bane only chuckled. "That's why we were inoculated for every disease known to man before we left, and why I've got a bag full of broad-spectrum antibiotics and anti-virals." He took another sip and sighed happily. "For this, I'll take my chances."

There was a knock at the door. Bruno pulled his pistol from under his jacket and stepped to the door. He peered through the peephole for a moment, then, keeping the gun ready but out of sight, opened the door a crack.

Bane heard him talking quietly, and a man's voice responding. Then he opened the door, and the man stepped in.

He was dark, short, slender and middle-aged, his cheeks pockmarked, and he had a bulbous nose over a thick moustache. He wore a tattered, stained white suit and scuffed black shoes. He clutched a straw hat nervously to his chest, and frowned as though he expected something distasteful to happen. "I am Geoff Krago. I was told you might have need of a guide. I was told you can pay in gold, not the government scrip." He glanced over at Bruno, and his eyes widened in alarm as he spotted the chrome-plated automatic that the big man was slipping back under his coat. But he did not bolt. He merely swallowed, looked back at Bane and clutched his hat a little tighter.

"I may have need of your services. I am told you are a knowledgeable man, that you know much about the city and its people. You know how things work. You know how to get things done."

Krago flashed a weak smile. "It may be true that I have some skill in such things. An expertise of sorts. I will help you if I can."

"You recognize that I need complete confidentiality. You must not speak of my concerns with others, not even your wife. Especially not your lovely children."

The man's mouth sagged a little in surprise.

Bane was careful not to let his satisfaction show. He had made many inquiries before summoning Krago. The man had not been chosen merely for what he knew, but also for his vulnerability to threats. Family men were, by definition, subject to persuasion. "I am willing to pay quite well for this consideration and, as you suggest, not in the local currency. If you accept these terms, you will find me quite easy to get along with."

Krago blinked nervously and licked his lips. "Of course. This is acceptable. What may I do for you?"

"I need to get into the capital. I need to meet with Galaxy Commander Isis Bekker."

The man looked alarmed. "I must know what this is about. I cannot be party to— There are things I will not—"

"Mister Krago, I am paying you to answer my questions. How do I reach her, personally and privately, or failing that, the provisional governor?"

"You—You could make an appointment."

"I've investigated that possibility. Assuming I could even get on the list, the first available appointment is six months from now. I require more immediate access. For that, I will have to operate . . . outside channels. How do I get access?"

The man looked down at his feet, chewed his lower lip. "There is no way, sir. The provisional capital is a fortress, much more so than the old one. You know what happened?"

Bane nodded. "Someone dived into it with an aerospace fighter loaded with explosives. The kinetic energy was such that the explosives were almost unnecessary. Most of your government was wiped out in a single stroke. Perhaps a suicide attack, though some speculate that the pilot tried to eject and could not. Several groups have claimed responsibility, but the true identity and affiliation of the pilot may never be known."

Krago nodded. "Then you can understand, sir, why they are paranoid. There is a two-kilometer security perimeter, very tightly controlled. The building itself was built as the headquarters of MyoMaxx Corporation, on the assumption that it might one day come under military attack due to the company's strategic importance. The walls of the building are armored like a 'Mech, hardened against all but the most intense and sustained fire. There are almost no windows. The air system is filtered against poisons and toxins. There are escape tunnels and bunkers, traps and countermeasures, antiaircraft defenses on the roof and at several outlying sites.

"These are only the defenses that I know of. I have little doubt there are more. The senior officials live there as well as work there. You will not get to them, no matter what you have in mind."

"I will require maps, details of the security perimeter and any other security measures that you can document."

"They will not help you."

Bane sighed. "Let me decide that. Can you do this"—
he pulled one of the little gold bars from his pocket and
held it up for the man to see—"or shall I find someone
more forthcoming?"

"No. No. I can do it! It may take a few days though.
Perhaps a week."

"Two days." He held out the bar, and the man
snatched it like a starving dog stealing meat. "If the information is satisfactory, there will be more."

"Yes, I will get you what I can. Two days."

Bruno caught the man's eye and jerked a thumb towards the door.

The man nodded, and allowed Bruno to lead him out.

As the door closed behind the man, Bruno turned
back to Bane. "You really think he'll keep quiet?"

Bane shrugged. "He might. He might not. I suspect
some word of our activities may leak out."

"That doesn't bother you?"

"If the powers that be become aware of our activities,
they may come looking for us. Under the right circumstances, that could suit my needs just as well. If Moham-
med will not go to the mountain . . ."

The former headquarters of the MyoMaxx Corporation had become something of a prison to Isis Bekker,
and she resented her confinement intensely. It was unbe-
coming of a warrior to cower in a fortification, avoiding
conflict rather than seeking it out.

Yet she knew that, for now at least, this was the unhappy duty of her position. Those around her recognized
it as well, and so she seemed unlikely to be relieved of
that responsibility anytime soon.

Still, it was not a prison without amenities. She had no
interest in the posh executive living quarters that most
of the senior Vega delegates now occupied, nor in the
executive dining hall, with its carved hardwood furniture,
fine china and crystal. Many things had changed for the
Ghost Bear society during their time in the Inner Sphere,

but they had not lost their taste for the spartan, their distaste for waste and frivolous luxury.

But the long-gone executives of the company had also provided for themselves recreational facilities with a more practical use, including a full health club located in the subbasement. There was a competition-sized pool, weight-training facilities and sports courts of various types. Though she was proficient in several sports, her favorite was four-wall handball.

She enjoyed the one-on-one intensity of the sport, the lightning speed of the action, and the physicality of striking the ball with her bare hand. The formal rules, of course, called for gloves, but she always waived that point, and nobody had the rank to contradict her. "A privilege of command," she would often say.

Her most frequent opponent was Star Colonel Conner Hall. Since the younger warrior was effectively her military commander on Vega while she attended to political matters, she had to consult with him regularly. Their handball games at least sometimes spared them both the boredom of sitting around an office looking at deployment maps.

With two paramilitary police guards as escorts, she took a private elevator, once reserved for the MyoMaxx CEO, down to the gym area. The two guards stood behind her, trying to be as invisible as their looming, black-armored presence would allow. She was sure Security Chief Ricco would not approve of this, after the assassination attempt, but she refused to live as any more of a prisoner than she already did. Assassins be damned.

She consulted her watch on the way down. A conference call with several of the senators over nagging details of the Articles had delayed her, and Conner was likely already there, probably waiting impatiently. Though she was certain he enjoyed their games, he disliked being away from the base for any length of time, unless it was on a mission. The attack on the MechWarrior barracks would doubtless only multiply his concerns.

She couldn't blame him. She ached to be there herself.

She should have died that day, ramming those missiles down Jedra Kean's throat. That would have been a proper ending for her career. If she believed in fate, she would think it had a sense of humor, and she was the butt of the joke. Maybe that was part of her reason for continuing her routine, despite the risk. She wondered if she had a death wish.

As she rounded the corner past the locker rooms, she was not surprised to see someone standing there. Given the confinement of those who occupied the building's inner reaches, the facilities were always in use. She could tell it was a senator by the special green, hooded sweat-jacket the person was wearing, still a sign of station even though it was a bit ragged around the edges. But only when he turned and smiled his thin-lipped smile did she recognize Chance Elba.

So did the guards, who immediately drew their side-arms and held them pointed at the ceiling. The threat was not immediate, but it was clear.

Elba's smile only widened, and he showed no trace of fear. He nodded his head in greeting. "Galaxy Commander. Out for some exercise, I see."

It wasn't the first time Isis had seen Elba at the facility, but she was always surprised. He did not have the look of a man who ever exercised, except perhaps to lift a glass to his lips. For a labor leader, he was a surprisingly unphysical man. She casually took a step closer to him before speaking. "I was not aware your privileges down here had been restored."

"That unfortunate scuffle with Senator Lee was some time ago. The suspension of privileges was only for a month."

She asked dryly, "Is that all?"

Senator Elba chuckled. "I confess, I had it coming. I am a man of considerable passions when it comes to matters of importance. I can overreact at times."

She raised an eyebrow, and frowned at him. "Is that so?"

"Which is why I'm glad I ran into you this morning. I understand there was an unfortunate attempt on your person last night."

She suppressed an impulse to sneer. He asked as though it were some rumor to be confirmed, but she had little doubt that the details of the encounter were being discussed as fact all over the building. In such confines, something like this could hardly be kept secret. This assumed, of course, that he hadn't sent the assassin himself. "As I am sure you know, there was. Nothing came of it."

"Fortunately."

"There was nothing fortunate about it. The would-be assassin was little more than a child, and I assure you, Senator, I am a good deal more formidable than I appear. I could, just as an example, mind you, kill you right now, with my bare hands, in any number of ways, very quickly or"—she paused suggestively—"or very slowly."

He chuckled and shook his head sadly. "You misunderstand me, Galaxy Commander. We've had our differences, certainly, and while I'd like nothing better than for you and your Clan brethren to leave my planet and return it to the control of free Vegans, I wish you no personal harm. And I wish to assure you that I had absolutely nothing to do with this unfortunate incident."

She reflexively wrinkled her nose. "Even having lived in the Rasalhague Dominion all my life, I still find lawyers a curious and unpleasant means of settling disputes. But they have created some interesting and useful terminology. I believe they would call your statement a 'disclaimer,' a formal denial of responsibility having little or no basis in fact."

He tilted his head. "Is that an accusation, Galaxy Commander?"

"Not at all. I merely state that you would say the same thing regardless of your responsibility in the matter."

He grinned slightly. "In that you are probably correct. But I am *not* responsible. And much as I regret the incident, I hope some good may come of it. I hope that you may come away from it having learned something."

"And what would that be?"

"That there are many people on this planet who resent your presence here with every shred of their being. That they will resist your unlawful occupation to every last man, woman—and child. Nothing you can do will change that, and it is beyond anyone's ability to control, even mine. I'm in communication with these people every day, Galaxy Commander. I hear their concerns. They fear the Clans, fear the Ghost Bears and they want you off their world."

"And perhaps, in the course of these communications, you have suggested a few activities for them."

His brow furrowed, and his eyes narrowed with anger. "You don't understand us at all, and you never will. You may share your bed with a Vegan, but you will never know our hearts. And that—that is why you will fail!" He turned and stormed into the men's locker room.

Isis proceeded to the handball courts in a sour mood. As predicted, she found Conner Hall already waiting. She ducked through the low doorway and closed it behind her.

The Star colonel glanced at her, reacting to her angry expression. Rather than question her, however, he simply stepped back out of the way.

She pulled a black rubber ball from her pocket, bounced it once on the floor and slammed it viciously with the palm of her hand. It bounced off the far wall with a loud report and returned to her.

She slammed it again.

Slam. Report. Bounce. Slam. Report. Bounce. Over and over, until finally she let the ball fly past her to bounce off the rear wall, return almost to the front wall before bouncing off the floor, back and forth in a shrinking series of arcs. She watched it with grim fascination. She sighed. "I am not much in the mood for a game today."

"I heard about the assassin."

She bent down and scooped up the ball. Her right hand stung from repeated blows. She squeezed the ball, savoring the pain. It reminded her she was alive. "I have had a bad morning, Star Colonel. I suggest we get on with making it worse. Your report?"

He leaned his broad shoulders against the rear wall of the court and shrugged. "My warriors maintain a high state of alert, but lacking any clear objectives or identifiable targets, we are limited to responsive action against enemy attacks. In that, they are always one step ahead of us, the destruction of our barracks being the latest example. It is like fighting shadows."

"In other words," she said, "little has changed."

"We have sent a few more body bags off to the crematory, and my MechWarriors are sharing quarters with the Vegan warriors, but essentially, that is correct. I ask again that we recall the rest of our forces to Vega. We simply do not have the resources to secure one planet, much less three."

"Our orders are to secure key worlds in this prefecture, in order to begin restabilizing the Inner Sphere. That is 'worlds,' plural, not singular."

"I understand that, but we are still spread too thin. Without the HPG network, our off-world forces on Cebalrai are essentially on their own, and in turn cannot be counted on to back us up should the situation here turn hot."

"We have had this argument before."

"Not since the latest intelligence inventory."

She blinked in surprise. "What?"

"For some time I have had our civilian intelligence people going over records of the battle, interviewing survivors of battles that took place before we arrived, inspecting prewar arms inventories, as well as identifying and cataloging battle wreckage based on orbital surveys. The goal was to determine how many 'Mechs may have been on the planet, and how many were destroyed. As you can imagine, it has been a monumental task."

"I would think there is a great deal of room for error."

"There is, but they have made considerable progress in crossing destroyed and captured 'Mechs off the pre-war inventories. But it has been some time since they have been able to remove one from the list, and there are still units unaccounted for."

She frowned. "How many?"

"Thirteen. Thirteen that we know of."

"But there could be errors in the records, or misidentified wreckage. Perhaps they are dead on the bottom of a river or lake somewhere, or covered by a landslide."

He nodded grimly. "That is possible, but we have been very thorough, to the point of examining battlefields with ground-penetrating radar and sonar units. I think it's likely that some of these thirteen, if not all of them, are still out there."

"In the hands of insurgent forces?"

"Almost undoubtedly."

"Then why have they not used them? If they are out there, we should have seen them by now."

He shrugged again. "Perhaps they are undergoing repairs at some hidden location, or in need of ammunition before they can be brought into play."

"But you do not think that is the case."

"No. There has been ample time to make field repairs, and with all the wreckage scattered around there is no shortage of parts. Even ammunition would not be that hard to obtain. Our field teams found considerable evidence of scavenging. This survey, of course, only attempts to account for the largest and most important resource, the 'Mechs. We can't even begin to account for all the conventional armor, powered armor, light weapons, explosives and so on.

"What can we do to stop this loss of resources to the enemy?"

"Recall all our off-world forces, for a start. We do not have the manpower to even catalog all the potential war salvage out there, much less collect or secure it. In effect, we are arming our enemies through neglect. In some ways they may be as strong as the day you killed Jedra Kean, and we are far weaker."

She frowned and wiped her mouth with the back of her hand. "I cannot recall the off-world units. Our mandate in this mission was made quite clear to me when we won the bid. I do not have to tell you how tenuous the Raging Bears' status in the Clan is at the moment. This is our one chance for redemption."

He nodded grimly, but said nothing.

"Conner, I am trapped here, but I cannot see why you do not put in for transfer to another Galaxy. We may be hanging on the verge of Abjuration, but a MechWarrior with your codex and battle history would be welcomed by any commander in the Clan. I certainly could not justify standing in your way."

He looked at her. What was that in his eyes? He almost looked hurt at the suggestion.

"Galaxy Commander, I am loyal. I am loyal to you. I am loyal to the Raging Bears. I am loyal to my troops." He seemed to consider for a moment. "And I am loyal to this world. Despite the chaos and the infighting, I think there is something special here. Something worth fighting for."

She studied him. Something worth fighting for? What hold did this godforsaken world have on him?

6

From the Great Work of
Galaxy Commander Isis Bekker

With the unexpected and very public death of Jedra Kean, our opposition seemed to deflate like a pricked balloon. Though I and my forces had been wounded, and were now outgunned and surrounded, the enemy forces began to fall back. Those who stayed we were able to fend off until reinforcements arrived, our own troops and the local forces that would come to be known as the First Vega Regulars.

It was immediately obvious that, except for scattered pockets of resistance, the major fighting was over. The only enemy forces we saw were on the retreat, and chasing them around the mountains become a losing proposition. The opposing 'Mechs and units we pursued were not defeated so much as that they disappeared.

We concentrated on rounding up the surviving warlords and their most notorious associates, and in that we were more successful. Our paramilitary police arranged for two hundred and thirty-seven swift trials and public executions.

The era of the warlords was over.

My long nightmare had begun.

I was left with a hollow shell of a planet, a world no further from chaos than when we had arrived, and perhaps a little closer. It had no government, no police, no center. Only factions vying for control. And though the high-ranking warlords had been eliminated, for each of them there were still a hundred thugs waiting in the shadows, each with dreams of taking their fallen master's place. If we withdrew, it would be as though we had never come. We had to stay and find some way to rebuild the framework of civilization.

That task fell to me, and I felt ill qualified. I am a soldier and a commander, not a politician or a diplomat. But I did not shirk the task. I faced it as I faced every battle, by marshaling all the forces at my command and using them as effectively as my skills would allow.

I quickly realized that my warriors could not begin to achieve the task alone, that they would only be one leg of a tripod consisting of the military, the paramilitary police, and a growing force of civilian specialists and advisors. I located a suitably fortified building in which to form a new government, dug in and rolled up my sleeves.

It was not hard to find leaders within the various factions, bring them together and form an interim senate. But getting them to agree on anything beyond that became the most difficult battle of my career.

This, to me, was the bitter lesson of Vega, the horror that shook me to my very core. I had always believed that civilization was strong, that it would survive any trial and always rise up from the ruins. But now I knew differently.

Civilization is fragile, delicate, like a soap bubble. It seems solid enough, but, in an instant, it can be gone. And there I was, gathering up what few glittering droplets I could find in the mad hope that the bubble could be restored.

Hope, too, is like a bubble.

*Paramilitary Police Headquarters, East Central
   District*
Nasew, North Nanturo continent, Vega
24 November 3136

Field Security Chief Ricco walked through the hallways
of the bustling building that was his domain, past uni-
formed officers rushing to duty from their briefings, technicians hurrying to file intelligence or investigation reports,
and cuffed prisoners being dragged to interrogation
rooms. His forces now outnumbered the Clan military on
Vega three to one, and more police were arriving with
every new DropShip. Still his forces couldn't keep up.

Not only did they have to keep order on the streets
and gather intelligence about insurgents, they also had
to rebuild and train local police forces and keep tabs on
the growing Clan civilian population. It was an overwhelming, impossible task.

God, how he loved it. God, how he loved Vega. He
hoped they would never leave.

There had been a time he had cursed his life, when
he had failed his Trial of Position and his true destiny
as a warrior had been lost to him. He had later learned,
through his own investigation, that the simulator in
which he had taken the trial had been sabotaged by a
jealous rival. He applied to the Clan Council for another
trial, but was refused. Rather than being a warrior, he
had found himself relegated to the laborer caste.

The injustice of that day had scarred him. He felt less
than a man, less than Clan. He had neglected his training
and duties, fallen in with members of the Clan who expressed their discontent by associating with the criminal
elements of Policenigo, and very nearly had gone down
a much different road.

But it was this criminal contact that first brought him
into the sphere of the paramilitary police. When he
found he could not accept some of the activities of his
new friends, he went to the police and agreed to act as

a mole. He was instrumental in bringing down a major smuggling operation and, to his surprise, was offered a Ritual of Adoption, a second chance to join the warrior caste.

Even then he had faced another Trial of Position, this one with live firearms in a combat tailored to the paramilitary police specialty. He had been wounded, but he had prevailed against three of his opponents, gaining him the official rank of Star captain. After all that effort, he found it ironic that his rank was rarely used. He wore the insignia, but in the department officers were usually addressed by position rather than rank. Not only was it their custom, but it also reduced tensions in interactions with military warriors, who considered the paramilitary police inferior, even those officers of superior rank.

He quickly learned that many in the paramilitary police were like him, bitter outsiders, existing on the edge of the warrior caste. But here, in the brotherhood of the badge, they pulled each other back from the dark abyss and then joined to fight against it.

The day he first put on the uniform of a law officer had been, other than the day he took up his command on Vega, the finest day of his life.

Unlike the other warriors, the paramilitary police did not boast of being the Clan's best and brightest. They knew they existed on the edge of Clan society and would never truly be accepted as part of the warrior caste. But they served as the perimeter defense against what lay beyond. Uncelebrated and unappreciated, they knew it was they who kept the Clan together, kept Clan society in order, and held in check the dezgrate—Clansmen who behaved dishonorably, even criminally, but did not entirely violate the core Clan tenets.

If the warriors and Clan society as a whole held them in some degree of contempt, well—they did not need the recognition of the masses. Their brothers and sisters in the force knew what they did, and that was enough.

But the life of a paramilitary policeman in the Rasalhague Dominion had been far from ideal. Their jurisdiction overlapped with that of local civilian police forces charged with enforcing law on the non-Clan freeborns who formed the great majority of the population. The criminal activities of the dezgrate were often tangled with those of non-Clan criminals, and so jurisdictional battles were frequent. Often a Clan criminal who would otherwise have been swiftly executed or punished was instead held indefinitely as a witness in some civilian trial. On occasion, Clan members were even placed under the authority of the civilian courts, where justice was slow, and punishments maddeningly mild.

All that had changed on Vega.

The planet had been under martial law since their arrival, with no end in sight. Criminals and injustice were everywhere, but the only impediments to justice were time and manpower, and his resources increased by the day.

If ever a world had needed the firm hand of Clan justice, it was Vega, and Ricco was glad to provide it for them.

Moreover, he had found an unlikely ally in Galaxy Commander Isis Bekker. While Clan society, especially the military, tended to hold the paramilitary police in contempt, Bekker had always treated him and his officers with respect, and insisted her officers and troops do likewise. She had the vision to recognize the importance of the police to the rebuilding of Vega, and she had welcomed them into her fold.

He had been surprised to learn that she had personally investigated his Trial of Position, and agreed that he had been wronged. "You may not hold the place of honor in the warrior caste that you might have wished for," she told him, "but in your heart, you know your true worth, and I know it as well. I hope that counts for something."

Even more surprisingly, he realized that *did* count for something. For centuries, the paramilitary police had been, in his opinion, the backbone of Clan society. Only here and now were they finally getting the recognition they deserved.

He passed through the briefing room, stopping for a moment to scan the war board, where supervisors posted arrests, special assignments and tactical alerts.

The latest DropShip from the Rasalhague Dominion brought with it the usual rash of arrests for minor offenses. The civilian workers being sent here were outcasts and marginals, he knew; he'd once been considered marginal himself. His men came down hard on the newcomers, charging them on offenses to Clan law that outsiders would hardly have considered a crime. The large public jail that they'd inherited was generally filled to capacity and beyond, and the worst offenders were sent to Prigione, the hellish prison facility and former warlord stronghold located just south of Nasew. There was a two-week wait, even for a flogging.

But Ricco felt the importance of their mission to establish order. First among the Clansmen, then among the general population of Vega. By quickly showing the Clan newcomers that they couldn't get away with things here, he kept them in line, and by keeping them in line, they set a good example for the general population.

He exited the other door of the briefing room and crossed the hall into the intelligence office, perhaps the most vital part of his domain, perhaps even more important than the dispatch center. As he walked in he could see a dozen officers at work monitoring security cameras, reviewing intelligence reports, watching recorded interviews with informants. The security officer on duty, Watch Captain "Flash" Teho, stood next to a desk in the corner, arms crossed over his chest, watching the men and women work. He looked up as Ricco entered and nodded a greeting.

"What's the latest, Flash?" The use of "watchnames," nicknames awarded by other officers, was a recent development in his force. It was a common practice among non-Clan police organizations, but the Clan taboo against taking unofficial names had kept this informal custom out of the paramilitary police.

Even now, it was of critical importance to avoid using a watchname in front of a nondepartment warrior. They were proud of their Bloodnames, and justifiably defensive of anything that might be seen as diluting the importance of those names. Ricco himself believed that the labnames, awarded to themselves by the scientist caste and now openly used by some members, were an insult to all warriors.

But watchnames were different. Rather than being used as a formal surname, as in Bloodnames or labnames, they were casual alternatives to given names, given by fellow officers in recognition of basic competence and as a sign of acceptance.

Not all watchnames were respectful, and they were subject to change. The watchname given to an officer often said a great deal about the officer's competence and the areas in which he or she could improve.

As the man in charge, Ricco didn't have a watchname. That too was a sign of respect. Before his promotion, he had been known as Slab.

Teho picked up a noteputer from the desk and began to page through the reports. "We are following up on reports of an insurgent safe house in the northwest sector, just outside the beltway. Surveillance has been assigned, and we've got people on the street working contacts."

He scrolled down. "We located an insurgent weapons cache in a shuttered flower shop on the north end of the commercial district: sidearms, grenades, a mortar. Small stuff, except that we are sure the mortar came from offworld, possibly courtesy of our friends in the Draconis Combine. I cannot prove it, but the signs are there. The owner of the building has been arrested and interrogated. He is a known associate of the Labor Party but, to be honest, I do not think he knew the weapons were there. We will give him a few more hours in the sweat-box, just in case."

Several more taps of the stylus. "Sixteen more reports of Freeminder graffiti appearing in the last twenty-four hours. They've been logged and requests turned over to the removal team, but the clean-up teams are now up to a six-month backlog. We've also identified two potential Freeminder meeting locations, if you want to set up raids."

Teho looked up and made eye contact with Ricco, who considered for a moment before answering. "I don't think so, Watch Commander. I don't see them as an immediate threat. If anything, the meetings will serve as gathering points for troublemakers, so we can round them up all at once when we are ready. File these as they come in, and push them down the priority list other-wise. The insurgents and their puppet masters are our immediate threat."

Teho looked less than delighted with that pronounce-ment, but didn't protest. He knew as well as anyone how thin their resources were spread. "We have the usual crime reports, updates from the police militia training camps—all positive by the way—and one oddity that you should see." He looked around. "Step into my office, and I'll show you."

They stepped into Teho's small, glass-walled office in-side the intelligence center. Teho closed the blinds over the glass, then stepped to the concrete rear wall where an ugly painting of a horse hung, obviously left by the person who occupied the office before the arrival of the Clans. Teho swung the painting back on hidden hinges, revealing a wall safe with a digital lock. "It took me months to guess the correct code, but now that I have it, the safe has proved quite useful."

"So what *was* in the safe?"

Teho chuckled. "Naked pictures. Can you imagine it? That somebody would bother to lock naked pictures in a safe?"

Ricco grinned. "Our ways are not the ways of everyone. It's good to be reminded of that sometimes."

Teho punched in the code, opened the safe and removed a clean but ragged piece of cloth wrapped into a palm-sized bundle, perhaps a scrub rag borrowed from some janitor. He laid the bundle on his open hand and unfolded it carefully. Whatever the rag had been hiding glittered under the office lights. Teho turned and held out the object for Ricco to examine.

It was the shape, and perhaps half the size, of an ident card, though thicker. One edge appeared to have been chopped off cleanly in some kind of shear, so Ricco assumed he was looking at only half of a larger, oblong piece of metal. He gingerly reached over and lifted it, feeling the cool heft of it in his hand. "Heavy," he said, looking at Teho. "Is it . . . ?"

"Gold? Yes, it is. Solid, very pure, about fifty grams. We took it from a black marketeer we picked up near the spaceport this morning. There is a thriving black market in precious metals and gems, so it wasn't the gold itself that was so unusual, it was the shape and markings."

Embossed in the top of the ingot was a word that read "3ANNSON." The *3*, however, overlapped the cut mark, and he assumed it was actually a *B*. He looked up at Teho. "Bannson? As in Jacob Bannson? Bannson Universal? Bannson's Raiders?"

"That would be my assumption. There are plenty of people named Bannson, but few rich enough to pass around gold ingots with their name stamped on top."

"Is he operating in this region of the Inner Sphere?"

"Not that we're aware of. Our latest intelligence reports show him in league with House Liao. But those same reports indicate the relationship has soured. Bannson may be looking for a new base of operations."

"Or new allies." He handed the ingot back to Teho, who returned it to the safe. "Or perhaps this is only a chance occurrence. The piece could have arrived from off-world by any number of means—smugglers, Draconis Combine agents, or even with a Clansman, by way of the Dark Caste. It may be a coincidence that it has shown up here, but keep your eyes open for any indications of Bannson activity, and let me know immediately if you find any."

"Will you tell the Galaxy commander about this?"

He considered for a moment. "The Galaxy commander has a lot on her plate right now. We should keep this in the department until we have something solid to hand over to the military."

Ricco left the office, exited through the intelligence center and strolled down the stairs to the squad room to continue his morning rounds. He couldn't get Bannson's name out of his mind.

Bannson was a medium-sized fish in a big pond; a rich industrialist, but also a thug. If he had been Clan, he most certainly would have been Dark Caste. Clan Ghost Bear would never consider him a useful ally. But Ricco was no fool, and he could see the fractures in Clan society all around him. There might be subsets of the Ghost Bears who would see Jacob Bannson as a very useful ally indeed.

Conner Hall strolled down the corridors of the clean, modern Clan hospital located near the center of the base. Looking around at the many wounded warriors being treated, he was suddenly glad that the bombers had chosen the barracks as their target rather than here. The casualties would have been far higher, and logistically, barracks were vastly easier to replace than the hospital, a cluster of memory-metal modular buildings that had been brought with them from the Rasalhague Dominion. He made a mental note to look into security precautions, and see if there was any way they could be improved without interfering with the hospital's operation.

Following instructions given to him by a nurse at the

entrance, he turned left at the next juncture and into a ward. He walked down the row of beds until he found Jorgen. The young warrior was a sad sight, flat on his back, his body in heavy traction, his head and neck immobilized in some contraption that looked like an ancient torture device. He seemed to be able to move his arms a little, but that was all.

Various tubes and bags were attached to his body by snakes of plastic tubing, and neatly bundled wires ran from under his sheets to an electronic device that Conner recognized as a Clan-designed bone growth stimulator.

Jorgen smiled weakly as he recognized Conner standing over him. "Star Colonel! You honor me!"

He nodded in greeting. "It is nothing special, warrior. I visit all of my people wounded in honorable battle."

Jorgen's smile faded. "There was not much honor in it, Star Colonel. I fell in a hole, damaged my 'Mech, and nearly killed myself before the shooting started. It was a poor showing."

Conner grinned at him. "There will be better days, better battles and better wounds, I assure you."

"It could be worse." He paused and took a deep breath. "I heard about the barracks." He swallowed. "That is no way for a warrior to die."

Conner nodded in agreement. "It is not our place as warriors to choose how we die. It is our place only to choose how we live. They were good warriors. They fought well. They lived well."

"That is not what their codex will say."

He had no answer to that, and there was a long silence between them.

Finally, Jorgen spoke. "What is really hard for me though, is waiting. They tell me it will be a long time before I am allowed in a 'Mech again."

"I cannot argue with you on that. I hate hospitals. I hate medical leave. Warriors are born to fight, not sit around—or lie around—in a place like this. But though it will seem to take forever, it will be over soon enough, and they tell me you will return to full combat readiness. I have confidence in the doctors, and in you."

He walked over and patted the bone stimulator, a pedestal-mounted plastic box covered with dials, numeric displays and plugs for electrodes. "These things, for instance, work great. The first time I had one used on me was my Trial of Position to Star commander. I made my rank, but ended up with my jaw broken in six places. Even with the help of this machine, I walked around for weeks with my jaw wired shut. I kept telling people"— he shifted to speaking through clenched teeth—"'you should see the other guy.'"

Jorgen laughed, which was the intent, but his expression quickly turned dark again. "You know, Star Colonel, that is part of the problem. I never did see the other guy. I heard from the nurses that you got them?"

"Dead center, while the cowards were trying to run away."

Jorgen pursed his lips thoughtfully. "That is good then, I suppose. I hear some of the FVR MechWarriors were here too, but they had been released by the time I was conscious."

Conner chuckled. "Too bad, in a way. Misery loves company. But they made a good accounting of themselves. I often wonder how they would do given real BattleMechs."

"What about Huntsig, sir? How did he do?"

Conner considered a moment. "He is a seasoned warrior. He handled himself professionally. I would expect no less of him. I will expect no less of you when the time comes."

Jorgen's eyes looked away, and Conner could see sudden anger there. "It should have been him, sir."

"Excuse me?"

"It should have been him in that pit. You ordered him to the tail-cap position, and he refused, so you sent me instead." His jaw clenched. "I don't think he's a good Clan warrior."

Conner noted Jorgen's sudden lapse into contractions, and took it as a sign of the depth of his anger. "Why do you say that?"

"He—he talks about you, sir. In the barracks. I mean, when there was a barracks. He spoke of you with disrespect, and challenged your authority. He said he would have your position one day."

"That is his right, if he thinks himself a better leader than I or thinks me incompetent, to challenge me to a trial. That would be his duty. It is the Clan way."

"But you are better than him."

Conner grinned. "This is true, and that is why I would defeat him in any such trial."

"Then why should you waste your time fighting him at all?"

Conner's grin turned into a concerned frown. "Jorgen, you have the potential to be a fine warrior one day. Why are you asking these questions? You sound like—" He looked around to see if anyone nearby was listening, then lowered his voice. "—like a Freeminder."

"I am sorry, sir. It must be the painkillers. I told them not to give me any, that I did not want to be doped up, but they would not listen." He wrinkled his nose. "Still, it should have been him."

As he walked out of the hospital, Conner considered the warrior's words, and concluded that Jorgen was right. It should have been Huntsig. The man had good skills as a warrior, but he lacked the mind or the instincts of a leader. The shame of it was, those skills would probably eventually lead him to a promotion for which he really wasn't suited.

Then it would be the men and women who were unlucky enough to serve under him, people like Jorgen, who would be the ones to suffer.

Driving back to the FVR barracks, he passed along the

back side of a rarely used repair hangar. Something caught his eye, and he rolled the utility cart to a halt on the empty road, looking at the weathered wall of the hanger. "Even here on the base," he said to nobody. He was looking at more Freeminder graffiti. First, in red, was the familiar, "Think the unthinkable." Then, next to that in green paint, were the words, "Obey the Final Codex."

The Final Codex? He'd heard rumors of such a document, a mythical lost writing of Nicholas Kerensky that supposedly described his final plan for the Clans, their ultimate purpose in restoring the Inner Sphere.

Or something.

He'd heard several different versions of the myth, most of them during his childhood in the sibko. He'd never given them any weight. Some of the myths were mystical and vague. Some bemoaned the loss of the one document that would show them their true purpose. Some actually included details of that secret purpose. One especially fanciful one he'd heard suggested that they were to seek out the descendents of Star League founder Ian Cameron, collect their genetic material and, using advanced Clan molecular biology, literally recreate the man gene by gene. It was all perfect nonsense.

Or something.

He wondered if the Freeminders were so deluded that they believed in children's stories. Or did they really know something that the rest of the Clan didn't? How was one supposed to obey the Final Codex if it didn't exist, if it couldn't be read?

He restarted the car, and drove on. He'd alert maintenance when he reached the barracks and have them clean up the graffiti. But as he drove he mused, how could he *not* think the unthinkable?

The unthinkable was all around him.

7

*From the Great Work of
Galaxy Commander Isis Bekker*

It is said of the Ghost Bear Clan that we change slowly, and this is true. But slow change is still change, and a journey of a thousand kilometers still is made up of single steps. The Clans have had over three hundred years to evolve and change. Despite our devotion to tradition and doctrine, we have changed. Changed greatly.

Single steps.

The first step was when the Great Father Aleksandr Kerensky led the Star League Defense Force on its exodus from the Inner Sphere to the Pentagon worlds, fleeing the crumbling Star League. Certainly, he would not have imagined how far we would come. His writings suggest he expected a rapid return to the Inner Sphere to restore the Star League, perhaps even within his lifetime. That was not to be.

The next step came when Aleksandr's dream crumbled, the Pentagon worlds fell into chaos, and it fell to his son, Founder Nicholas Kerensky, to lead yet another exodus, this time to fabled Strana Mechty, in the Kerensky Cluster.

There, he built a new society from the ashes of the old, a society forged in hardship and strife, built on the principle that promotion and position must always be made on the basis of ability and merit. Nothing else, and nothing more. It was this new society that became the Clans.

The step that followed came when the Clans returned to liberate the Pentagon worlds from chaos and unify the children of the first exodus under Clan rule. The process that followed was long and complex, as the Clans struggled to define their new purpose. Ultimately, that step led to a failed invasion of the Inner Sphere. The Clans were driven back but not humbled, and gained some holdings in the Inner Sphere.

The next step would belong to Clan Ghost Bear alone. With great secrecy and stealth, the Clan built great ark transport ships, and moved its entire population to the Inner Sphere, to rule over the worlds conquered from the Free Rasalhague Republic and the Draconis Combine. They named their holdings, melded under Ghost Bear rule, the Rasalhague Dominion, then began a series of smaller steps that would continue for generations.

At first, the Clan tried to force their ways on the people of their occupation zone, but these efforts went badly, and eventually were abandoned. The Ghost Bears decided instead to hold themselves separate from and above the society of native freeborns. Most Clansmen, especially those of the warrior and scientist castes, lived in Clan enclaves, relatively isolated from the freeborn societies around them.

But the walls they built were imaginary, and those of the lower castes often crossed them. As many in the laborer caste lived outside the enclaves as within. Freeborn practices crept into Clan life. The use of contractions became more common, even accepted in some lower-caste circles. Even among the warrior caste, Clan slang fell out of use. This was especially true of the Raging Bears, who worked closely with spheroids and found it necessary to adapt their communication style.

Still, vulgar language was the least of the transgressions that became increasingly common. Though the practice was repugnant to Clan purists and was severely punished when discovered, some in the lower castes secretly intermarried with native freeborn, even to the point of maintaining homes and families separate from their genetically matched Clan marriages.

Some said we Ghost Bears were losing our identity as a Clan. As more Clansman embraced change, forces aligned in response to forcefully crush it. It was in this jostling between the forces of unbridled reform and rigid oppression that the first Freeminders were born. They advocated a freedom of thought and change that most Clansmen considered wrong and found frightening. Three times the Freeminders rose up as a secret force for change. Three times they were swept away by hard-line Clan traditionalists.

When for decades they did not return, it seemed that the days of the Freeminders were done. But change was not. Despite all efforts to the contrary, Ghost Bear society could not survive unchanged in such close proximity to the much different society of the native freeborn.

As time passed, larger divisions appeared in every stratum of Ghost Bear society. Something had to change, or civil unrest, even civil war, would be the result.

How did so many Clan misfits and malcontents become attached to my beloved Omega Galaxy, the Raging Bears? That began long before my time, when the newly formed Raging Bears took a step of their own. As with the first exodus, it was a step whose ultimate outcome could not have been foreseen or imagined.

The Galaxy was created because, as ever, the Clans found themselves in conflict with forces of the Inner Sphere, forces who did not follow Clan traditions and rituals or practice honorable combat—traditions and rituals and practices that sometimes put Clan forces at a disadvantage. From their inception, the Raging Bears were schooled in the tactics of the Inner Sphere, including massed fire, deception and tactical retreat.

From the beginning they were outcasts in some circles, considered to be a necessary evil for the survival of the Clan, but also a group to be shunned. Though The Raging Bears have maintained a proud tradition of upholding the spirit, if not the letter, of Clan values, our stock has risen and fallen over the years. It was shortly after I assumed command that a new Khan, a rigid traditionalist, was elected, and that stock fell as drastically as it ever had.

I will not bore you with the political details. Let it simply be said that almost overnight, the Raging Bears had fallen so far from favor that we found ourselves in danger of dissolution, even Abjuration. My loyal allies in the Clan Council could only do so much to support us, and the situation was deteriorating.

Then another step was made for us, the controversial decision to send three Galaxies to occupy and stabilize selected planets in the Inner Sphere. From the beginning, many on the Council described it as a misadventure, and few commanders were even willing to bid seriously on the mission.

But that is the one step of this long road that I took myself. I bid the Raging Bears on this fool's mission because it would remove us from the sight of our enemies and perhaps give us one last chance to prove our honor, our skill as warriors and our loyalty to the Clan. It was a desperate decision, and one without immediate rewards.

The new power bloc in the Council used this as an opportunity to drive out the elements in our evolving society that they found offensive. Suddenly, we were attached to a movement that we were not part of, and of which most of us did not approve.

Still, I was determined to make the best of it, to achieve our difficult task and restore honor to our Galaxy.

It was barely a week after the major fighting stopped on Vega that the first Freeminder graffiti began to appear.

How could I have know the consequences of my one, small step?

How could Nicholas Kerensky have known, so long ago?

And yet there are those who believe that he did, that everything that has happened since, all the trials, divisions, wars, victories and defeats: they are all part of some greater plan, part of the true purpose of the Clans.

Even in my most respectful and charitable thoughts of the Founder, I find this difficult to imagine.

But this is a basic premise of the Freeminders, that a lost writing of Nicholas Kerensky known as the Final Codex exists, and that it somehow supports Freeminder doctrine and desires. They believe that long-lost, perhaps suppressed, work offers us our final deliverance, the revelation of our true purpose and destiny.

It seems unlikely. Incredible.

I do not believe.

Yet, I cannot bring myself to entirely dismiss it.

We have wandered far from the point where we began. But a journey of a thousand kilometers can still form a circle, and the beginning and the end can still be one.

Krottenwik residential district
Nasew, North Nanturo continent, Vega
25 November 3136

Taylor Bane reflected, as they ("they" being Bruno Vic, their guide Geoff Krago and he) moved on foot deeper into the ghetto called Krottenwik, that it was like walking back in time. On the periphery, apartment buildings still stood, and despite visible damage from blast and fire, provided homes for struggling families. But as they moved on, the buildings became hollow shells, half-crumbled walls without roofs, window openings looking down at them like empty eye sockets.

Amid these ruins, people lived in homemade tents and makeshift shacks constructed of castoff and salvaged building materials. The imaginative roof of one hut, from which a gaggle of dirty children watched them pass with wide eyes, was constructed entirely of road signs, the metal and plastic sheets overlapping like large, colorful shingles. Bane was bemused by the number of animals obviously brought in from the countryside; chickens and domesticated emus picking through garbage heaps, feral cats stalking the mice that were everywhere, and horses, which took the places of trucks and tractors. Some resourceful souls grew sickly looking vegetables in garbage-can planters, and vendors sold clear plastic bags of murky-looking drinking water on what once had been street corners.

Beyond this, the situation became even more grim. Here even the walls had fallen into heaps of broken rubble. There were few buildings here, or even tents, and people lived huddled under tarps or sheets of tattered cardboard. The people themselves were huddled piles of refuse, strewn across a scrap heap of humanity.

At one point they passed a bonfire, and it was a moment before Bane realized that it was a funeral pyre. No mourners stood to mark the passing of the dead, and black smoke curled up towards the heavens unheralded by song, prayer or a single tear.

They'd left the car a kilometer back, parked on a barely passable street under the watchful eye of a shopkeeper Krago trusted. The bribe required to ensure its safety had been relatively modest. Bane had spent more for valet parking at a downtown hotel on other planets.

Bane felt incredibly conspicuous walking through Krottenwik, and he felt confident that was the case. He'd dressed down for the day's meeting, wearing a plain, cheap suit that he kept for such occasions and carefully divesting himself of his ordinary, modest jewelry. But he was walking among people dressed in rags.

Everywhere they went, he could see people watching him, feel their eyes as they examined him from the shadows. Some watched with the intense interest of predators, some with curiosity and a few with fear. They rounded the crumbled corner of a building and nearly ran headlong into a cluster of children playing a game that involved a battered can and sticks.

The children screamed and ran to cower behind a large, red-haired man who wore a look of authority. The man calmly stood his ground, making no threatening move, but his silent message was clear: "Don't touch the children, or face my wrath."

Bane raised an open hand of truce, nodded and led the others on a wide circle around the man before continuing on their way.

Once they were thirty meters or so away, Bane glanced back. The children burst into motion and continued on their collective way, like a school of tetras in a fish tank. The big man just stood, watching them, thick arms crossed over his chest.

Taylor Bane thought of himself as a hard man, but he had a soft spot for young children. He didn't think any child should have to live like this. He wanted to figure out who was responsible, and start breaking heads.

Krago looked nervous. "I wish you would reconsider this, Mister Bane. I cannot guarantee our safety here. These are dangerous people you are meeting with."

Bruno cracked his knuckles. "*We're* dangerous people, too."

"It's not," said Bane, "like we're going to rob these guys, or take them down. We're here to make introductions. We're here to do business."

Krago shook his head. "One does not do business with a rabid dog."

Bruno looked around skeptically. "A rabid dog would probably have better digs than this. If this guy we're going to see is so powerful, why is he living under a blanket in a pile of rubble?"

Krago sighed. "Because it is a very good place to hide, and because he is a very wanted man. In any case, he is not precisely living under a blanket." Krago veered off the street and into the ruined foundation of a building. The ragged stumps of a few walls remained standing in the otherwise blasted area. As they walked closer, a pair of men appeared from behind the walls, assault rifles trained on them.

As the party raised its hands, another pair of men with rifles appeared behind them. Bane never saw where they came from. Whatever their hiding places had been, they were well camouflaged.

"Please," said Krago, his hands held high over his head. "These gentlemen have come to see Gustavo. We are expected!"

One of the men in front of them, who appeared to be in charge, nodded to the men behind, who stepped up and patted them down. They removed two handguns and two knives from Bane's clothing.

From Bruno they retrieved five guns, two knives, a dagger, a blackjack, four throwing stars, a taser and an especially large pair of nail clippers. Even so, Bane knew for a fact they had missed another small dagger, two more throwing stars, a straight razor and a small canister of tear gas.

Bane was surprised to discover that Krago was unarmed. Bane had half expected the man to double-cross them at some point during this expedition, perhaps pull a gun and try to take all their gold, as though they wouldn't have it safely hidden somewhere that he would never find it. Evidently he was a more honorable man than Bane expected.

That, or he simply couldn't afford a gun.

They were led around the ragged walls and into a

narrow space between two parallel sheets of masonry. There they found a narrow stairway leading beneath the rubble. One of the guards went first, turning and waiting for them at the bottom, gun at the ready.

Bruno, Krago and Bane were directed down next. Two more guards followed them, with the final guard remaining at the top. At the bottom of the stairs they followed the first guard into a dark, narrow tunnel that sloped downward. Bane estimated they had traveled twenty feet or so when the tunnel began to brighten. They turned a corner and passed through a doorway into a much larger chamber.

Bane was surprised to see that the room, probably part of the basement from the collapsed building, had electric light. Possibly buried power lines had survived the destruction of the neighborhood above, or perhaps there was a well-muffled generator hidden somewhere nearby, or possibly the whole thing ran off batteries.

In any case, this simple amenity in these tortured surroundings suggested somebody with considerable resources at his disposal.

The room was dry and clean, suggesting the building had been new at the time of its destruction. The walls were stark concrete, but the space was well furnished, with thick carpets unrolled on the cold floor and expensive, if not tasteful, furniture.

Two more men with guns stood on either side of a large, overstuffed chair with matching leather ottoman. The chair didn't look much like a throne, but Bane understood that was its intended function.

The man in the chair didn't look much like a warlord, either. To Bane he just looked like a thug. He guessed the man's age at thirty, though the effects of hard living might put that number closer to twenty. His face was narrow and angular, his dark brown hair long and stringy, his beard trimmed short, but not neatly. His wiry arms were covered with vulgar tattoos that started somewhere inside his black tank tee shirt and continued across his hands. He wore green work pants and a worn pair of high-top boots. He sprawled across the chair at an angle, one skinny leg draped over the chair's arm.

The man was watching a scratchy transmission of a soccer match on a small tri-vid screen, an incongruous jewel-handled cane dangling from his fingers. He looked up, and used the head of the cane to click off the tri-vid's power switch.

Bane stopped a few yards short of the man's chair, at the precise moment when the guards on either side started to stiffen and raise their assault rifles. "Am I addressing Mr. Gustavo?"

The man pushed himself up out of his slouch and sniffed. "They call me *Warlord* Gustavo, or they don't call me at all."

"I was under the impression that the Ghost Bears had rounded up all the warlords and executed them."

"Well, see, those were the old warlords. One of them was my brother."

"That's supposed to impress me?"

"It should. What was his is now mine."

Bane looked around. "He left you this basement? Wow."

"You have brass, for one of two guys in bad suits. I have to keep a low profile, obviously, but with the old warlords gone, the pie that's left is cut in pretty big pieces. I've got my fingers in everything in this city."

"Is that so?"

"It is. You want to play, you've got to play with me."

"Well, there's an old saying back on Northwind, where I come from."

"What's that?"

"A man who has his fingers in everything, ought to wash his hands."

Gustavo's eyes narrowed. "Is that supposed to be a joke?"

"Do you know who *I* work for, Warlord Gustavo?"

Gustavo fished in his pants pocket, pulling out one of

the little gold ingots. "Jacob Bannson." He chuckled. "Now, my man, am *I* supposed to be impressed?"

"Frankly, yes."

He laughed. "Well, let me tell you, Bannson is a long way away from here, and as far as I'm concerned, you're just two guys in bad suits."

"We put on the bad suits special, just to meet you."

Gustavo stared at him.

"No, seriously. We're slumming here, and its obvious we didn't slum far enough." He jerked his thumb toward the ceiling. "Bad neighborhood you're in."

Gustavo chuckled. "See, in the good old days, the neighborhood upstairs was in my brother's territory. They gave him trouble, so he sent me to give them trouble back. Now, they know better than to mess with a Gustavo. I say jump, they're a meter off the ground before they can ask 'how high?' "

Bane tilted his head. "I see. Well, *Mister* Gustavo, are we going to talk business here today?"

Gustavo chuckled again. "Well, like I said, Jacob Bannson is a long way from here, and I just can't see what kind of business I would have to discuss with him. You, on the other hand, are right here, and word is you've been passing these"—he held up the ingot— "around pretty freely. So the business I'd like to discuss is, where are the rest of them, and can you tell me before my boys start cutting you up too bad?" The guard closest to Bane shouldered his rifle and pulled out a nasty-looking switchblade knife, which he snapped open and held in front of Bane's face.

Bane glanced at Bruno, who was standing with a gun muzzle held inches from his side. "I'll give you your answer, if you'll give me one simple answer first. Are there any more Gustavos waiting in the wings?"

He shrugged. "Just me."

Bane casually touched the cheap cuff link on his left wrist. "Good," he said, snapping his head to one side, grabbing the guard's forearm, striking the inside of the wrist with his other hand and slipping the knife into his own hand. He continued his momentum, spinning the man around, twisting his arm back to control him, putting the knife to his throat and using him as a shield.

It was at this kind of moment, Bane considered grimly, that you have to wonder, just how well do your opponents like each other? With the weapons they carried, the guards could shoot through two bodies as easily as one. He hoped they liked his prisoner well enough to hesitate for maybe two seconds, because Bruno was already in motion.

The big man had reached back and casually deflected the gun barrel away from his side. The guard holding the gun fired off a burst, which hit the third guard, who had had his gun trained on Krago, in the knee. The guard dropped to the floor screaming, and Krago dropped to join him, cowering in fear.

Bruno stepped backward towards his guard, planting himself on the man's foot to hold him in place, then sent his elbow deep into the man's solar plexus.

The fourth guard appeared at the entrance to the room. Bane drew the knife across his prisoner's throat and pushed him forward, snatching the rifle away from him as he fell. By the time the fourth guard had a clean shot, Bane had the gun in firing position, and strafed a burst of bullets across his position without aiming.

Out of the corner of his eye, Bane saw Gustavo pull a large automatic pistol from under the cushion of his chair. Bruno put a burst of bullets into his chest and stomach.

Bane heard a movement behind him, and spun to see two more men brandishing rifles enter from the far side of the room.

They didn't see Bruno standing to their left, or the guard doubled over in pain at his feet.

Bane rushed behind Gustavo's throne as bullets bounced off the concrete behind him, and he felt the stinging impact on his arm of what he hoped were splinters of concrete.

Bruno made a noise and jumped back. The newcomers fired at the noise, instead striking the man doubled over on the floor. Bruno returned fire, and one of the men flew back.

Bane popped up from behind the chair and strafed another burst across the remaining man, before taking more careful aim at his chest.

The man whose throat he'd slit gurgled and thrashed around on the floor. Bruno quickly put a mercy bullet in his skull. *Thoughtful of him.*

The room was quiet. They listened carefully for other attackers, but there was nothing. Bane sniffed. "Guess the warlord's private army isn't what it used to be. Wonder if he mentioned that to the people upstairs?" He looked at his arm, inspecting the ripped sleeve and the spatters of blood, none of it his.

Bruno looked at him with concern. "You good?"

"Ruined a perfectly cheap suit."

Krago looked up from the floor, his eyes wide at the carnage around him.

"I told you," said Bane. "We're dangerous men."

They gathered up the half-dozen automatic rifles and Gustavo's expensive pistol, plus all their own weapons and climbed the steps. Most of the rifles were slung over Bruno's broad back, but Bane carried one. Krago had refused any weapon.

As they emerged, they found a crowd of curious bystanders watching from behind piles of rubble and the few ruined bits of wall still standing. Bane saw the children he'd scared earlier. He also saw the red-haired man whom the children trusted as their guardian. Bane lowered his weapon, and he and Bruno walked up to the man.

He nodded to Bruno, and he divested himself of his excess weaponry, handing the guns over to Big Red. "I guess you're in charge now," Bane said. He removed his jacket and pulled out the removable shoulder pads, peeled open the hook-and-loop closures, and removed three gold ingots from each. He put them into a stack, handed them to Bruno, reassembled the jacket, and put it back on.

He recovered the gold from Bruno and passed it to Big Red. "I want you to buy food and hand it out to the children. Eat some yourself if you want, but the gold, all of it, is for them. Understand?"

Big Red's hard face slowly spread into a grin. He nodded.

Bane looked around at the crowd. "Mr. Bannson would appreciate it if you would remember today's generosity. He may be around this way someday."

Bruno and Bane returned their own weapons to their proper places, and with Krago stumbling along after them, they began the hike back to the car.

"Well, Bruno," said Bane after they'd walked awhile, "we came to talk to the people in charge. Looks like we haven't found them yet."

Isis Bekker looked at the thick pamphlet sitting on her desk as though it were a venomous serpent. She looked up at Vincent Florala. "Where did you get this?"

He turned away from the simulated window, where he had been studying the financial district to their north and the buildings rising there with frustrating slowness. "One of my intelligence people got it from a small printing shop near the old capital in Neucason. We were looking for insurgents and found this instead."

"Then these were not distributed?"

"I didn't say that. This was a proof of some kind, found laying on an art table. The woman operating the shop freely admitted that five thousand of them were printed and picked up two weeks ago, presumably by your Freeminder friends. She had no loyalty to them, and as far as we can tell, no reason to lie."

He must have seen the look on her face at his use of the word "Freeminder." He nodded. "I've played dumb on the subject in the past, Isis, so as not to make you uncomfortable, but we've been looking into the movement for some time now, and I've kept my briefings current. Frankly, many. of my people are sympathetic to their cause, and I think support is even stronger in the Labor Party. They see themselves and your laborer caste as kindred spirits, both oppressed by the tyranny of the Ghost Bear warrior caste."

Those last two sentences were nonsense and she nearly said so, but it wasn't Vince that she needed to argue the point with. He surely knew better.

She once again reassessed the man who stood before her. He made it so easy to underestimate him. He successfully projected an image of a pleasant and congenial man, fiercely devoted to his people and his causes. Articulate, but far from brilliant.

That, she knew from experience, was a mask that hid a good mind, a resourceful nature and a streak of ruthlessness that could come into play when the stakes were high. *He is much like a bear himself: soft and furry to the touch, but one must never forget that he has teeth and claws.*

She had to wonder, too, at his comment about withholding his knowledge of the Freeminders so as not to "make her uncomfortable." She had to remember that he was not Clan, and that his statement, even coming from someone she trusted as much as he, could not be taken at face value.

Polite deception, even between lovers, seemed to be the norm among the people of the Inner Sphere. And as closely as they worked together, and as much as they agreed on, Vince had his own agenda, and his agenda was not her agenda, nor that of her Clan.

Her attention returned to the pamphlet. She reached out and touched the cover. It was printed on heavy, slick paper, the background designed to make it look like the cover of a leather-bound book. Gold letters in the center of the cover read, "The Lost Words of the Founder." And below that, "Know the truth of Nicholas Kerensky's Final Codex, and the lost destiny of the Clans."

She picked it up and opened it. Her eye was drawn to scaled-down reproductions of a series of ancient-looking pages, curled and blackened around the edges as though they'd been snatched out of a fire. Her gaze returned to the introductory text at the top of the first page, and she began to read.

> *The fragmentary pages pictured here come from one of the few existing copies of the Final Codex, written by our founder Nicholas Kerensky. Though these authenticated pages are not dated, they were most likely written between 2822, when the last rebel forces in the Pentagon worlds were quelled, and Nicholas' death at the hands of Clan Widowmaker. These documents state that it was the Founder's intention that the document be kept secret until 3019, the two hundredth anniversary of the Clan eugenics program, and that it then be released to all the people of the Clans, so that they could know and embrace their true destiny.*
>
> *Why did this not happen? It is possible that the Final Codex, which was to be placed in the archives of each Clan for safekeeping, was lost during the struggle with the Not-named Clan before it could be distributed. But we, the Freeminders, who have had the courage to study these instructions, believe that the document was distributed. We have evidence that it was suppressed from release by a conspiracy of the Khans in power at that time, and that this conspiracy continues to this day!*
>
> *Know the truth! All of Clan history since 3019*

*has been a mistake, a blight on the memory
of our honored Founder, and a denial of the glorious destiny that he set forth for the Clans!*

*Read for yourself and learn! The Final Codex
tells us that, in our Founder's name, the eugenics program must end, and the caste system
must be dissolved. The day of our glorious
reunification with the Inner Sphere is more than
a century overdue. Yet even without this critical guidance from the Founder, Clan Ghost Bear
has returned to the Inner Sphere and stands
poised to fulfill this destiny. We can lead the way,
and set an example for all the Clans.*

*We are, flesh and bone, the Founder's gift to
the future. It is time to deliver this gift to the
Inner Sphere. Only through this gift can the long-
lost legacy of the Star League be restored.*

Isis Bekker looked up at Florala. "This is nonsense.
A complete fabrication. Obviously, this document is a
clever forgery designed to fool the weak-minded of the
lower castes."

Florala looked at her with a raised eyebrow. "Is it?
Why are you so sure?"

She frowned at him. "If you have studied the Freeminder movement at all, then you should be able to see
how this document is nothing more than wish fulfillment
for them. They are mostly a collection lower-caste malcontents, grown soft during our time living in the Inner
Sphere. They romanticize the lives of the native freeborns and wish to become part of that culture. They
wish to see themselves as equals of the higher castes,
even warriors. They wish to freely intermarry with the
native freeborn and breed like animals. This is abhorrent
to us, Vincent. These people belong in the Dark Caste.
And that is where I should put them!"

As she spoke, a frown appeared on Florala's face, and
deepened with every word. "I think you're being far too

quick to dismiss this. You haven't even read the entire pamphlet. I have, by the way. The concept of the Final Codex may be 'convenient' for your Freeminders, and it's possible they're bending the contents to suit their agenda, but from what I know of Clan history and the personality of Kerensky, it makes a fair amount of sense."

Her jaw hung open in surprise. "That we should abandon everything that makes us Clan? We have changed, Vincent. We have adapted to our new situation, but this nonsense proposes an end to everything we are!"

His head tilted, like someone trying to explain a difficult concept to a child. "Isis, this gives purpose to everything you are, all your centuries of sacrifice and deprivation."

She laughed. "Sacrifice, perhaps. But deprivation? Deprivation of what?"

"Of *family,* Isis. I've heard you speak of your Clan's founders—" He struggled to remember the names.

"Hans Ole Jorgensson and Sandra Tseng."

"Right. You told me the story of how they rebelled against Kerensky when he tried to separate them. They were willing to die in a frigid wilderness together, rather than let him tear them apart."

"This is true. But what is your point?"

He laughed, but she heard an edge in the sound. "Do you think they wanted so desperately to stay together because of their genes? Because some damned Keeper in a eugenics program put them together based on a computer printout? They did it because they were soul mates, Isis. They did it because they were in love, so deeply and fiercely that they would die to preserve their relationship. Your entire Clan is based on love, the very emotion your Clan nature tells you to deny." The whole thing seemed to disturb him profoundly, in a way she didn't understand.

"You couple when and where you please, with whom you please, but you're denied the joy and pain of seeking someone worth giving your life to. You're denied the hope of finding a life partner, and together having children. Your children, that you can raise and care for, and teach, and go to the grave knowing they'll carry on for you. Yes, I call that sacrifice. Yes, I call that deprivation."

"Those in the lower castes do care for their freeborn children."

"Children born of eugenically arranged, loveless marriages. And this is only true of your so-called lower castes, not the warriors."

"Not the warriors," she agreed, unsure why that was an issue.

He pointed at the pamphlet. "That document says that all that sacrifice was *for* something, and more importantly, it says it can end!"

"Why should we want it to end?"

He threw up his hands in frustration and spun away from her, then back. "Isis, you can be so oblivious at times, it drives me insane! This isn't some alien concept we're talking about here. This is a central, core value of your Clan, *your* Clan above all others. The Ghost Bears were founded on love, born of the union of a man and a woman, and they have always espoused the concept of family."

She blinked. "What you say is true. We have family. The family of our sibko, of our caste, of our unit, of our fellow warriors. *That* is family to us."

"And that's good, but it's a shadow of what your founders shared. And notice that Kerensky, he didn't separate them. Once they demonstrated their bond, and how strong it made them, he let them stay together. Isn't it just possible that a few years later, when he sat down to write his ultimate plan for the Clans, he thought regretfully of his decision to try to separate them, and of what he was asking his fellow Clansmen to give up in the name of necessity? Wouldn't it be logical that his final gift to them would be to restore to them what they'd lost?"

She shook her head and pushed the pamphlet away. "You are still talking nonsense, Vince. We don't need any of the things you speak of. We have lived without them for centuries."

He bowed his head and shook it sadly. "You just don't understand, do you? I wish I'd never brought it up. You and your damned Clan bluntness. Some truths I could live without knowing."

She looked at him, puzzled. "What?"

"That business about 'intermarrying with native free-born and breeding like animals.' That hurts, you know."

"Hurts? How could that hurt you?"

"We've been—as you so romantically put it—coupling for nearly a year now. Is that still how you think of me? Is the idea of mingling your precious genes with mine, even hypothetically, so horrible a concept?"

She frowned. "It just is not done, Vince. It is wrong."

He looked at her, and she saw something new in his eyes. "*I* don't think so, Isis. I think you and I could make fine children together. I honestly wish we could."

She felt her face go red. "Vince, what you are talking about is perverse."

"Not to me it isn't. It shouldn't be to you either, if you were actually true to the legacy of your Clan's founders. You claim not to know love, Isis, but I—" The words seemed to hang in his throat for a moment. "I love you. I love you enough for both of us."

She just looked at him, dumbstruck.

He went on. "Look me in the eye and tell me you feel nothing in return."

She looked him in the eye. "Vince, I find your company enjoyable and stimulating. I find our work together satisfying, and our clashes to be challenging. You are very important to me. But I'm not even sure I know what love is, and I don't see how you can be in love with me."

He laughed harshly. "A bold pronouncement, if you

don't know what love is. If you don't think I mean it when I say I love you, then try this on for size."

He walked around her desk, got down on one knee, and took her hand. His actions seemed impulsive, seemed to surprise him as much as they surprised her, but he did not hesitate.

"Isis Bekker, I'm asking you to marry me!"

8

From the Great Work of
Galaxy Commander Isis Bekker

The origin story of the Ghost Bear Clan is as powerful and fantastic as that of any of the ancient gods and heroes of Earth. In the same way as those ancient stories, I cannot say how literally this tale is to be taken. The events described are not impossible, but they stretch the bounds of credibility almost to the breaking point. Some of my Clan would criticize me harshly for questioning its truth, but in my mind, that shows only the weakness of their beliefs.

Personally, I do not think it matters. I have always found comfort and wisdom in the story and the lessons it teaches. I have always found strength and purpose in the teachings of the Bear.

Truth is not merely an assemblage of facts that can be broken down like a wall, brick by brick. Truth is what we can learn from the story, and the value of those lessons. If the lessons are strong, the individual facts do not matter.

This is truth of the heart, not truth of the mind, and it is far more powerful.

So I will tell you my truth. I will tell you the origin of my Clan.

Hans Ole Jorgensson and Sandra Tseng were among the mightiest warriors of Nicholas Kerensky, and among his most energetic and vocal advocates in the events leading up to the formation of the Clans. They were also married, and as many people forget, had a son who was killed during the violent incidents that led to Nicholas Kerensky's Second Exodus to the Kerensky Cluster.

But as Kerensky put into motion his plan to create the Clans, he made a fateful decision. Individually, Jorgensson and Tseng were too valuable to give to any one Clan. He decided to place them in two separate Clans, ending their marriage and partnership.

That, they could not abide.

Of this part of the story there is little doubt, and if one studies the details of the pair's life before the formation of the Clans—their time as soldiers under Aleksandr Kerensky, their transition to peaceful family life on the planet Babylon, the death of their son, their return to military service under Nicholas and their critical role in the creation of the Clans—it is possible to see the beginnings of all the principles that our Clan holds dear.

But there is nothing mythic about it, nothing grand, and its lessons are subtle and subject to interpretation. And, therefore, there is more to the story, and the facts of this part are subject to question. But that does not matter. This part of the story is as necessary as the rest, for it is powerful and mythic, and anything but subtle.

It is said that, rather than be separated, and rather than directly refuse the orders of the Founder, the pair chose to die together. They traveled into the antarctic wilderness of the planet Strana Mechty, expecting never to return. They wandered the frigid wilderness for three weeks, until their supplies ran out and their demise seemed certain.

They sought refuge in a mountain cave, made peace with themselves and each other, and waited for death.

Suddenly, it seemed that death had come to them in literal form. A Strana Mechty ghost bear, a predator five meters tall and weighing over eight hundred kilograms, appeared at the entrance to their cave and roared its challenge. In this moment, when others would have run in terror, or given in to despair, they stood their ground, defiantly roaring back.

If death had come for them, it would not take them easily.

The bear could have killed them with one swipe of his huge claws, and yet he did not. He dropped down on all fours and circled them, sniffing curiously. Once again the bear roared a challenge, and again they roared back.

Standing back to back, Jorgensson and Tseng defied the bear, but lost their battle for consciousness: frozen and starving, they slipped into a blackness from which neither of them expected to return.

But then a miracle occurred. They awoke some time later. Hours or days, who can say? But they awoke, warmed back from the brink of death by the huge ghost bear, which now curled around them as it might protect its own cubs.

When they began to stir, the bear rose and left the cave. It returned soon thereafter with a fresh kill in its mouth. It laid the kill before them, quickly devoured half of it, and then stepped back, watching the two humans carefully.

Cautious but desperate, they claimed the other half of the carcass. When they had finished eating, they fell back into sleep, again aware of the great bear warming them with its body.

For three days this continued, the bear bringing them fresh meat and warming them against the cold. They regained enough of their strength to emerge from their shelter.

There they made an amazing discovery. The ghost

bear was not a solitary hunter, as had been believed; Jorgensson and Tseng had been cared for by an entire family of bears. They now understood that the ghost bears hunted in packs and shared their kills equally. In the clan of the ghost bears the strong ruled the pack, but each member of the pack was provided for.

They were family, and in family they were strong.

Inspired by this discovery, Jorgensson and Tseng resolved to return to the Clans and argue for their right to stay together. When they at last emerged from the wilderness, they had long been given up for dead, and it is said that none was happier at their safe return than the Founder. He listened carefully to their tale of survival and the lessons they had taken away from their ordeal, and their appeal to bring the strength of those lessons to the Clans—together.

Kerensky granted their request, and in honor of their great trial he named their Clan Ghost Bear.

Of course, they did not become the first leaders of Clan Ghost Bear by appointment. They had to prove themselves all over again through Trials of Position. Each defeated all of their opponents, earning the right to become the first leaders of our Clan and assuring that their names would live forever.

And that, true or not, is the story—or at least the essential part of it.

And from that story, from the lessons of the bear, come the fundamental principles by which the Ghost Bears have always lived.

We value strength. As with the bear, strength allows us to weather challenges and misfortune from without, and the errors that we may inflict upon ourselves. Strength is the key to stability and the path to prosperity.

We value patience. The Ghost Bear hunts by patience and stealth, burrowing into snowbanks where its white fur makes it almost invisible and waiting for its prey to pass. Only then does it spring out with great ferocity and overwhelm its kill. By this means, the bear saves wasted effort in a land where food is often scarce.

Like the bear, we do not rush to exploit the apparent weakness of our enemies, nor are we quickly drawn to new and unproven ways. We practice caution, not out of fear, for we fear no one, but out of wisdom. We study each new challenge and opportunity before acting. We know that for every opportunity we may miss, two more will come our way if we only wait.

But like the bear, when the time comes for us to move, to act, we do so swiftly, with great energy and without hesitation. At those times, though we are normally bound by our love of tradition, we may act in ways that seem to others impetuous and rash.

So it was when our Clan quietly moved entirely into the Inner Sphere, over the potential objection of the other Clans. So it was when we came to Vega and the other weakened worlds of the crumbling Republic. The move might have seemed sudden, the decision rash, and yet there can be little doubt that our leaders have been discussing such a possibility for years.

Finally, the Ghost Bears value the concept of family. Perhaps this is not family as Jorgensson and Tseng would have known it, but it has served us well. We believe in unity of purpose, hard work and dedication to our causes. We believe in the strength that is gained when we bond together in groups, be they children growing up together in sibko, the comrades in a Star of warriors or the laborers in a work group.

We are a hard family. We challenge each other relentlessly and expect much of our siblings. Yet in the friendships that grow from such bonds, we believe we are stronger.

As I consider the story of our founders and the lessons they handed down to us, I feel that my commitment to the Ghost Bear Clan and its ideals has never been stronger. And yet I also find myself examining the dogma that has grown from those lessons. How much of what we do is necessary to those core values? How much was once a matter of harsh necessity, but now only a matter of "how things have always been done?"

Like the bear, I do not move, do not act quickly.

But in this moment of stillness, I consider, and plan for what may come my way.

The time for action may yet come, and still I am not sure what I will do.

*Office of Galaxy Commander Isis Bekker, East
   Central District*
Nasew, North Nanturo continent, Vega
26 November 3136

Isis Bekker put down her pen and carefully closed the volume on her desk. It was bound in red leather, and bore her name in a plain font upon the cover. The book's blank pages were now roughly half filled. When she had completed the last page, it would join the first fourteen volumes in a locked trunk that she kept at the foot of her bed.

She had been writing in the books since passing her first Trial of Position, and the books formed her Great Work, the traditional artistic expression of a warrior's devotion to duty and cause. It had taken her nearly ten years to fill the first volume, and when she looked back at it now, the words seemed to have been written by someone else. Its pages formed little more than a ledger, a dry recording of training, trials, battles, challenges and accomplishments, as though a warrior's life were a merchant's balance sheet, to be totaled and tabulated.

But as she rose through the ranks, took on more responsibility and was forced to confront the complexities of command in the real world, her writing had became more complex as well. She had completed the second volume in five years. The third in three. The fourth in a year and a half. For some time, she averaged one volume a year. But in the year since coming to Vega, she had filled one volume and was well into another, and still the speed of her writing was accelerating.

She had long since stopped wondering if anyone would read these after she was dead. She had stopped wondering if they would be displayed at her funeral, or recorded in her codex, or displayed in a place of honor in her Bloodname chapel. Perhaps that was the true lesson of the Great Work, its true value. Now, she wrote only for herself. Putting her thoughts down on paper gave her peace and clarity of thought, and that was a priceless gift.

There was a knock at the door and she looked up, wondering if it would be Vince, then feeling relieved when it was not.

She still could not believe that he had asked her to marry him. It was an absurd proposition, and yet she had not, for reasons that remained unclear to her, done the obvious thing and said no.

Perhaps it was simply the Ghost Bear tradition of caution and deliberation. Never rush into anything, even if the action seems obvious.

And so the question still stood there between them. They had not spoken of it since, yet it was there, and hung over them like a cloud anytime they were together. *Why do they always have to complicate things so? Life is complicated enough without adding these emotional games.*

She shook herself. Her visitor was her chief advisor, Trenton. She could forestall the issue of Vincent for a little while longer.

"Come in, Trenton. I was just finishing some personal business." She wondered if he was going to be contentious about the name-and-title business, but apparently he had other matters on his mind today.

He glanced curiously at the book on her desk, but said nothing. He'd seen the books many times before, but had never asked for an explanation, and she had never offered one. Though Clansmen rarely lied, they still managed to have secrets. He put his computer pad on the desk, spun it around so she could see it right side up, then tapped it with his finger. "Blah, blah, blah," he said.

"Very amusing. I know you do not share my attitude toward all this." She waved her hand at the pad. "Still, I am sure that you have handled all the day's routine business well, and that everything is in order. Now, sit."

He pulled a straight-backed chair out of the corner of the office, placed it in front of her desk sideways, dramatically flipped the tail of his lab coat out of the way over the far side of the seat, and then settled down facing her, his right elbow propped on the back of the chair.

"Have you been working on the special project I gave you?" she asked.

"Researching the Freeminders. Yes, I have, and I've come to some conclusions, though there's doubtless much more to learn."

"Let me have the overview."

"Well, first of all, they're big, and they're growing in all the lower castes, but especially the laborer caste. Only a little of that growth is coming directly from recent civilian immigrants from the Rasalhague Dominion. They are, however, being recruited almost as soon as they arrive, and those new arrivals are very receptive to what the Freeminders have to say."

She frowned. "Why so?"

"Newly arrived civilians are an unhappy bunch, not just because many of them were already operating on the fringes of acceptable Clan behavior. You were aware that many, especially in the laborer caste, had begun to secretly marry native freeborns?"

She could not help her expression of distaste. Of course she had heard rumors, and hoped they were not true. "I have heard such reports, yes."

"Well, many of those workers are now here, trans-

ferred against their will and without their unacknowl-
edged families. They've been forced to leave behind
wives, husbands, homes and children. Given the illicit
nature of these relationships, to complain is to invite
punishment."

Her first impulse was: *Good! It serves them right!* Then
she thought of Jorgensson and Tseng, and their sadness
at being separated. It was a strange quandary, for her to
feel a conflict between being Clan and being a Ghost
Bear.

He continued. "For whatever reason, the paramilitary
police have chosen, or perhaps have been instructed, to
look the other way regarding the Freeminders, except in
the most flagrant cases. The level of enforcement also
varies by caste. Laborers rarely suffer punishment, while
technicians can maintain their second lives only through
extraordinary secrecy. The Freeminders advocate open
and unrestricted marriage between Clan and non-Clan,
with no punishment or loss of rank. They also advocate
that families, Clan or not, be allowed to travel together
whenever there is a transfer or reassignment."

She shook her head. "This is monstrous!"

Trenton looked at her strangely, but said nothing.

She continued. "It goes against all our traditions and
customs. There must be some way to stop it."

Ever restless, he jumped up from his chair, slid it back
to the corner and began to pace the length of the office
as he spoke. "Not *all* our traditions and customs. Regardless, this isn't some cult isolated to a single caste
that can simply be eradicated. Malcontents or not, these
civilians are key to your stability efforts. The warlord
purges targeted managers, technicians, engineers and so-
called 'intellectuals,' the very people needed to keep
things running. We have no shortage of local workers—
when they aren't on strike for their own reasons, of
course—but we need people to manage, direct and supervise their efforts. Ultimately, we'll need to train and
educate local replacements if we hope to turn a func-

tional society back over to the locals. But that could take years."

She sighed. "But what you are talking about concerns higher castes—technicians, scientists, maybe even merchants—but not laborers. Can we control this movement at the level of the laborer caste?"

He shook his head. "Your problem, Galaxy Commander, is that you spend too much time with warriors"— he grinned—"and scientists. When's the last time you even spoke with someone in labor caste?" He held up his hand. "Never mind. The point is, all the Clan staff here in the capital, where you spend most of your time, are higher caste than laborer."

"Specifically as a security precaution, specifically out of concern for the Freeminders."

"I think any such threat is overblown. But what I was getting at is that the laborer caste has changed in recent decades from its traditional roles. Since the Ghost Bears moved back to the Inner Sphere, more and more of the work traditionally done by the laborer caste has been relegated to Inner Sphere workers. This has accelerated over the last few decades. The average laborer caste worker now has as much education and training as a low-grade technician or merchant of twenty years ago. In some places, they even supervise native workers. Any genuinely creative work or position of serious authority calls for a higher caste, of course, but these are not the sort of knuckle-dragging, mouth-breathing rock-breakers that fulfill your stereotype of the caste."

"I said no such thing."

He rolled his eyes slightly. "You didn't have to. You're warrior caste: deadly on the battlefield, largely oblivious to the 99,999 lower-caste workers who make your glorious victories possible."

"Now who is talking in stereotypes?"

"Perhaps, but there's a grain of truth to it, and I verify my stereotypes by close observation. You can't say the same."

"So you are saying there is nothing we can do? That is absurd."

"There are things you *could* do to discourage them, at a minimum. I'm simply saying that there's nothing you *should* do. The Freeminders are a threat to nothing but certain traditions, and none of these traditions are central to our core beliefs, not as Ghost Bears anyway. They espouse the virtues of free thought and nonconformity, but in my opinion they have more interest in the *freedom* to do these things than in actually doing them. They are, at heart, still Ghost Bears, and still Clan. Creating new freedoms will eventually lead to change, but it could take decades or longer. I think that the contamination resulting from living in the Inner Sphere leads to such change anyway. Perhaps by openly acknowledging this, we can guide and control it."

"They should seek you as their publicity agent."

"I'm simply stating facts as I've seen them. The Freeminders are a greater threat if we try to suppress them than if we simply continue to look the other way. Certainly they run contrary to practices of the Clans as a whole, but we are already regarded as outcasts and Inner Sphere apologists, even by many in our own Clan. Ultimately, they do little harm, and may do much good."

"But they *do* harm the Clan. They disrupt the breeding programs."

"This isn't the warrior's eugenics program we're talking about—it's much less critical. And it appears that most Freeminders still participate in the marriages arranged for them by the scientists. The children of such marriages are usually sent to crèches that offer full-time care, and as such are raised in more typical Clan tradition than most lower-caste children.

"In turn, by breeding with the locals, they're introducing superior Clan genes into that population, resulting in a stronger and more effective workforce in the Dominion."

Trenton shrugged. "As I said, the locals have largely

supplanted the original tasks of the laborer class. It seems only appropriate that they have the benefits of our superior genes. After three hundred years of guided breeding supervised by the scientist caste, even the lowest-grade laborer has something to offer the Inner Sphere."

Isis leaned her head forward, and rubbed the bridge of her nose. "Enough. I will read your report, and forestall any rash action against the Freeminders. 'Haste makes waste' is at least a respectable Ghost Bear principle, and little about this situation is clear to me."

He stood looking at her expectantly.

"Is there something else?"

He frowned, and his expression turned dire. "There is. Military intelligence doesn't fall under my normal purview, but assembling odd and unrelated facts does. My security clearance gives me access to military material, and I often review it on my own initiative, as a form of recreation."

"You have found something of significance?"

"I may have. Vega's deep-space tracking systems were badly damaged prior to our arrival. There are still gaping blind spots in our coverage of the sky. We've not officially been aware of any unauthorized traffic in the system since the end of major hostilities, and thus we've assumed that any Draconis Combine agents or materiel supplies for the insurgents were already here when we arrived.

"But I have collected a series of seemingly unrelated anomalies: unconfirmed deep-space radar returns, possible fusion drive-flare sightings, unexplained radio traffic. And I have connected the dots."

She stood and leaned forward on her desk. "You found a DropShip?"

His expression turned even darker. "Possibly multiple ships over the last several months. I think they may have entered the system using a pirate jump point, then maneuvered using short fusion burns and low-energy orbits to make them harder to spot."

"Even so, and even with the holes in our tracking network, we should have spotted them as they approached the planet. One or two ships might slip through undetected, but not ongoing traffic like you're describing."

"They could evade us if they knew enough about the planet's radars and sensors to tailor the ECM against them. And if they knew the details of the gaps in our tracking system, they could schedule their JumpShip arrivals and DropShip fusion-drive burns."

"Blast it! We have been worrying about a handful of unaccounted-for 'Mechs, and the Combine could have been dropping in shiploads of reinforcements for all we know."

"The good news is, I doubt they have been able to get much to the surface. It is possible they have set up a staging area elsewhere in the star system, on a moon or asteroid. When they deploy en masse, they won't be able to hide themselves. They will not have far to come, but at least we will see them coming."

Ricco's patrol strike sled easily crossed the rubble-covered streets of the Krottenwik slum, but he was forced to keep his speed to a crawl to avoid the pedestrian and horse traffic that seemed to wander randomly across the broken cityscape. It took him ten minutes to cover the distance from the last navigable street to his destination.

He homed in on a tracking signal until he found a demolished building with another strike sled and three hoverbikes parked on top. He popped the canopy on his hovercraft and stepped out. Inquisitor Janine, a tall, blond woman with shoulders so broad she could have been an Elemental, stepped up to greet him.

He nodded in greeting. "What do we have?"

"This way." She pointed. "Bunker in an old basement. Pretty nice setup. Seven adult, male Vegan bodies currently in residence."

She led him down the narrow stairs, removing a flashlight from her pocket and turning it on as they descended into darkness.

She stopped, removed a small bottle and a handkerchief from her pocket. She opened the bottle, dumped a little on the handkerchief, and held it over her mouth and nose. She offered him the bottle. "Cheap New Egyptian perfume," she explained. "Smells like a camel's ass to me, but it is just the thing for covering the corpse-stink."

He shook his head. The bullet he had taken in his first Trial of Position had struck him in the face. The Clan medics had patched him up so that he didn't even have a scar, but somehow his sense of smell had never been the same. He doused his meals with garlic and hot-pepper sauce just to taste them at all, and crime scenes had never bothered him.

He pulled out his own flashlight and followed her around the corner. Work lights on stands were set up in the corners, casting harsh shadows across the large space.

"We suspect there was a generator in a hidden chamber up above, but it is gone now. All we have are the mounting brackets and connecting wires."

The place was a mess of overturned furniture and emptied cabinets. Drag marks on the naked concrete floor suggested that several large items had been removed, and dusty outlines were all that were left to suggest that rugs and carpets had been taken as well.

There was one body faceup just inside the doorway, and six others on the floor in various positions around the room. A seventh sat in a large lounging chair now splattered with blood. None were recognizable. On several, the faces were completely missing.

"Somebody left the door open, and all kinds of scavengers apparently came down here for a picnic. There are mice, cats, dogs, even birds that could be drawn down here by the smell."

"Things were taken, and for the Krottenwik, these

guys obviously had a lot to take. Do you think this was a robbery?"

"Evidence suggests that some of the larger items at least were removed well after time of death. I think what we see here is the result of scavengers of the human kind. I also think these guys were armed when they were killed. We have powder residue and shell casings for a number of conventional assault weapons, none of which are here. Maybe the scavengers took them."

He inspected one of the casings. "Are you sure this is not a robbery? In this place, any of those things—the weapons, the generator, the rugs, and most anything else that was down there—could have been sufficient motive."

"But if so, they would not have taken any one of those items, they would have taken everything. Besides, there is other evidence, which I will explain shortly. First"— she pointed at the man in the chair—"we have a probable identification on this body. The cane and the long hair are known trademarks of a small-time thug named Tim Gustavo. His older brother, Sean Gustavo, was a high-ranking warlord killed during our arrival. The younger Gustavo managed to recruit some of his brother's former soldiers along with some of their weaponry, setting himself up as the self-styled 'Warlord of Krottenwik.' He has been on our radar, but we had been unable to locate his headquarters."

Ricco looked around. "Well, I suppose we know where it is now. Whoever did this to Gustavo did us a service." He turned towards the stairs. "Let us get out of this rat hole."

They climbed back into the sunlight and relatively fresh air. Inquisitor Janine removed the handkerchief from her face, folded it and replaced it in her pocket. "We do not have any witnesses to the killing, but we do have reports of two well-dressed men entering Gustavo's enclave early yesterday before gunshots were heard. The men later emerged and created quite a commotion."

"More gunfire?"

She shook her head. "No. This is where it gets interesting, and why I called you in. The men handed out some gold ingots or bars, stamped with the name of Jacob Bannson. Of that much we are relatively certain. We have not located any of the actual gold, but one woman did take a tracing off one of the gold pieces." She reached into the other strike sled and produced a tattered piece of paper. Made using some kind of colored chalk or crayon, the tracing was obviously a complete version of the partial ingot being held back at the station.

"What else did you find out?"

"Not much. From there the stories get interesting and contradictory. Several people insisted that they drove in by limousine, which is clearly impossible. Several people, perhaps confused by the name on the bars, have insisted that Jacob Bannson himself was here. Others insist that he is coming soon, to help the people of Krottenwik, or at least the children, or perhaps even to drive the Ghost Bears off the planet."

He nodded. "We have seen the gold before. Somebody, possibly somebody in Bannson's employ, is making the rounds of the city, dropping gold as they go. They are not going out of their way to be inconspicuous."

She looked at him. "If Jacob Bannson is involved, this could be a matter for military intelligence. Should you alert the Galaxy commander?"

He considered for a moment. He was almost certain that the information would interest Galaxy Commander Bekker, but he also knew it would be even better if he could deliver Bannson's agents themselves, and that certainly seemed within the realm of possibility.

"No, I think we should hold on to this information for a while. Without providing them with any more information than necessary, I want all our patrol officers looking for more of these gold ingots. And anything else related to Jacob Bannson."

He turned back towards his strike sled, kicking a broken bottle out of his path. "I want very much to meet Mr. Bannson's agents, and following the gold may be our key to finding them."

9

There is a footnote to the origin story of the Ghost Bear Clan, one I have always considered ill-fitting. It seems somehow out of place, as though it were added as an afterthought, and even as a child I could see this incongruity. I asked my instructors about it, and was sternly warned not to allow my mind to wander into such troublesome areas. "That way, Isis, lies the path to dishonor, and even to the bandit caste. A warrior does not question."

And so I put my thoughts about that part of the story aside, and later even came to embrace it. But my concerns only lingered in some dark corner of my mind, waiting there, like the Ghost Bear, hidden and ready to spring.

This is the part of the story that troubles me so: as Tseng and Jorgensson returned from their time in the wilderness, it is said that they witnessed two young ghost bears battling in a territorial dispute. This sight so impressed them that they resolved to return and test themselves against a ghost bear after they had recovered from their ordeal.

A year later, they led a hunting party into the frigid wilderness and were soon confronted by a large male ghost bear. The great bear reared up and roared a challenge. Hans Jorgensson stepped forward and roared back his own challenge. And then, as his wife and the hunting party watched, Jorgensson engaged the animal in single combat, armed with only a crude spear that he had made himself during the journey.

It is said the battle was short, that Jorgensson used his superior speed to evade the bear's blows until he could drive his spear into the bear's eye socket, instantly killing it. Now, an outsider might question the idea that a hundred-kilogram man could so easily defeat a six-hundred-kilogram bear possessing more than twice his reach and claws the size of bananas. But as Clan, I cannot dismiss the possibility. When skill and luck are on a warrior's side, impossible things can happen, and Tseng and Jorgensson were seemingly gifted with both.

The story goes on that the party soon encountered another bear, a female, responding to her mate's death call. This time it was Tseng who stepped forward with the spear and drove it through the female bear's heart.

This was the birth of a sacred ritual in our Clan called the Clawing.

In the early days, the Clawing required an actual return to Strana Mechty, but with that world lost to us in the War of Reaving, that is no longer possible or, fortunately, necessary. When the Ghost Bear Clan moved to the Inner Sphere, they brought with them preserved embryos of our beloved namesakes.

When suitable habitats were found on several worlds of the Dominion, cubs were brought forth from special iron wombs created for the task, and breeding pairs were released in likely hunting grounds. Some worlds were not suitable for the great bears, but on others, they thrived, pushing out native predators and adapting to new prey.

Each year a few of the very finest warriors travel to the arctic wastes where the ghost bears live. The Loremaster of our Clan leads them into the hunting range of the ghost bear, so that they can relive the trials of Tseng and Jorgensson, and then test themselves in a fight to the death with a ghost bear.

That one warrior might achieve such a miraculous victory is not impossible. That two should in a single day calls the matter into greater question. But I still maintain that it is not impossible, and in the universe, anything that is not forbidden is, at some point in history, mandatory.

No, I do not question the possibility that our founders actually accomplished what it is said they did. The part that bothers me, that makes me question the truth of the story, or to suspect that it has been altered over time, is that they would seek to hunt the great bears at all.

Unworthy though I am, when I try to place myself in the mind of Tseng or Jorgensson, I see only their love and respect for the bears.

The bears saved them from death and nurtured them back to health. The bears made them part of their family, The bears shared with them their lessons, and sent them back to the world of men to carry these lessons to others.

That they would have been drawn to return to the bears at some point is almost certain. That they might have killed a bear in self-defense, and that such defense might have been necessary against such savage predators, that is also credible.

But that they would have set out on a calculated mission to murder our brothers and benefactors, that I find difficult to imagine.

Surprisingly little is known about the ghost bear. It is

such a sacred animal that our science caste hesitates to study it.

I have read and studied what is known, and I can tell you this. Ghost bears fight almost constantly among themselves. They fight for territory, for mates, for dominance, for food. But they fight for cause, not sport. And they almost never fight to the death, or even to the point of severe injury. Once a bear has proven his or her superior strength, the other bear prostrates itself in a show of submission and the bears each go their own way.

To kill another bear, to do it great injury, would be to weaken the entire pack. Evolution craves efficiency even more than do the Clans. In nature, little is wasted, and the penalty for violating this rule is extinction.

Every year, new hunting parties set out on the Clawing. Less than half return, and less than half of those are successful. And yet, as I consider it, even that is too many.

That one warrior might best such a bear is possible. That two might in a day is barely credible. That one in a thousand might do it throughout the march of history, that I can also believe.

But a quarter? Even one success per year seems too many.

And that is where dark thoughts creep into my mind. I have heard rumors, whispers, of hunts conducted without honor: with powerful weapons, with traps, with poison bait. I do not wish to believe such stories, but it is otherwise difficult to explain the numbers. It sickens me to imagine warriors, not even deserving of that name, would so dishonor our Clan and our most sacred totem. But like the victory of Tseng and Jorgensson, it is not impossible.

Though I once and again questioned the story of the first Clawing and the practice of the ritual itself, there was a time when I, like any young warrior caught up in the passion of our traditions, craved to be a part of it. I dreamed of stepping into an icy land, not unlike the place where it all began, walking in the footsteps of Tseng and roaring my challenge to the great bear.

It was not to be. I had one opportunity, but I was outranked by Ivan Gurdel, a warrior from my sibko, and he went instead.

I was not bitter. I had known Ivan Gurdel all my life. We had been playmates. We had fought side by side and back-to-back. We had been friends, and we had been family, and we had coupled joyously.

In honesty, he was a better warrior and a better leader than I will ever be. No one I have ever met was more deserving of such an honor. I know with as much certainty as I know any single thing in this world, that Ivan Gurdel faced his Clawing with honor, that he faced the great bear alone, with but a spear in his hand, and that he fought with courage, strength and skill.

Ivan Gurdel did not return from the wilderness.

In my darkest thoughts, in my most troubled dreams, I think of Ivan. I wonder, what is a ritual that may reward our weakest and most dishonorable, and sends many of our greatest to their wasteful, unnecessary doom? We were always taught that the Clawing was a purification ritual, that it returned to us only the strongest and most worthy, and made our Clan always stronger.

But what if that was wrong? What if it returned to us the weak and deceitful? What is it doing to us then?

Nasew Spaceport, Southwest Industrial District
Nasew, North Nanturo continent, Vega
27 November 3136

Conner Hall watched from the front stoop of the barracks as the *Confederate Mk III* DropShip, a gleaming, inverted pear shape, descended from the sky on a tail of fusion flame. As it grew larger, panels slid back on the ship's lower flanks and four sturdy landing legs unfurled. Thrusters fired around the ship's "waist," rotating it so that it was aligned with one of the landing pads scattered across the field. Even from a kilometer away, the roar was deafening, and a blast of hot air washed over him like he was standing in front of an open furnace. Then the ship's engines throttled up slightly and it slowed, settling over the flame pit before touching down with a ground-shaking thud and shutting down its engines.

The sudden silence was stunning. Conner continued to gaze at the big ship, engine nozzles still glowing red with heat, gasses and steam venting from dozens of ports. Just looking at the ship made him feel better. It was going to solve a lot of their logistical and deployment problems, and take some of the pressure off their thinly spread forces.

Karen Tupolov stepped up behind him and looked at the newly arrived craft. "What's this, then?"

He turned and grinned at her. "A welcome gift from Galaxy Commander Bekker. For the moment, it is a shipment of badly needed spare parts and a few new VTOLs to replenish our depleted air units. But once the DropShip is empty, it will be assigned to detached duty here. It will allow us to deploy a Star of our 'Mechs to any trouble spot on the planet in approximately forty-five minutes, or call in reinforcements from the outlying units on short notice."

"That's wonderful."

But there was a hesitation in her voice that gave him pause. He thought for a moment. "Your unit has never made a DropShip deployment, has it?"

She shook her head and flashed him an embarrassed smile. "As I've often said, the FVR is low-rent, low-tech and local. I've never even been off this continent, much less to space."

"Trust me. In this type of deployment, you will be in and out of the atmosphere so quickly that you will hardly know it."

She laughed, and absently brushed a wisp of hair back over her ear. "Oh, that's *very* reassuring."

He smiled at her. "I have every confidence that you

will do fine, but you and your people should be trained on DropShip procedures. I would like to do a practice deployment soon, if we can arrange things so that it does not endanger city security." He looked at her curiously. "You are not afraid, are you?"

She laughed again. "I know it's foolish. I've been piloting IndustrialMechs since I was fifteen. I've watched my world fall apart around my ears, and I've battled warlord assault 'Mechs with not much more than a glorified steam shovel. Nothing should bother me by now. But yes, I'm a little afraid."

"Fear is not a warrior's enemy. Recklessness is not his friend."

"That's nice. Where did you read it?"

"On a bathroom wall on Pomme De Terre, I think."

She laughed and put her hand on his arm. The touch didn't seem to carry any special meaning, but he liked it nonetheless.

"There is more good news on that ship as well. Among the spare parts is some war salvage traded with Alpha Galaxy on Alrakis. With these parts, we should be able to put several of the warlords' 'Mechs we salvaged back into service. Just think, you could be in the cockpit of a real 'Mech soon!"

That did make her smile, big and unreservedly, and he could not help but smile back.

"That would be wonderful! I've always wanted to—" She blinked and shook her head. "No, this isn't about me. This is wonderful for Vega. With real 'Mechs, we'll finally be able to start rebuilding, have some hope of taking over our own defense and security again. That would be a great day for us."

"That will be a great day for everybody. But these 'Mechs still put you a long way from planetary security. Even our combined forces aren't enough to stabilize the major cities on North Nanturo continent. We haven't even begun the job of securing and rebuilding the original capital in Neucason."

She frowned slightly. "You make it sound like you could be here almost indefinitely."

He glanced at her. "Are you that eager to be rid of me?"

"No! Of course not. It's nothing personal, Conner. It's just that my MechWarriors and I have been working so hard, for so long. We're eager to begin really carrying our weight, to take back responsibility for the safety of our own world. It's a matter of pride. Just for a minute there, I let myself hope that we could be close to that. You just dumped a big load of obvious reality on that hope."

"That was not my intention."

"Nope"—she pouted slightly—"just good old Clan bluntness."

Taylor Bane sat in the back of the car, absentmindedly inspecting a cigarette burn in the seat cushion, as they bounced slowly down the broken pavement on one of Nasew's secondary streets. He glanced up at the back of Bruno Vic's head where it towered above the driver's seat. "Hey, Bruno, do you have to actually aim for the potholes?"

"No, boss. You just point the car down the road, and it falls into 'em naturally."

He thought maybe Bruno was making a joke, but you just couldn't be sure with him. Anyway, he knew the rough ride wasn't Bruno's fault. Even in the more civilized parts of the city, the roads had not been patched since the warlords first took over. "How much farther?"

"If I read this note right, just a couple more blocks."

The note proposing a meeting had been delivered to their hotel. There was no indication of who the note was from, though it was written on the stationery of one of the city's top law firms. Of course, the fact that the warlords had purged most of the lawyers made this a dubious distinction. When Bane had called the firm for more information, they had been willing to say only that the message came from an important client.

Bane looked around. They were in the financial district, just north of the primary security zone. He could occasionally see the security wall and watchtowers equipped with gun emplacements when he looked down the north-south cross streets to his right.

At last the car slowed in front of a medium-height office tower, its simple Bauhaus-style facade still bearing scars from the recent conflicts. The car turned onto a down-sloping ramp leading into a parking garage.

An armed guard stood at the locked gate. He approached and tapped on the window with a billy club.

Bruno held the note up to the window. The guard inspected it for a moment, then walked back to an electronic box mounted on a post. He inserted a key card, punched in a code and the metal gate began to roll back.

They pulled into a dimly lit and nearly empty parking structure of a type that could have been on any office building on any planet. Bruno drove around randomly for a while. They had been instructed to look for a green door and to drive through it.

Near the back of the building they finally located it, a large overhead door that opened at their approach, revealing a relatively tiny room. It took a moment for it to dawn on Bane that it was a freight elevator.

The car pulled inside, clearing front and rear with only a few inches to spare. Bruno's hands flexed on the steering wheel as the door rolled shut, and with a lurch the elevator began to move up. Bane watched the numbered lights flashing on a panel mounted on the side wall until the elevator stopped with another lurch on the tenth floor.

There was a short delay, and then the door rolled open. Surprisingly, since it was daylight and they were on the tenth floor, the area beyond the elevator was mostly dark. A man appeared, casually carrying an assault needler in his hands. He walked up to the rear passenger window of the car and bent down. "Mr. Bane, please come with me."

Bane unlocked the door and stepped out.

Bruno started to open his door as well, but the man quickly pointed the muzzle of his weapon at the big man. "I'm sorry, but only Mr. Bane is invited to this meeting."

Bruno obviously didn't like this, and he scowled up at Bane, looking for orders.

"It'll be fine, Bruno. I've got a better feeling about this guy."

The man with the needler let Bane go first. They walked out into a large space, as though the entire floor had been gutted. Here and there shafts of light cut into the space, but largely it was black. Bane got the impression that most of the windows were simply boarded over. There was a noise behind him, and he turned to see the rolling door close again over the elevator.

"Mr. Bane," said the man with the gun, "I'm certain that you're armed. I'd be grateful if you didn't make any sudden moves for those weapons during your meeting. It would be awkward if I had to shoot you."

He smiled slightly. "For both of us. Which way?"

The man directed him with a sweeping motion of his gun barrel.

Bane dutifully trudged into the darkness. As his eyes adjusted, he became aware of a dim red light set over a windowless, office-style door. Needler-guy directed him to open the door, and followed him inside.

The room was small and functional, perhaps a former construction office. The bare walls were painted white and the floor was industrial laminate tile. A small plastic table had been set up in the middle of the room, and there was a chair on either side of it.

In one chair sat an older man, hawk-nosed, nearly bald. He was thin, almost frail-looking, but Bane could immediately tell that he was not weak. The man held himself with the confidence of a fighter with countless bouts under his belt.

Bane had seen men like this before: gang leaders, CEOs, union organizers, patriarchs, leaders of seasoned mercenary units. Men who had remained on top of the heap long after their prime, and kept younger and stronger men and women in their thrall.

The man looked up at him and smiled, his expression a strange mixture of pleasure and contempt. He did not stand.

"Mister Taylor Bane, I presume. Very little happens in this city that I'm not aware of; I knew almost immediately when you landed, and I know the identity of your employer. If Jacob Bannson is seeking alliances here on Vega, we should talk." He waved at the other chair. "Please, sit down."

Bane spun the chair around backwards and straddled it, crossing his arms over the high back.

The old man watched him carefully. "Not an unnecessarily formal man. A man who likes to feel he's in charge of his own situation, especially when he isn't. I like that."

He stuck out his hand, and Bane took it. The hand was bony, the skin like dry parchment, but the grip was surprisingly strong. He shook once and then released.

"My name is—"

"Chance Elba," Bane interrupted, "senator and Speaker of Labor to the Provisional Congress."

Elba looked at him steadily.

"I've been reading the newsfaxes since I got here, watching news broadcasts. My reason for coming here is to make contact with people of power and authority, so naturally I've needed to identify who those people are. I've got to say, figuring out who those people are here is a lot more difficult than on most planets I've been to."

Elba smiled. On him, the expression looked slightly poisonous. "Then I'm glad we could meet, Mr. Bane.

Vega is a very complicated world these days. It wasn't so when I was a boy. Things were very different. Some would even say idyllic. But I'm a 'the glass is half-full' sort of person, so let's just say that it was boring."

"You don't impress me as a man who's lived a boring life."

He laughed heartily. "You should have seen me ten years ago, Mr. Bane. I was quite fit for a man my age. I still had a full head of hair. I'd made my fortune in ways that let me sleep at night. I raced novaboats off New Egypt. You know what those are? Ocean-racing boats powered by surplus high-time fusion cores pulled from BattleMechs when they're too old for service. Even when they are used and nearly worn out, it's impossible to use full throttle on the boats, because you'll just tear the hull apart.

"So the question is always just how close you can go to the edge. And, of course, these days they don't swap a 'Mech's fusion core until it's on the ragged edge of exploding anyway, so it's like driving a runaway monorail with a bomb in the back."

Elba laughed. "God, I miss those races. But who knows now when or if they'll ever run them again? New Egypt has remained relatively stable, but most of the racers, and the money, came from North Nanturo." The man looked sad, almost wistful.

"The tensions were already there when Devlin Stone abandoned The Republic and allowed it to fall apart. Did you know our hyperpulse generator was one of the first in The Republic to fail? Whatever happened to the rest of the HPG network, the attack on ours was special. It was destroyed in the same wave of suicide attacks that took out the capital. We were cut off from the rest of the Inner Sphere. It was like somebody pulled a switch on chaos. It all went to hell."

Bane nodded, saying nothing.

Elba looked up as though suddenly remembering the other man was there. "I'm boring you. You didn't come here to hear about history."

"Actually, in a way I did. The information that has come out of Vega since the HPG net fell has been sporadic and contradictory. And, of course, the Rasalhague Dominion has tightly controlled access by the media since they entered the picture. I've listened to several versions of the story of the fall since I've arrived, but from common people, merchants, hotel workers. None of them have the perspective you do."

Suddenly Elba looked annoyed, and he leaned forward. "Well, you may have all day to chat about these things, but I didn't come here to educate you about planetary history. I will educate you a little about *me*. I lost my fortune in the bank collapse of 3131 and '32. During the reign of the warlords I negotiated trades, pacts and surrenders between many of their enclaves by day, and worked with the resistance and refugee relocation the rest of the time.

"I was declared an outlaw by Jedra Kean two years ago, and I was one of many resistance fighters trying to form a shadow government when the Ghost Bears arrived. When they decided to go through the motions of creating a puppet government, they had little choice but to turn to me." He laughed. "To their eternal regret.

"Have you noticed I use a lot of contractions? You know why? Drives the Clanners crazy. I'll, I'll, I'll, don't, can't, won't." He leaned a little closer. "You want to know how to *really* get to them? Y'all. Lord, they hate that. Y'all."

Bane wasn't amused. "I'd think you'd be more favorably disposed toward the Clan people. Seems to me they rescued you from a dangerous life as an outlaw and installed you in a public position of power, when they certainly didn't need to."

Elba looked at him critically. "The Ghost Bears—I dislike calling them the Rasalhague Dominion; that's a smoke screen, like sugarcoating a horse apple—have come here for the same reason so many others have throughout history. We have resources. We have mines.

We have factories. And we have skilled workers who are the best in the Sphere, and have never been given their due. They've come to take advantage of our weakness, to rape our industry and enslave our workers, just like they did on the planets of their so-called Dominion."

The corners of Bane's mouth curled down in disapproval. He had a good feeling for when a person dropped out of stating their core beliefs and lapsed into rhetoric. Elba had just done so. "Mr. Elba, I'm not sure we can do business here."

Elba blinked at him in surprise. "What? You're making a mistake, Mr. Bane. If you really want to deal with the key people on Vega, you need to start with me."

"The Labor Party? From what I can see, you're important, but you don't even hold a political majority."

Elba smirked. "As I was under the warlords, I am still the focus of many powers not immediately visible." He nodded at the dusty room around them. "It isn't unusual for me to be meeting people in places like this. I've got clandestine locations all over the city, and even scattered elsewhere on the continent.

"The government the Ghost Bears have put together is a sham. Those of us granted even marginal freedom to speak are those they somehow imagine to be less dangerous, and less offensive. They're quite wrong in my case, but that was their intent.

"Though it pretends to be a democratic body, many of the Vegan people lack true representation. Some of them dare not even speak their minds in public. Many of those people talk to me."

"Terrorists?"

"Freedom fighters, some of them. Not all."

"They share the ideals of the Labor Party, then?"

Elba frowned. "Not exactly. But we're united in our opposition to the Ghost Bear occupation."

"Brothers in the principle of biting the hand that feeds you." Bane stood. "My employer greatly values loyalty.

Favors returned for favors done. I don't think we can work with you or your people, Mr. Elba."

The guard tensed, raising his weapon slightly, looking to Elba for guidance.

There was a polite knock at the door.

The guard glanced sideways at it, conflicted as to his next action.

Bane carefully kept his hands in plain sight, raising them slightly above his shoulders, palms forward, so the guard could see that he offered no threat.

The guard slid sideways and opened the door, pushing the muzzle of his weapon into the opening.

A meaty hand reached in to grab the barrel and yanked the guard who, unfortunately for him, had the weapon's heavy strap over his shoulder, out into the darkness.

Elba leaped to his feet but found himself looking down the barrel of the snub-nosed needler Bane had pulled from under his jacket.

Bane sniffed. "This is rude, I know, but I didn't want there to be any misunderstanding about our leaving, and you've made it clear to me that you're not a man who can be trusted."

Elba glared at him, his eyes like black diamonds. "I wasn't eager to let you run off so quickly, but you were in no danger."

"So you say. Me, I like some insurance."

There was a thud, like a body falling against an outside wall, and then Bruno Vic stuck his head through the door. "You good, boss?"

"I'm good. Just finishing up our conversation."

A hint of fear crept into Elba's expression. "You won't get away with shooting me."

Bane smiled, enjoying the moment. "Yeah. The Clan paramilitary police will be all over me if you go down." He chuckled. "They'd probably make me a Star colonel." Then he raised his weapon so that it no longer pointed at Elba. "I'm not sure we can be friends, but I hope there's no reason we've got to be enemies." He looked at Bruno. "You kill anybody, Bruno?"

Bruno shrugged. "Busted a few heads." He shrugged again. "Probably not."

"Good." He looked back at Elba. "You just send us a bill for the expenses."

"This is outrageous! You'll regret this."

"Probably less than you will." He considered for a moment. "There is one opportunity to keep the lines of communication open. Just help me out on a little thing. Get me a private audience with Galaxy Commander Bekker."

Elba laughed. "Even if I wanted to, you know there's no love lost between Bekker and me. I can do many things. That isn't one of them."

"How about Provisional Governor Florala?"

"That turncoat? Same difference, Bane. He's sleeping with the enemy. Literally. That isn't happening."

Bane frowned. "Too bad, Elba. Or can I call you 'Chance'? See, I know your kind of operator. Enemies or not, I don't doubt for a minute that you could put that meeting together to happen an hour from now, if you really wanted to. But you won't do that, because you're afraid that we'll do an end run around you if we make contact with them, which now"—he flashed a sour little smile—"is exactly what will happen."

Isis pulled her fur-trimmed coat tighter against the cold of the howling wind. Snow blew into her face and stuck, freezing to her numbed skin, building up like leaves falling on a grave. There was just light enough to see, but the sky was so dark and gray that she could not be sure if it was dusk or high noon.

Her gloved fingers tightened around the wooden shaft of the spear, and she held it ready, marching steadily through the maze of passages between the jagged slabs of broken pack ice and dark gray outcrops that marked the boundary between the frozen land and the frozen sea.

She stopped suddenly and kneeled, reaching down to put her hand in the footprint she had just spotted. Her hand was lost in the track, a deep oval depression in the snow nearly a meter long. She could see the outlines of the huge toes, and the gouges where its saberlike claws dug in as it walked.

Ghost bear!

Then she heard the roar.

It was deep, terrifying, haunting. It echoed through the maze, so that it could have come from a kilometer away, or ten meters. She couldn't tell.

Ahead, she saw another track. She stood up and began following the trail.

She tracked the bear for what seemed like hours, sometimes losing the trail on bare rock, but always able to pick it up again.

The trail seemed to end at a frozen lake.

She scanned the far shore, looking for the bear, but saw nothing.

Then came the roar.

Behind her.

This roar did not echo. It was close.

The bear had doubled back on the ice. Tricked her.

The hunter was now the hunted.

She turned to face the bear, a big male. He looked at her, reared up to his full five-meter height, and roared. The sound hit her like a shock wave, so that she felt it shaking inside her rib cage, vibrating in her chest.

She was in the open, exposed. This was no place to stand her ground.

She turned and ran. The bear dropped and came after her on all fours.

She zigzagged through the maze, taking the sharpest turns, the narrowest passages, to slow her pursuer. But she could hear the bear behind her, see it, when she dared look back. Bounding after her, great jaws open, small eyes glittering at her from under heavy, arched brows.

There was no rage there, no hatred, only grim determination.

Kill to eat.

Eat to live.

She was no enemy to the bear. She was only meat.

She ran. Ghost bears were supposed to hunt by ambush; strong sprinters but quick to tire. Not this one. Her heart pounded, her legs ached, her chest burned with every breath of frozen air. She felt she might die before the bear ever touched her.

She had to turn and fight.

Ahead, she saw a cave opening in a hillside. She scrambled up the rock, hearing the bear's thudding stride as it came after her. Just at the mouth of the cave, under an overhang, a slab of rock provided a kind of platform. There, she could face the bear eye to eye. There, she might have a chance, if she could get the bear to rear up and give her a target.

She turned, raised her arms to make herself look as big as possible, and roared her challenge at the approaching bear.

He did not stop. Did not respond. Did not return her challenge.

She was beneath his notice.

Except as meat.

Except as prey.

She ran into the cave, barely a step ahead of the bear. Cracks in the roof had allowed water to seep down during the rare summer thaws, and great stalactites, stalagmites and columns of ice decorated the chamber. Light came through from somewhere, refracting through the ice, turning blue and green, magically bathing every corner in soft color.

It was a beautiful place to die.

The bear reared enough to grab at her with its front

paws. She spotted a narrow space between two ice columns, and ducked under the bear's front legs, its bristly white hair actually brushing her face as she dived for cover. She slipped into the narrow opening and pushed herself backwards as far as she could, until her shoulders were jammed against the stone wall of the cave.

She could see nothing. The only sound was the bear breathing, the sniffing as he sought her scent.

Then the bear's paw shot into her hiding place with terrifying suddenness. It was like being struck at by a cobra the size of a small horse. The claws swept past her, shredding her jacket and cutting a gash in her arm.

The bear drew back slightly, then struck again, trying to find a way to reach deeper into the hole. She jabbed at the paw, stabbing the point of her spear deep into the pad.

The bear roared in pain, jerking the paw back and ripping the spear from her hands. She could glimpse the bear through the opening. It sat on its haunches examining the injury, then shook its paw violently until the spear flew free and clattered away to the floor of the cave.

The bear licked its paw for a moment, then looked back at her hiding place. It roared. This time it was angry, and with just cause.

She pushed herself as far back as she could, just as the bear's paw passed within inches of her leg. And she discovered that she could push herself upwards, that the ice and the cave wall formed a small chimney.

She jammed her back against the ice, digging her toes and fingers into whatever openings she could find in the rock, and pushed herself upwards. Centimeter by centimeter she ascended, all the while listening to the unhappy bear searching for her just beyond the ice. She had little doubt that the bear, had it been determined to do so, could have smashed the ice columns to reach her. If it became any angrier, it might yet do that.

At last she reached a kind of ledge and another narrow passage out between the ice columns. She crawled through the gap. The opening was nearly blocked by a thick stalactite of ice. She looked down, and she could see the bear pacing just below her.

She shifted her weight, and a crust of frozen blood cracked and broke off from her tattered jacket, landing on the floor next to the bear.

The great animal stooped, sniffed the frozen blood and suddenly looked up directly at her. It bellowed, reared up towards her and almost seemed to leap as it flailed its front paws just below her. The animal seemed to lose its footing, and fell heavily against the column below her.

The world seemed to tremble. She saw jagged cracks race like black lightning through the ice around her. Chunks of ice and loose stone rained down on her from above. She struggled to keep her footing on the narrow ice ledges that supported her.

The bear stared up at her, then reared up.

Again it missed. Again it reeled into the column. She almost fell forward out of the hole, catching herself on the stalactite. It cracked loudly, and shifted slightly under her weight.

The bear glared at her from below.

She was unarmed against the mighty ghost bear. The only weapon she had was her brain.

It would have to be enough.

She carefully placed her feet, and leaned out to shove on the stalactite. She pushed and shook it. Again, she heard cracking. Small bits of ice rained down. She had to break loose the hanging ice, and do it when the restless bear was directly underneath.

Her first attempt failed. The bear moved into position and she pushed, but the ice did not break.

When she looked down again, the bear was off to one side. She waited as he paced the room, finally settling down beneath her again, sitting back on his haunches, looking up.

She threw her weight against the ice.

It gave but did not break.

The bear, seeming to sense danger, started to move.

She pushed harder.

The ice snapped, suddenly falling away, throwing her off balance.

She teetered for an instant, the ice falling below her. Then she tumbled out into empty space, falling right toward the bear's waiting maw.

The blunt point of the ice struck the bear directly between the eyes. The bear grunted and lurched forward.

She landed directly between the bear's shoulder blades, thick layers of fur and fat breaking her eight-meter fall. She rolled, struck the stone floor with enough force to knock the air out of her lungs, rolled again and ended up sprawled facedown, gasping, on the cave floor.

She waited for the death blow.

It did not come.

When she regained control of her breathing, she lifted her head and saw before her a rolling mountain range of white fur and flesh. The bear lay sprawled on its back, chest barely rising and falling as she watched, pink tongue hanging from its mouth.

Helpless!

She moved, trying to get up. Her hand fell on something solid and round.

The shaft of the spear!

She struggled to her feet, took the spear in both hands and, marshaling her strength and courage, climbed onto the bear's belly. She stood over it, spear held high and aimed the point for the spot on the chest from which she could actually hear the great heart beating.

Then she saw the woman.

She was tall and looked strong, dressed in leather and fur. Not bear fur, Isis noted, but from the arctic hares and snow grazers that were the ghost bear's most frequent prey. She stood inside one of the great ice columns. Isis had seen that face a thousand times in history books and in official paintings.

It was Sandra Tseng.

Yet there was one startling difference from every picture of the woman that Isis had ever seen. The hair of the woman before her was snow-white, the color of the ghost bear. The look on Tseng's face was one of deep concern. She looked at Isis with compassion in her dark eyes. "Will you kill the bear?"

Isis looked down. Under her feet, she could feel the bear's breathing, the thudding of his heart. His life was her firmament.

"Will you kill the bear?"

She stood frozen, indecisive. A bear does not act in haste. A bear does not hurry. The bear twitched, the head moved, the tongue drew back into the mouth.

"Will you kill the bear? It will wake soon. You must decide now." Her eyes looked deep into Isis' soul. "Will you kill the bear?"

Before she could answer, she heard a man cry out—

She sat up in the darkness, her eyes wide, but the woman was gone. The bear was gone.

She was gasping, her heart pounding. It took her a moment to orient herself, to realize that she was in Vince's apartment rather than her own.

She remembered now the impassioned proceedings on the congressional floor, the awkwardness afterwards, and the moment when longing had overcome their mutual confusion.

She rarely slept in his bed. Usually they would couple, enjoy each other's company for a while and she would return to her own quarters. She was never really comfortable in Vince's apartment. It was too large, too ornate, too full of useless, inefficient clutter.

From across the room, a small fish tank gurgled, and in its dim light she could just make out her surroundings. She glanced over and saw Vince staring at her, rubbing his wrist. Suddenly, for the first time in her life, she felt naked and clutched the sheet, damp with her own sweat, to her chest.

"Are you okay? I thought you were going to break my arm."

She swallowed. Her mouth and lips were dry. She wanted water. "I just had a dream."

"A nightmare?"

She twitched. Nightmares were for children, not warriors. But certainly, the dream had disturbed her. "I dreamed about Strana Mechty, and the ghost bear.

"I dreamed about Sandra Tseng."

She could just see his eyes reflected in the dim light. "Are you saying you had some kind of vision?"

She laughed nervously. "I'm Ghost Bear, not Nova Cat. I don't believe in visions." She hung her head, letting her hair fall across her face. "But we used to say back in the sibko, sometimes a dream can be a message.

"A message from yourself."

10

I will never see Strana Mechty, where our Clan was born. That world was lost to us in the horror that was the War of Reaving.

This saddens me, not only that I will never see this place, but that none of our warriors will.

I cannot help but feel our Clan has lost something, something more important than land or territory, and I am not even sure what it is.

The life spans of warriors are traditionally short. It has been more than eighty years, almost two average warrior lifetimes, since the Ghost Bears abandoned their worlds in the Kerensky Cluster and moved nearly all their people and possessions to the Inner Sphere.

For the young warriors under my command, the time in the old Clan territories is ancient history.

Though we have struggled to maintain our traditions and ways, we are not the same people as the Ghost Bears who traveled back along the Exodus Road. I wonder if they would recognize us now, if they would look at us as our Clan brothers back in the Kerensky Cluster now look at us, and wonder if we can still be of the same body.

As I see it, two great forces have reshaped us in those eighty-plus years. The first is that we have lived among non-Clan people all this time. The natives of the occupied worlds far outnumber our people, and though our Clan's population has continued to grow, even our laborer caste remains a minority on the worlds we call our own.

We have struggled to keep ourselves above and apart, to maintain our rigid traditions and our warrior-bound honor.

But every day our young Clansmen and -women see people around them who do not share their discipline and, more importantly, do not labor under their responsibility. It is not the way of the Clans to believe the quality of one's life is measured in material possessions or in hedonistic pursuits, but these things are seductive, and we have been exposed to them for a very long time.

And along with those things comes a lifestyle of free—some would say lax—thinking and independent action.

In retrospect, it hardly seems surprising that many of the lower castes, especially the laborers, succumbed to those temptations. They did not have the benefit of a warrior's rigorous training, the fellowship of the lifelong bonds of the sibko, or the release of the rituals and trials of blood. And it is also not surprising that we, as warriors, increasingly isolated from those other castes, did not see what was happening until it was too late.

But the warriors had their own problems, and their true crisis arrived in slightly more recent times. In the 3080s, The Republic of the Sphere was formed under the leadership of Devlin Stone. So shining was his vision for his new republic that many factions within our Clan began to believe he held the key to forming a new union that would be the rightful successor of the Star League.

And so, despite much controversy, the Ghost Bears threw their full support behind his effort.

When Devlin Stone called for the Great Houses to decommission most of their 'Mechs and build a new, peace-driven economy, the Ghost Bears felt compelled to support him, much as it ran contrary to their instincts. They made a great show of being among the first to disarm, tearing down their OmniMechs and parting them out for scrap, and converting the factories that made them to other goods. Or so it seemed.

Their efforts were successful. Shamed that Clansmen would choose to lay down arms before they would, the other Great Houses followed suit. But what they did not know was that many of the 'Mechs were not destroyed. Some were stripped down to shells, which were hidden or buried against future need. Some were partially scrapped, with parts from different 'Mechs collected so that they might be reassembled into a single functioning unit on short notice.

Some 'Mechs were simply hidden, placed in caves or abandoned bunkers, or sunk to the bottoms of lakes.

Though we lost countless 'Mechs and most of our immediate production capability, the Ghost Bears were never as helpless as we made ourselves appear. Though we believed in Devlin Stone, we did not trust the Great Houses, and we felt we had to be ready to defend The Republic if and when the time came.

Our fears, of course, were justified.

But while we waited for that inevitable betrayal, we faced the second force that would change our Clan. Our tradition of trials by combat was thrown into disarray: MechWarriors faced trials with no 'Mechs to fight in.

There existed a whole generation of MechWarriors who had never sat in the cockpit of a real 'Mech. Some warriors were diverted into conventional armored forces or infantry, but such forces have never held much prestige in the Clans, and even these forces were greatly reduced during the peak years of The Republic.

During that time, it became common for trials to be fought in simulators rather than with real 'Mechs, tanks or aerospace assets. In a way, it seemed an ideal solution.

Clan simulators are stunningly realistic, and a warrior can get far more cockpit time in a simulator than they ever could hope to experience in a live 'Mech or other high-value combat vehicle. Using simulators, both training and trials could be carried out in secret from the rest of The Republic, maintaining the illusion of the "peaceful" Ghost Bears. Many warriors thrived in this environment, spending countless hours in simulated battle, honing their skills to a razor's edge.

It can perhaps be said of the MechWarriors of that period that they were the most technically skilled in our Clan's history.

Skill alone does not matter.

Warriors need far more than skill in battle. They need courage. They need composure under fire. They need the ability to fight through pain and injury.

Some warriors are born with these things, but despite three centuries of the eugenics program, the scientists have yet to isolate those particular genes. Some warriors must learn these qualities. Still others will never possess them, and should be culled from the ranks before they can endanger others in combat.

Those things cannot be determined in a simulator.

After Devlin Stone withdrew from The Republic and the need to rearm became clear, there were too few 'Mechs to allow for any but the most important and high-profile trials. The average warrior still settled disputes or fought for rank in a simulator.

When I assumed command of Omega Galaxy, I set out to end all that. I declared that all trials must be trials of blood, all combat must risk mortal injury.

For many Ghost Bears, that meant hand-to-hand combat, as our long-standing emphasis on such skills has made most of our warriors deadly in their use. But trials by knife, sword or even using small arms became more common. Warriors facing a Trial of Position were required to prove their technical skills in simulator trials, yes, but that was only a preliminary to the trial of blood.

During this time I began wearing my ceremonial sword in public as a sign of my devotion to the principle of mortal combat, even for MechWarriors. I participated in my share of trials as well, and in each, I prevailed.

The effect on warrior morale was immediate, and I felt that the core of my forces became immeasurably stronger. Other Galaxy commanders obviously thought so as well because they also adopted the practice, and at last it was endorsed by vote of the Clan Council—even if by then others had attached their names to the idea.

But I also faced criticism. Warriors died in trials, and this potential for fatal injury was a new phenomenon to this generation. The ranks were thinned further by warriors testing down to lower castes. I accepted that these men and women should never have been warriors, and believed that we were stronger without them, even if our numbers were reduced.

Not everyone agreed. I made enemies. It was then I discovered that, in the upper power structure of a Clan, strength can be weakness.

I have always had a talent for working with individuals outside the warrior caste and with those outside the Clan. I suspect this is why I was placed in command of the Omega Galaxy, the Raging Bears, which has a long tradition of adopting Inner Sphere tactics and being deployed only to fight against, or even alongside, non-Clan forces.

This principle of fighting fire with fire has been quite successful and given us some glorious victories, but the Omega Galaxy has always been held in low regard by more traditional Ghost Bear units. It has traditionally been treated by the Khans as a necessary evil, useful to have around but never to be celebrated. There have always been those who felt the unit had gone too far from the traditional ways and should be dissolved, or even completely Abjured from the Clan.

Still, I took my position with pride and have always strived to meld its unconventional traditions with the true honor of the Ghost Bear Clan. For my enemies, that would never be enough. The taint of the Omega Galaxy was on me, and I soon realized that I would never be free of it.

And so began the seeming decline that eventually led us to Vega.

You might wonder how we, least favored of the three Galaxies sent to stabilize those six worlds of The Republic, ended up with the two planets we did.

Cebalrai is rather obvious. The planet is a hellhole, desirable more for its strategic location than for any advantageous characteristic. The disturbances there were minor, and the planet required a simple police action rather than a war.

Our assignment to restore Vega likely seems more of a mystery to you. Of the six worlds, it was where the fiercest early resistance could be expected, and was therefore the source for the most glory to the unit and its warriors. Of the six worlds, it was the most important on any number of counts. Not only was it a former prefecture capital, a rich source of raw materials and historically a great industrial world, it was also regarded by many as the birthplace of the Star League.

But it is this last characteristic that likely discouraged the other Galaxies from bidding on Vega. Certainly, great glory would adhere to any Galaxy that could restore order to a planet of such importance to all Clans. From the vantage point of our occupation zone, we could see that the task would be long and difficult. Even before we arrived, some said it was impossible.

And if restoring the home of the Star League would bring glory to the Galaxy that accomplished it, to the Galaxy that failed it would bring eternal shame.

Nasew Spaceport, Southwest Industrial District
Nasew, North Nanturo continent, Vega
28 November 3136

Star Colonel Conner Hall walked the catwalk running
the length of the 'Mech hangar, observing the activity as
the 'Mechs along each wall underwent repair and service.

Everywhere sparks flew from welders and grinders.
The overhead cranes cycled back and forth constantly,
carrying weapon pods, complete arms, myomer bundles,
actuators, jump-jet assemblies. The recent influx of parts
had sent the unit's technicians into a frenzy of repairs.

It was good to see.

Lack of parts had sidelined many of the Clan 'Mechs
and left the technicians with little to do but organize
their repair bays and scrub up the odd oil spot. He heard
many complaints, most not intended for his ears, and
knew that morale had been slipping.

Doubtless this discontent and lack of work accounted
for some of the Freeminder graffiti he'd been seeing.
But now, looking down at the technicians, who outnumbered the warriors in his unit a hundred to one, he saw
only busy hands and happy faces. Surely the Freeminder
activity would subside.

If even he, in the warrior caste, had been feeling frustration and doubt, how must it be for the worker ants
teeming below?

He tried to put himself into their minds, and found it
a curious place to be. A warrior always had some control
over his destiny. A warrior responded to order and discipline, of course, but they were the claws of the Ghost
Bear. When the time came to act, they were the ones in
action. A warrior was in control of his skills, of his emotions and, ultimately, his destiny. How would it be to
work your whole life as simply a cog in a greater
machine?

A technician could repair a 'Mech. A scientist could
design one. A laborer could build one. A merchant could

secure the materials for one. But they would never sit in the cockpit and take one into combat. They could never experience the thrill of victory, except vicariously.

How did one exist like that? It was tempting for a warrior to believe that the other castes were simply different, that they did not have the interest or inclination to enter combat.

Yet often, late at night or when most of the warriors were out on missions, Conner had discovered technicians in the 'Mech simulators, fighting with great enthusiasm and energy if not a lot of skill. They would quickly explain that they were simply recalibrating the screens or some such nonsense, but he knew better. Some warriors would have been infuriated. Conner was secretly pleased, though he could not admit it to the technicians. He wanted his techs to have spirit, to want the kill as he wanted the kill.

Of course, as Isis Bekker was fond of pointing out, simulators were not combat. To sit in the safety of a simulator and fire at an enemy that cannot truly harm you is nothing like facing death on the battlefield. But there too, Conner had seen things that made him think.

During their landing on Vega, two descending Drop-Ships had been knocked down by unexpected ground fire, a loss of resources from which the Raging Bears had yet to recover. One of the ships had come down in a zone saturated in heavy fire, and Conner had led a salvage and rescue mission to the crashed ship.

His column included a force of technicians in service vehicles and unarmed loader 'Mechs. They'd found the spherical DropShip looking like a dropped melon at the edge of a salt marsh. The lower half of the hull had been crushed, and the broken and burning dome of the upper hull loomed over them.

While the warriors took up defensive positions and laid down covering fire, the technicians had waded into the wreckage through snake-filled marsh water, pulled out the few survivors and delivered them to the MASH units. Then they returned to the ship for salvage, hacking apart wrecked 'Mechs while mortar shells fell around them and lasers melted off what little armor their IndustrialMechs carried.

Several fell to enemy fire, but none had faltered. None asked to retreat; Conner himself gave the order to withdraw. There were those among the technician ranks who did not lack for courage or nerve.

He wondered how they saw him. He knew that every man and woman down on that floor knew his name and the name of every other MechWarrior in Omega Galaxy. He knew the lower castes avidly followed the missions and victories of the warrior caste, as much as security allowed. Children collected and traded cards printed with warriors' pictures and combat statistics.

He had heard some compare this activity with the way spheroids followed football or soccer, and there were parallels. But it was not the same. The Ghost Bears had their own sports and were quite fond of "American" football. There were leagues, and games were broadcast over the tri-vid nets.

But while there might be some small matters of personal honor at stake in the outcome of a game, football was just an entertainment, like an Honor Play or a Clan Spaniel cartoon. The accomplishments of the warriors were the lifeblood of the Clan. They were the measure by which all castes judged their value, and the success of their work.

A lift rose up to the catwalk ahead of him and jolted to a stop. A female technician stepped off onto the steel grating, oblivious to Conner's presence.

Conner recognized her as Chief Machinist Joanna, one of the ship supervisors. He stepped forward and announced himself. "Chief Machinist!"

She turned and, seeing him, snapped to a respectful attention. "Star Colonel! I was not told you were on the hangar floor."

He grinned. "Technically, I am forty meters above it. I came up here via the outside stairs. Sometimes I just like to stand up here and watch, especially when your teams are busy."

"Yes, sir. We are certainly busy today, and glad of it."

"How is the progress?"

"Warrior Jorgen's 'Mech is fully operational again. I anticipate that you will reassign it since he will not return to duty for some time. With the new parts, we expect to complete the overhaul on the two other 'Mechs in the bay within five days. They have been out of service since the final battle with Jedra Kean. I think the one on the end may actually be the machine in which the Galaxy commander brought down Kean's *Atlas,* though by now it is about sixty percent swapped-out parts. It was in bad shape when they brought it in."

He looked down to the end of the near row of 'Mechs, where four non-Clan units, two *Spiders,* an *Uller* and a *Rifleman* at least appeared to be coming together well. "How about the salvage units? How are they going?"

She glanced at them and wrinkled her nose. Clan technicians generally felt that non-Clan tech was inferior and barely worthy of their attention. "We are still missing a few small but critical parts. I have been in contact with our units in other cities, and we are engaging in another round of battlefield salvage as schedule and hostile action permit. We think we know where to find the parts, but we have to collect them, and then they may have to come from as far as Neucason. It could take us two more weeks."

"Make it a priority. I want to start moving the FVR MechWarriors into real 'Mechs as quickly as possible."

She gave him a strange look, and he flashed back to his curiosity about how their minds worked.

Making a guess at her question, he added, "Chief Machinist, though they are not Clan, the FVR is central, vital even, to our mission here. Perhaps if you ask your technicians to think of their victories as our victories, that may make working on these 'Mechs a little less distasteful."

She smirked. "Yes, Star Colonel. Perhaps a little."

"Get to it then."

"Yes, sir!" She turned and walked rapidly away.

Conner caught movement from the corner of his eye and realized a lone warrior standing on a connecting work platform had overheard his conversation. The warrior stepped closer, out of the shadows, and Conner could see that it was Duncan Huntsig, a dark expression twisting his broad features.

He walked up to Conner, planted his feet apart, and crossed his arms over his chest. "Why do we waste our resources on them, Star Colonel? You plan to give these 'Mechs to the Vegan freeborn, when many of our own MechWarriors lack functional 'Mechs. You allow the freeborn to fight with us, when their worthless Industrial-Mechs only slow down our formations and make us convenient targets for our enemies."

He studied Huntsig, considering how he should respond. He was glad to finally have the man's concerns out in the open. His resentment had been simmering too long. "Rebuilding the Vega forces so that they can defend and police themselves *is* one of our primary missions here, MechWarrior. We cannot do that without putting them into combat and, for the moment, that means fielding them in the best equipment we can spare.

"These are not Clan 'Mechs. Our MechWarriors would not feel comfortable in them, even if I were to assign them to our units. Parts for them are not available through our supply chains, so their operational readiness will never come up to our standards. In effect, I am using them as training 'Mechs, which is their best application at this time."

Waves of anger and disgust warred on Huntsig's face. He literally quivered with suppressed emotion. Finally, the true reason for his anger came out. "You will put them in 'Mechs, and they will take the few real targets available on this forsaken world!

"There is no *glory* here! All around us The Republic is crumbling and its territories are in question. There are battles everywhere, and we rot on this world, facing invisible enemies without the honor to face us in honest combat!"

Conner sighed. He did not blame Huntsig for his attitude, because part of him felt the same. Loyalty kept Conner here, because loyalty was as much a part of Conner Hall as his bones.

"Put in for a transfer to another Galaxy. I will not stop you."

Huntsig laughed harshly. "When was the last time another Galaxy accepted a transfer request from the Omega Galaxy? A year? Two years? Such a request would only put me at the end of a long line that no longer moves. To be part of Omega Galaxy is to carry a taint on one's reputation. Without an outstanding battle record, there is no escape, but without escape, there is no chance to achieve such a record. No, what glory I can bring to my codex is here, and I swear I will find it!"

"Have patience—there may yet be opportunities for proper battle. Our intelligence sources continue to find evidence of Draconis Combine agents on Vega. They have a long-standing interest in this world, and its instability has not escaped their notice."

"Why then has it escaped ours? We should not be engaging in a futile effort to repair this broken world. We should be claiming it in the name of the Rasalhague Dominion, or more properly, for the Ghost Bear Clan! They need order and we can give them order, but on our terms, not those of idiotic Inner Sphere politicians."

Huntsig's anger seemed to diminish. "I will not be placated with rumors of spies and saboteurs, Star Colonel. We have enough of those here without imagining shadowy threats from off-world. As for patience—how patient were Laumer, or Bruce Tseng, or any of the others who have fallen without glory?"

Conner experienced the dead calm of acceptance he always felt entering a battle. "If you find my command incompetent, MechWarrior, you know your right. You know your duty.

"Do you wish to challenge me in a Trial of Refusal? For I would welcome it."

Huntsig considered. There was no fear in his eyes, only the hesitation of someone thinking through his best course of action. "No, Star Colonel, I do not. For if I bested you in trial, my next challenge would have to be the Galaxy commander herself, and I do not wish to attain her position."

He turned as if to walk away, then turned back. "I will not die in my bed, Star Colonel. I will not rest until I have earned honor for my codex by laying down my life in battle. So I swear."

Conner watched him march to the nearest stairway and begin the long climb down to the hangar floor. Then he turned away, and left by the same door he'd entered.

Huntsig only said what many other warriors dared not, at least not to their commander's face. Huntsig only wanted to be the best MechWarrior he could be, to bloody himself in service to their Clan. There was nothing wrong with that.

The problem was that Huntsig said all this and yet refused to properly challenge him. Now was perhaps not the best time for a trial, but at least the matter would be settled according to Clan tradition. The spheroid military had a term for this situation that seemed to apply. *Insubordination.*

He stepped through the door and out onto the landing. As the door swung shut, a hissing noise above and behind him caught his attention. He turned to see a small man in maintenance coveralls hanging from the roof by a narrow cable and a leather harness. He stared at Conner, eyes wide, a paint wand in his right hand and a small control box in his left. On the wall in front of him were the words THINK FREE. The last *E* was not quite complete.

They stared at each other for a moment, and then the man pushed a button on the control box. Somewhere above, an electric motor whirred and the man ascended rapidly up the wall of the hangar, his feet leaving smears in the wet paint as he bounced past, until he scrambled over the lip of the roof and disappeared.

Conner looked at the not-quite-completed graffiti and blinked in amazement, not entirely able to accept what he had just seen. Who did he think had been painting graffiti on the walls? Laborers? Janitors, or perhaps groundskeepers?

But the coveralls proved this was one of his own mechanics. One of the people he and his MechWarriors trusted with their lives every time they climbed into their 'Mechs.

And though he didn't know the man's name, he had seen him before. He knew that face!

Security Chief Ricco stood in the middle of the empty hotel suite as his officers searched the abandoned rooms, pulling out drawers, turning over mattresses, moving furniture, looking for any evidence of who the occupants had been or where they had gone. So far, they had found nothing. The room's occupants had been thorough.

This carefulness extended to their vehicle. They had registered a car when they checked in, and records showed it leaving and returning several times since. But the vehicle registration system had been destroyed in the Warlord Massacres, and there was no way to trace ownership through the recorded license.

In any case, Ricco was sure that would be a dead end as well. They'd put out an alert for their patrols to watch for the license number, then discovered the car was still parked in the garage, empty and just as clean as the room.

Not that they had left no evidence. There were plenty of fingerprints. Hairs on the sink and bathroom floor. A used tissue in the wastebasket. But the care with which gross evidence had been removed suggested to Ricco that this was not an oversight. He suspected that he would have no luck identifying the men using fingerprints or DNA.

A man wearing a white housekeeping uniform entered the open door to the suite, followed closely by Inquisitor Janine. Since Ricco was keeping quiet the possible involvement of Bannson on Vega, and Janine already knew about the gold that had been found so far, he had decided to keep her involved in the investigation.

Ricco studied the man. He was tall, round-faced, dark of hair and complexion, with a neatly trimmed goatee. He looked curiously at the activity in the suite, but did not give the impression that he was particularly nervous, or that he had anything to hide. He looked at Ricco, clearly choosing him as the man in charge. He pointed a finger accusingly. "Are you *sure* you have the authority to do this? Because my people are going to have to clean all this up."

When the man spoke, there was a slight accent that Ricco couldn't identify. Probably not a native Vegan then, and that caught his interest. Could this possibly be a Draconis Combine agent? He discarded that idea. Ricco's reading of Inner Sphere criminology texts told him that hotel work was always a magnet for immigrant labor, so there was no likely reason to be suspicious. "We are acting under the authority of the Provisional Government. We have the authority to burn this place to the ground if we can think of even half an excuse."

The man seemed taken aback, but not intimidated. "Well," he said, "okay then."

"You have a name?"

"Yes." He stared at Ricco. "Oh! That was a question!"

The man was playing dumb, Ricco was sure of that.

"Reese Fentun. I'm in charge of the housekeeping staff at the hotel, what there is of it."

"You saw the men who last occupied this room?"

He smiled. "Oh, yes! Many times. Mr. Smith and Mr. Jones, they were very nice guests. Good tippers." He looked around at the demolished room. "I don't suppose you are going to be leaving a tip, are you?"

"You could identify these men?"

"Of course."

He looked at Janine. "I assume you checked with hotel security. Do they show up on any security camera records?"

She frowned. "Half the security cameras in the hotel no longer work, and most of those that do cannot record. The cameras in the lobby and by the desk record, but at those times when we know they were there, such as check-in, the cameras are not operational. The recording is just video noise."

"A jamming device."

She nodded.

Jamming even a halfway-decent security camera with a portable device was not easy. That told him only that the people he was seeking had access to expensive high-technology toys. People like employees of Jacob Bannson. He looked back at Fentun. "You could describe these men to a technician, so we can create a composite image?"

Fentun looked surprised. "Well—sure I could."

He looked at Janine. "Hold him until we can get a technician here."

Fentun looked annoyed. "I have work to do."

"It will have to wait. Go with the Inquisitor."

Janine started to walk back to the door, but Fentun just stood there, a slightly confused look on his face. "Don't you want to see the note?"

Ricco blinked. "Note? What note?"

Fentun reached inside his white jacket and drew out a sealed hotel stationery envelope. He presented it to

Ricco. "Like I told the nice lady, Mr. Smith and Mr. Jones checked out this morning. They told me that some people might come looking for them, and if so, I was to tell them everything they wanted to know, and give them this note."

Ricco took the envelope cautiously by the corner between his thumb and forefinger. He examined it, then held it up to the window, looking for signs of a letter bomb or some similarly dangerous content.

"Oh for the love of—!" Fentun's tone was scolding. "It's just paper! I watched him write it out and put it the envelope myself!"

He scowled at Fentun again and took out a folding pocketknife, which he used to carefully slit open the envelope. He held it over a white tablecloth as he pulled out the note, in case anything of interest fell out.

Nothing did.

The letterhead, like the envelope, was hotel stationery. He had a feeling it was written with a hotel pen, too. It read:

> *To whom it may concern:*
>   *Sorry we missed you. Leave a message at the desk.*
>   *Taylor Bane*

Bane watched through the heavily tinted windows of their new car—much nicer than the old one, a welcome fringe benefit—as Reese, the head of hotel housekeeping, was escorted to a waiting paramilitary police van. Doubtless they would shortly have reasonably accurate images of him and Vic, and a record of their actions while at the hotel.

That didn't bother him. The high-profile part of their assignment on Vega was over. They'd made their presence known and left enough bread crumbs for the concerned parties to follow them. Now they had potential enemies here as well as potential friends, and stealth was called for.

He wasn't much concerned about the paramilitary police. Clan cops were plodding and obvious, not really experienced with people actively trying to elude them. Clan criminals, from what he had seen, were prone to giving themselves up and invoking *surkai*—forgiveness.

Chumps. If you could still feel like you needed forgiveness for something, you should never do it in the first place.

He looked down at the two envelopes in his hand, which a hired agent had collected from the front desk shortly before the paramilitary police arrived. Collecting future information without tipping off the police would be slightly more complicated, but nothing he couldn't deal with. Many people at the hotel had collected big tips from him, with the promise of more for future service.

He imagined that Reese had turned over the his third envelope to the paramilitary police. That still left seven in the stack he'd given the man, assuming that they were still locked in his office and that the police didn't find them. If he lost access to those envelopes, that would be too bad, but hardly tragic. The two notes in his possession were as much as or more than he'd expected to collect from the arrangement.

He ripped open the end of one envelope—Bruno had already checked them with a bomb-detecting wand—and extracted the paper inside. He opened it and began to read. He smiled. "Good news, Bruno. One of the major players we came to talk with has finally entered the picture."

"That's great, boss."

"You bet it is. Because the package is on the way, and it's going to get delivered, one way or the other. The only question is, who's the lucky recipient?"

11

*From the Great Work of
Galaxy Commander Isis Bekker*

The fundamental principle of the Clans we do not owe to the man who founded them, Nicolas Kerensky. In fact, that principle predates the formation of the Clans, and is our gift from the Great Father, Aleksandr Kerensky. It is known as the Hidden Hope Doctrine, and as set forth by the elder Kerensky described how the Clans were destined one day to return to the Inner Sphere, bringing with them the enlightenment of the Star League.

In recent times, Aleksandr Kerensky's once-sacrosanct role in history has come into question. Certainly he made mistakes, and dark events took place under his command. But in the larger scope of our society it is the Hidden Hope Doctrine that may have caused the most trouble for the Clans.

Not the doctrine itself, which was clearly created with the most noble intentions and without which the Clans themselves probably would not exist. That there would one day be a return, a day when the Clans would come home to the Inner Sphere, was never in question.

The problem was that, over time, various Clans and

factions chose to interpret that doctrine differently, and also the meaning of the return. Eventually, this would develop into the one gaping fracture along which all the Clans were not-so-neatly divided, the division of Wardens and Crusaders.

The Wardens believed that the Clans should remain in their place of exile and wait patiently for an external threat that would endanger all of humanity. Then, and only then, would they sweep in to be mankind's deliverers and finally fulfill their destiny.

The Crusaders were not patient. It was their belief that the Inner Sphere had already fallen into barbarism, that its darkest hour was already at hand, and that only immediate conquest and domination by the Clans could rescue them from that darkness.

Ultimately, the Crusaders would have their way, convincing the Clans to return to the Inner Sphere not as rescuers, but as conquerors.

The Crusaders were wrong.

The Inner Sphere was not as weak as they imagined, nor were the Clans as strong. Though victories were won and conquests claimed, the Inner Sphere rallied against Clan aggression and ultimately ended the invasion through the trial that came to be known as the Great Refusal.

History had spoken, and declared that our destiny lay elsewhere.

In my opinion, however, most of the Warden Clans also were wrong. The only great threat to the Inner Sphere had proven to be the Clans themselves. Though some Warden Clans still wait to make this commitment, the return to the Inner Sphere has already begun. My beloved Ghost Bears are living proof.

Even now, most Clansman still define themselves and their Clans in line with those two camps, the Wardens and the Crusaders. As much as any Clan, in their long history the Ghost Bears have walked the line between these two camps.

Since the time of the Great Refusal, we have clearly defined ourselves as Wardens. Yet we were willing participants in the invasion of the Inner Sphere, and it is we who have most visibly profited from it. It is we who continue to occupy holdings in the Inner Sphere. The duality of our position is obvious.

Or, I should say, it is obvious if you define the world only in terms of Warden and Crusader. It is my assertion that history may judge the Ghost Bears to be neither Warden nor Crusader, but something new. Something important. Something that may reflect the true destiny of the Clans as it was intended by the Great Father, and his son who followed.

Could it be, by accident or by design, that we unknowingly hang on the ragged edge of our destiny?

The Ghost Bears have returned to the Inner Sphere, but what have we done here? It is true that we helped foster Devlin Stone's Republic of the Sphere and its era of peace. It is true we have brought the native people of the Rasalhague Dominion together and given them the dual gifts of security and prosperity.

But though we are in the Inner Sphere, we have never allowed ourselves to be of it. We have kept ourselves apart from the people around us, the people to which the Great Father said one day we would return.

How then, are we to deliver to them the "enlightenment" of which Aleksandr Kerensky spoke?

That is the riddle.

If it can be solved, then our Hidden Hope may be much closer than we ever imagined.

Confederate Mk III-*class* DropShip Vancouver
72 kilometers above North Nanturo continent,
  Vega
29 November 3136

Star Colonel Conner Hall hung in the harness of his command couch as the buffeting g-forces of reentry increased. His 'Mech shook mightily, but the clamps in the DropShip's 'Mech bay held it securely.

He glanced out through the ferroglass cockpit at Karen's AgroMech, locked into the rack next to his. Her cockpit was several meters lower than his, and he was surprised to discover that he had a clear view into her cockpit.

Usually, the thick ferroglass of a 'Mech's cockpit prevented two pilots from clearly seeing one another. But here, through some trick of light and angle, he could see her perfectly, like a fish in a bowl.

He felt like a spy, looking down on her from above. She sat rigid in her cockpit, a grim but determined look on her face, like someone enduring an uncomfortable but necessary medical procedure.

He thumbed up a private com channel. "Karen."

She started, glanced up toward his cockpit, and smiled. He suddenly realized that the trick of light worked both ways. She could see him as well. The smile turned sheepish, and she almost seemed to blush. "Hi, up there."

"Hi, yourself. You don't seem to be enjoying the flight."

"The good thing about this," she said, "is that it will make the part at the end with the people shooting at us seem so nice by comparison."

He laughed. "It will be done soon enough. I wish I could say the worst is over, but this is a combat landing, and we will be coming in hot and fast. The pilot will not hit full throttle until the last instant, and even then he will count on the landing gear to take up some of the shock. It could be a rough ride."

She grinned. "Well, thanks for that comforting preview."

"It is better to know what is coming."

"I'm not so sure about that."

He glanced at the flight status screen on his heads-up display, a glowing outline of the DropShip descending steeply toward a moving display of the terrain. Time was short, and Karen was not the only officer under his command. "I should go," he said, getting ready to change to the command-loop frequency. "Time to address the troops."

"Wait!"

She gazed up at him, a strange look in her eyes. She licked her lips, nervously. "When we get back to base—Well . . . that coupling thing." She swallowed. "We could have another talk about that."

He laughed softly. "I would like that."

"Don't sound so smug."

"That was not my intention. Actually, I had made some inquiries with the locals about your customs. I have had any number of dining and dancing establishments recommended to me. I only regret security concerns make them pretty much out of the question."

"We'll pop open some field rations and turn on some music. That's good enough for me."

"We will consider it a—date, then." The ship shuddered especially hard, reminding him that the landing was coming up fast. "I must go. Gravity waits for no man."

He switched over to the command channel. "Your attention, Star. The good news is, we are about to engage in the first 'Mech combat on Vega since the fall of Jedra Kean. The bad news is, we have not had time to practice DropShip deployment. Listen up, FVRs. Wait for external clamp release when we land. Fight them, and you'll damage your machines. Release them internally, and you might release too soon, which could leave you bouncing all over the inside of the bay, damaging yourself, the ship and the rest of the 'Mechs in the Star.

"Keep in mind that the DropShip is a flying fortress, with armor and lasers of its own. You will not need to protect it and, initially, it can protect you. The five laser turrets are located between the bay doors, so stay clear of their lines of fire. Let them cover you, and concentrate on disembarking and forming up. Once we are clear of the ship, I will take point. Captain Tupolov, you are left flank. Lieutenant Chow, you are right flank. Lieutenant Kortlever, you watch my back. MechWarrior Huntsig, you are end cap."

He heard an unhappy grunt from the radio and assumed it was Huntsig.

Conner ignored him and continued. He could hear the fusion drive kick in at minimum throttle, creating a plasma sheath that would reduce the amount the hull heated in the atmosphere. G-force was approaching maximum, but his training kept him alert and talking.

"We are responding to a report by a local militia patrol out of Fargo City, about four hundred kilometers from Nasew. That makes this a relatively short trip on a high ballistic arc, and a rough ride. The description of the enemy is a single light 'Mech, possibly an *Anubis*. If that is accurate, the unit will be light and stealthy, with long-range missiles and lasers. AgroMechs will need to be cautious. This 'Mech has light armor, so if we can corner it and hit it, we can take it out quickly and easily."

"Star Colonel, should not I be in the front of the formation with you? Our 'Mechs are a better match for this machine, and we can run interference for the FVR units. They could take damaging fire from those missiles before they can close to fighting range."

Well, that was unusually polite. Perhaps Huntsig is changing his strategy.

He heard the fusion engines throttle up even more. The pilot was scanning for their target and maneuvering to put them down as close as possible.

"Negative. Our intelligence here is uncertain. I will keep Kortlever close and take fire for him. The rest of the formation is to hang well back and cover us in case our target has friends. Huntsig, you are responsible for covering Tupolov and Chow. If a secondary target appears, draw fire and help them maneuver into fighting range."

"Secondary targets? This is the first 'Mech we have seen in almost a year."

The fusion engines cut and the g-force slacked off; Conner felt his stomach trying to leap up into his chest. The DropShip was currently a falling object.

A female voice spoke in Conner's headset.

"Pilot to 'Mechs. I'm having trouble getting a solid lock on your target, but I should be able to put you down within a few kilometers and give you a vector."

"Good enough," replied Conner. "Give us a deployment count as soon as you are ready."

The fusion drive rumbled to life again. For a moment it remained at minimum throttle, as though anticipating. Then it roared to maximum throttle, the roar deafening, the intense vibration causing Conner's vision to blur. The g-force was intense, and he knew the nozzle linings wouldn't survive more than a few seconds at this thrust. Either they were very low and the pilot knew what she was doing, or they were dead.

There was a teeth-rattling impact, a bang as the landing gear telescoped out and slammed against the stops before recoiling slightly. The fusion drive cut and it was suddenly quiet except for the turbine pumps winding down and the hydraulics in the landing gear shifting as the DropShip leveled itself.

"Pilot to 'Mechs. We have no visual with the enemy. Landing zone looks cold. Ten seconds to clamp release. Doors in twenty seconds. Ramps deploying now."

Conner heard the whir of electric motors as the loading ramps extended down. It was a critical moment. Often, if there was going to be enemy fire, the sudden movement would trick them into firing prematurely.

Above the 'Mech bay he could hear the whirs and clunks of the defensive turrets moving as they swept the surroundings looking for a target. But they did not fire.

"Zone is still cold," said the pilot.

This may be a quiet mission after all.

Conner stretched in his couch, feeling compacted by the reentry and hard landing. He shifted his 'Mech's systems out of standby, scanned all his system displays and armed his weapons. He took hold of the grip on his control stick and tested his feet against the pedals. Through his neurohelmet he could feel the 'Mech come alive, its weight and balance shifting.

"Clamps," said the pilot. "Three, two, one, release."

There was a loud clanking noise behind his head and Conner's 'Mech was suddenly free to move. He put his weapons on standby and let the sensors and targeting systems do a quick diagnostic; all green. "Huntsig, you and I are first out. FVRs, exit on a three-count. Kortlever, get close and stay close. Keep your eyes open."

"Yes, Star Colonel!" Kortlever was green, but a good marksman and sharp under pressure.

"Doors," said the pilot, "three, two one, open!"

The DropShip's 'Mech bay was a donut-shaped space surrounding the fusion drive. Five doors, one for each 'Mech, rolled up in unison.

Conner throttled up and walked his 'Mech rapidly forward. He could see Huntsig moving out of the bay to his right. They both strode down the ramps, the 'Mechs' feet thundering on the metal. Conner kept going, but Huntsig slowed at the bottom of the ramp. In his rear camera, he could see the FVR AgroMechs emerging from the other doors. Kortlever's immediately throttled up to a full run and pulled in behind him.

The rest of the formation fell in behind.

The DropShip had landed at the bottom of a shallow valley. A small river snaked along the valley floor through marshy grass meadows. Steep, rolling hills surrounded the valley.

"Pilot," Conner said, "you have that vector for us?"

"Turn course two-eight-zero. We estimate the target is six to eight kilometers on that vector, apparently with good ECM. I am sorry we are not closer, but terrain limited our choice of landing sites. We will stay here unless the site becomes too hot, and that seems unlikely. Remember that recall code is November Surprise."

Conner grinned. "Very good. Thank you, *Vancouver*."

They turned to the suggested compass heading and moved out of the valley along a narrower gorge. There were scattered trees at the bottom; tall, narrow hardwoods growing thicker as they ascended the walls on either side.

It was an easy path to follow, but it was also ideal for an ambush.

The topographical maps the Clans had obtained of the planet often had proven to be inaccurate, so he did not fully trust his map display. "Pilot, what did you see coming in? What are we headed into?"

"The cut you are in should take you close to the target. At about kilometer four, things flatten out a bit. At kilometer five, there is a small lake with forest that extends to the north along the shore. And at kilometer six there is the beginning of a burn, possibly a recent forest fire."

Conner throttled up his *Karhu* as much as he dared without losing Lieutenant Kortlever's slower AgroMech MOD. He had a momentary second thought about deploying the FVR units. They would be at a huge disadvantage against a fast 'Mech like an *Anubis*.

Of course, if the enemy 'Mech decided to run, the *Karhu* wouldn't be able to keep up either. If the *Anubis* stood and engaged them, the terrain might minimize the advantage of the target's speed and maneuverability.

As promised, the hills separated ahead of them, forming a shallow bowl with a quiet lake at the center. Beyond that, a saddle between two hills was marked by the blackened and defoliated trunks of trees.

Conner throttled back, continuing to move but scanning the surroundings and his sensor displays for their target. "Look sharp," he said. "It should be just around here."

"There!" It was Karen's voice. "Running along the ridge just to the left of the burn."

"I see it," agreed Kortlever. "It's an *Anubis* all right."

Conner brought the stick over and turned upslope, hoping the target was not yet aware of them—possibly the pilot would be a poorly trained insurgent and less than proficient with the use of his 'Mech's radar and other detection gear. "Let us go, Lieutenant. Keep me between you and the target until I give you the order to break."

"Roger that." Conner wanted to use his jump jets, but that would leave Kortlever exposed and might spook the *Anubis* into running. Instead, he tried to keep his 'Mech out of sight behind the trees as much as possible.

Suddenly a warning tone screeched; a flight of missiles streaked toward him. There was no time for evasive action, but the screen of trees in front of him caused the warheads to detonate prematurely.

The flash stung his eyes and chunks of wood bounced off his cockpit, but his systems indicated minimal damage. "The target has seen us!"

"He's running across the burn," called Karen. "We could move along the west shore of the lake and catch him if he doubles back."

"Go that plan," said Conner.

"Second 'Mech!" It was Huntsig. "We have a second *Anubis* coming out of the lake, southeast shore. It is making a run for it. I am heading to intercept."

Conner's brow furrowed as he struggled to get a weapons lock on the first *Anubis,* which was running and bobbing in his laser crosshairs. "Stay with your formation, Huntsig."

"The AgroMechs are too slow. If I wait for them, he will escape."

Conner's 360 screen showed Huntsig's *Karhu* making maximum speed along the lake, rapidly putting distance between himself and the AgroMechs. "Tupolov, Chow, turn back and try to keep visual on my position." He finally managed to get a targeting lock as his crosshairs centered on the fleeing *Anubis*, and he squeezed off a laser volley.

Metal along the 'Mech's upper right leg flared into incandescence and rivulets of melted armor ran down, and the 'Mech stumbled and slowed slightly.

Yes!

Suddenly, the enemy 'Mech's greatest advantage had been minimized. His superior speed was gone.

"We have another 'Mech!" It was Chow, sounding alarmed. "In the lake! It's big! It's big!"

"It's a *Catapult*," reported Karen, her voice tense but controlled. "We're taking fire."

Conner immediately turned away from his target. The *Anubis* was a minor danger compared to the *Catapult*, which was as big as his *Karhu* and an excellent distance fighter. "Karen, Chow, get out of there. You are no match for a *Catapult*. Huntsig, get back here!"

"On my way," said Huntsig, obviously upset that he had gone after the less formidable target.

The cockpit lurched violently as he ran down the uneven slope. He caught sight of Karen backing away from the shore, laying down covering fire with her autocannon that mostly fountained up water as the much bigger *Catapult* reared out of the far side of the lake. Conner knew her intent was to momentarily blind the *Catapult* pilot and delay his return fire.

"Star Colonel," Kortlever said. "You're losing me."

Conner swore. Kortlever might be in no immediate danger, but if the first *Anubis* doubled back— "I am throttling back, Lieutenant, but give it all the speed you have. You may fall back, but I will not leave you behind."

He saw returning autocannon fire from the *Catapult* as Chow slipped his AgroMech over a forested rise and gained some cover.

Karen's 'Mech reeled as armor-piercing slugs chewed into its thin armor.

Conner let loose with an on-target laser shot to the *Catapult*'s upper hull, and a wild burst of autocannon fire that missed its target, trying to draw fire away from Karen.

A burst of missiles fired from the big launchers on the *Catapult*'s back. Conner instantly recognized an entirely new danger; the way they moved marked these as streaks, homing missiles based on Clan tech. They arced through the sky and, despite his quick evasive action, several smashed into Conner's 'Mech. His ears rang from the explosions, and damage indicators appeared all over his status displays. He heard an unpleasant grinding sound and his entire 'Mech seemed to lean slightly before something popped, and then he was back up to speed.

A second volley of streaks vanished into the trees and exploded near Chow's last position.

A *Catapult* was bad enough, but this one had obviously been upgraded. Conner hoped the missiles were the only surprises it was packing.

Conner watched as more red lights appeared on his status screen, and there was a *chunk* as his right autocannon jammed. He flipped a switch on the panel to his left to run a clear-cycle, hoping to break loose the jam, and fired again with his lasers.

Karen's 'Mech was damaged, one leg dragging slightly in the sand as it slowly backed away from the *Catapult*. She was still firing her autocannon.

"Huntsig," Conner demanded, "where are you?"

"On my way. Taking fire from the second *Anubis*."

A flash of motion drew Conner's eye to his rear-view camera display just in time to see another missile slam into his 'Mech from behind and several others landing just short of him, probably from the first *Anubis*. Despite the noise-canceling feature of his neurohelmet, his ears rang from the detonation.

Then the clattering of the autocannon clear-cycle stopped and the gun froze completely.

The situation was so obvious to Conner. The two *Anubis* were simply escorts for the *Catapult*. Fortune had allowed them to detect the enemy as they were relocating the big 'Mech from one hiding place to another.

Suddenly Chow's AgroMech appeared, running past a break in the trees. The earlier attack had missed him. He nailed the *Catapult* with autocannon fire, then vanished into cover again.

Conner also locked his remaining autocannon on the *Catapult*, determined to do some damage to those deadly missile racks. His slugs flashed against the armor just below the missile ports, but he could not tell if he had damaged the launchers or not.

Huntsig appeared off to Conner's left at a full run, flames from a successful missile hit still dancing around his upper torso.

Conner maneuvered down to the lakeshore, trying to draw fire away from Karen. "We have to regroup and retreat. We do not have the distance weapons to take these 'Mechs!"

"I'm taking laser fire from the first *Anubis*," announced Kortlever. "I've lost my autocannon!"

"Get to cover," Conner ordered. "Chow, cover him and stay close."

"Yes, sir."

Conner saw that Karen's 'Mech was almost over the same rise that had earlier sheltered Chow.

The *Catapult* was now backing up the far lakeshore, and the second *Anubis* was angling over to meet it.

The first *Anubis* was nowhere to be seen. Perhaps it had lobbed its last flight of missiles at Conner and then made a run for it.

Conner kept moving, juggling stick, pedals and targeting controls, firing his remaining weapons at the *Catapult*. Huntsig did the same. Chow and Karen took targets of opportunity as they presented themselves, occasionally getting in a shot against the big 'Mech.

The *Catapult* was now completely out of the lake. It lobbed off one last missile at Huntsig, then turned and bolted north, the second *Anubis* keeping pace. Though he ached to set off in pursuit, Conner knew it was the wrong course of action.

"At least," said Karen, "we put them on the run. If only—"

Her voice was drowned out by the sound of autocannon fire chewing into her 'Mech.

"*Anubis,*" yelled Chow. "The first one doubled back!"

Conner saw it briefly between the trees and led it with a burst of laser, but it disappeared.

Karen's 'Mech was out of sight behind the rise to Conner's left. He headed towards her at top speed. "Karen, are you okay?"

"I—" The transmission dissolved into static.

Her antennas might have been damaged.

"I have it in my sights!" said Huntsig. He began to fire at the *Anubis* that Conner still could not see.

Conner topped the rise and followed the ridgeline, constantly scrutinizing his HUD for enemy attack. He spotted Karen's 'Mech.

The AgroMech teetered, its gun arm blown completely off and lying on the ground a dozen meters away. "Tupolov is hit bad! Where is that *Anubis*?"

The *Anubis* appeared on the ridge above the AgroMech.

Huntsig's *Karhu* appeared in the sky, riding on the flames of his jump jets, and dropped onto the slope just below it.

Conner watched as a flight of missiles arced away from the *Anubis*. Most went wide, exploding all around, but one homed in.

It plowed into Karen's 'Mech, swallowing it in flame. The 'Mech lurched forward, threatening to fall.

He shoved his throttle to the stop, trying to put himself between her and the enemy fire.

Too late.

A streak missile, a parting gift from the *Catapult,* bored into her from the other side.

Bits of her armor clattered harmlessly off his 'Mech.

Somewhere above them, Conner was dimly aware of Huntsig's lasers blazing and his chattering autocannon chewing into the *Anubis,* sending melted and shredded armor flying into the air. Dimly aware as the *Anubis'* reactor blew, immolating the enemy 'Mech in its own plasma.

But only dimly. He marched his *Karhu* up to Karen's fallen 'Mech, then throttled back, torso hard over, moving in a slow circle, searching for some sign of life. He looked down into the cockpit, but through the cracked and blackened ferroglass he could see nothing.

12

From the Great Work of
Galaxy Commander Isis Bekker

During the Ghost Bear's time in the Inner Sphere, there has been a growing concern among the highest ranks of our Clan, a debate among the Khans and the loremasters, that we have somehow lost our way.

To an outside observer, nothing could be further from the truth. Our greatest differences with the native freeborns of the Rasalhague Dominion had long been settled. Under our benign protection, their people and ours enjoyed an unprecedented period of peace, health and economic prosperity. Despite dire predictions that our Clan would enforce a military dictatorship, the Ghost Bears had nurtured a civilian government (though there are those who would argue that it was only a kind of limited return to Clan isolationism). The Dominion's quiet strength and subtle guidance helped Devlin Stone form and solidify his new Republic of the Sphere, allowing us, for a time anyway, to share our gifts with countless worlds not under our direct influence.

Though the Dominion's holdings did not include Terra, a few among our Clan even dared suggest that by acting as its ready guardian, we might be on the verge of some-how fulfilling the destiny of the Hidden Hope Doctrine.

In truth, our success gnawed at us. We had fulfilled so much of our destiny, yet there was no obvious path upon which we might continue. The Rasalhague Dominion was an economic and political power, but the greater purpose of the Clans was not to create a commercial empire.

Though we had been instrumental in forming The Republic of the Sphere, it constrained us. We could not readily expand our holdings, and the organization of The Republic helped to level the political playing field. As Vincent Florala has often pointed out to me, the way of the Clans rarely works to our advantage in our execution of Inner Sphere politics, or even in understanding them.

It was apparent, even before my birth, that the Ghost Bears needed to find new ways to act, new ways to advance our cause. Many secret councils were called. Cadres of scientists and technicians were assigned to this task, under the personal direction of the Khans.

Countless scenarios—military, political, technical and economic—were suggested, run as simulations and war games, evaluated and either discarded or filed for possible future application.

Our occupation of Vega and the other strategic worlds of Prefecture I: that was a plan first proposed in rough form at least fifty years before its execution. Though it must have seemed we acted quickly, it was truly only a matter of logistics and adjusting the existing plan to fit current circumstances.

Ghost Bears never act hastily if it can be avoided.

But while these great plans were formed, other experiments also took place. Some on a very large scale, such as the formation of my own Omega Galaxy with its goal to adapt Inner Sphere tactics and methods.

And some on a very small scale, such as Boerderijschool, the crèche of my sibko. Located in the mountains north of Reykjavïk on Rasalhague, Boerderijschool took the form of a self-supporting agricultural complex, mostly a ranch and farm. Most of the day-to-day work providing for our sufficiency was performed by lower-caste workers and by freeborn children, who formed a second, independent crèche. But all the members of our sibko were expected to learn the ways of the farm as well as the way of the warrior.

This may seem strange, even contradictory to the Clan way. In fact, many of us came to resent this indignity as we approached adulthood, and a repeated period of rebellion in this crèche probably contributed to the end of the experiment shortly after I graduated.

At the time, I felt very little about the end of that training style.

Now, I think it a shame that the Ghost Bears abandoned it.

What can a warrior learn on a farm? Many things, I believe.

For example, to ride a horse is to understand a 'Mech. Even a small child can learn to understand how a mount enhances its rider's speed, power and abilities. But the rider also learns that with these enhancements come dangers, responsibilities and limitations. A rider learns to respect his or her mount, to care for it, and to know what it can and cannot do. A rider knows that a good rider on a poor mount is better than a poor rider on a good mount.

These are lessons a MechWarrior can take to heart.

As in any sibko, we were educated. We honed our bodies, not just through combat drills and gym exercise, but also through hard, humble labor in barns and pastures. From the moment we could walk we trained to fight in all the standard Clan ways. But our emphasis was on unaugmented combat, simple and close to the earth. We learned to fight each other, but we also wrestled steers and rode bulls. We fought hand-to-hand, and with blunt and edged weapons. We learned to fight with farm tools. That may surprise you.

We learned to take the implements around us and turn them into effective and deadly weapons; not merely the obvious choices like the ax, the scythe and the whip, but also the rake, the hoe and the shovel.

Even a humble garden stake can be a very effective weapon for one who wields it with speed, power and surprise. I still have the scar on my left shoulder as a reminder of that lesson.

From this we learned that a warrior's most deadly weapon is his or her brain, and that no object, no matter how benign it seems, should be ignored by one seeking victory. Not all weapons have sights, or triggers, or blades or cockpits. Some are not even material objects.

This lesson serves me to this day.

But in my tenth year of life, we spent a season tending plants, and even I, normally the most willing of students, was driven to complain. At the time I could see no purpose to it, no lesson that would serve me on the battlefield. I was always bitter about that summer spent watering tomatoes and weeding carrots. Any lessons it carried seemed lost to me.

Only now, in the twilight of my life as a warrior and facing my greatest trial, do those lessons become apparent. Only now do I see the value in them.

I know now that a great army cannot be built, it must be cultivated. I know that the crop we reap may not always be the crop we sowed, and yet, there still must be food on the table. And there is more—

The great riddle of the Clans is that we have not been more successful in our goals. We have been trained and bred for three centuries to be the greatest warriors humanly possible, yet we have known defeat at the hands of our supposed inferiors many times. The Crusaders were turned back from Terra in the Great Refusal.

Some may say this last is only an example of how dishonorable outsiders turned our own honor and traditions against us. But I will write here that which cannot be spoken: our Honor Road is also our weakness.

There.

The deed is done, and I will gladly stand and be judged by any who read it. Draw sword against me if you will. This is my opinion.

Not that I value my honor any less, or that I would surrender it willingly, or that I would defend it with less than my life.

I am Clan.

But I seek to find purpose, for myself, for the Ghost Bears and for all the Clans. It is only through the blunt honesty that is our tradition that I can identify that purpose. Our own honor, our rigid traditions: these are potential weaknesses that can be used against us—and were, in the Great Refusal. Our enemies were not dishonorable in the choice to exploit them, but wise.

How does this relate to the lessons of the gardener?

Like Clansmen, many plants are the result of controlled breeding, not just for a few centuries but, for some plants, well over a hundred centuries. Many of these plants are outstanding in many useful ways when compared to their wild cousins. They bear more and larger fruit. They grow faster. They time their cycles to the needs of man, and not to the rhythms of nature.

Yet these plants have had ample opportunity to escape our fields, to spread their strength across the hundreds of worlds colonized by man. So why is the universe not full of planets jammed with beefsteak tomatoes, russet potatoes, sweet corn and winter wheat? Why do crops fail to insects, disease, drought or frost while their "inferior" wild cousins soldier through?

The answer should be obvious.

These plants were bred for certain useful traits to the exclusion of others. Their strengths are also their weaknesses.

In the artificially controlled conditions the farmer provides, they thrive; released into the wild, they fail. Even with all the farmer can do, conditions can still make them fail. And when these plants fail, the solution to

regaining their hardiness almost always lies in cross-
breeding with wild plants to select those survival traits,
those strengths, that the domesticated plants have lost.

Is that, then, the answer to the riddle of the Clans?

It explains so much, and for a time I sadly considered
that it might be true. If the principle of selective breeding were true, then at best the Clans are only living
weapons, tailored for war but ill-suited for the greater
role of humanity. As we learned at Boerderijschool, it
is easier to kill a man with a shovel than to dig a ditch
with a sword.

But upon further reflection I could not accept this dire
conclusion, and I turned to another lesson from the
fields: the lesson of the seed.

What is a seed? Some seeds can be eaten, and therefore used directly as food. That is a useful function, but
it is not their purpose. A seed is a legacy, a way of
passing the strength of one generation of plants along
to the next. A seed contains that which was best of the
generation that came before. A seed is patient, for it
must wait through the long winter for the growing days
that will come. A seed is strong, for at the first touch of
water and warmth it must be able to send down roots
and pull nutrients from below, and to push its way up
through unyielding earth to seek the sun. A seed is a
great and wonderful thing.

But a seed is not a plant. It is not a crop. It must
sprout. It must draw in strength and sustenance from
around it so that it can grow. Only then is its purpose
fulfilled.

Every farmer knows that some seeds do not sprout.
No matter how warm and fertile the soil, how generous
the sun and rain, for some reason these seeds fail. Are
those the seeds that say to themselves, "I am a great
and wonderful seed. I am proud, and a seed is what I
will always be!" Perhaps. And if so, these are the seeds
that wither, die and rot in the ground, their promise lost,
their legacy unfulfilled.

So a wise farmer plants many seeds. Some will fail, but others will grow. If enough grow, he can cull the weak so that only the strongest may go on. Did our Founder know this lesson when he made not one Clan, but many? Was he storing his seeds for the long winter, in hopes that one might find fertile soil and bring forth a new Star League, not just in name, or in form, but in spirit?

And what are we to make of the Ghost Bear Clan? It has returned to the Inner Sphere, basked in its rich fields, stood so close to Terra and to Sol, the sun that warms all the worlds of man. Yet its hull remains closed. It does not combine itself with the richness around it. It does not share its rich legacy of the past with a needful present.

That is my answer to the riddle of the Clans. We are great. We are strong. We are proud. But we are not the end of all things. Our destiny awaits us.

We are but seeds.

And it is time to grow.

*Mobile Military Hospital, Southwest Industrial
  District
Nasew, North Nanturo continent, Vega
30 November 3136*

Conner Hall stood in the ward of the Clan hospital looking down at Karen Tupolov through the plastic isolation curtain.

Incredibly, even after what had happened, all the pieces were there. But very few of those pieces were undamaged. She had burns, a dozen broken bones, whole-body concussion damage, multiple organ failures, and she'd been resuscitated four times before they could stabilize her. She looked more like a nightmare than a human being— a mass of tubes, metal braces and wires, all surrounded by machines that beeped and pumped and throbbed with a cold, parasitic life of their own.

He was aware that someone had stopped next to him, and he glanced over to see a doctor looking at him expectantly. "You wished to speak with me, Star Colonel?"

The doctor was a tall woman, dark, wide-shouldered and muscular. Doctors were scientist caste, but he figured her for a warrior test-down.

"What is the condition of patient Tupolov?"

She glanced towards the bed and almost imperceptibly wrinkled her nose. "Since you were here last, we removed the spleen, located and stopped several areas of internal bleeding and strapped together six ribs. Physically, she is stable and about as well as can be expected considering the extent of her injuries." Again, that subtle look of disgust. "Though I do not understand why this freeborn is in our hospital getting this level of care."

Conner glared at her. "She is here because I *ordered* her sent here. Your triage people downstairs tried to deflect her to the civilian hospital. If she were there, she'd be dead by now!"

Even if the local hospitals had been fully staffed, equipped and functional, which they were not, Clan medicine was far in advance of Inner Sphere technology, at least in matters of trauma and battlefield injury repair.

The doctor gave him a puzzled look, but did not respond to his outburst. She examined the chart hanging next to the isolation tent. "That would account for the delayed treatment noted here. The delay could be the cause of the potential brain damage, but that might have happened anyway."

"Brain damage?"

"Did they not tell you? She flatlined four times—twice before she even got here. That creates oxygen deprivation, which can result in brain damage."

"But you can fix that?"

The doctor cocked an eyebrow at him. "You said she would be dead by now in a local hospital. Well frankly, if she were one of our warriors, she would be dead as well. We can repair almost any bodily injury if we can get the patient here alive, but the brain is somewhat lesser-known territory."

"So there is nothing you can do?"

The doctor seemed to consider. "I did not say that. There is an experimental treatment, a drug designed to regenerate damaged nerve tissue. In animal trials, regular infusions of the drug into the cerebrospinal fluid resulted in massive brain regeneration. But we would not administer such a treatment to a Clan warrior. There is very little point for any upper-caste Clansman, and the treatment is too inefficient to be worthwhile for the laborers. Human trials have never been done."

"Why not?"

The doctor shrugged. "I would think that was obvious. Even with a healthy, regenerated brain, most of what the warrior was would be lost. Memories, skills, reflexes, personality. It is unlikely much would survive the process. A warrior simply would not be a warrior anymore. Or a scientist a scientist for that matter. Or— I suppose even a freeborn would not be a freeborn."

"You say 'most' of what the warrior was would be lost. But not everything?"

The doctor studied her patient. "It would depend, I suppose, on the extent of the damaged tissue that is replaced by new growth. But even if I were more sure about the effects of the drug on human tissue, there is no way that I could guess the results in this particular case. The damage she has suffered is extensive, but the brain is a varied and plastic organ, and still something of a mystery. Frankly, if we knew everything about how the brain works, you would be piloting your 'Mechs completely through your neurohelmets, with no manual controls at all. And that clearly is not the case."

He looked at Karen lying there, his heart tight in his chest, grieving her already. "But you could try this?"

The doctor gave him a small smile. "Normally, no. This is not an approved or authorized treatment. But the fact that she is not Clan bypasses some of the standard protocols, and with authorization from a senior officer . . ."

He stared at Karen's face, bruised and barely visible under all the bandages and the translucent breathing tube. He felt selfish for his own thoughts. His concerns were not "would she be an effective warrior?" or "could she be retrained to pilot a 'Mech?"

He was wondering only if she would remember *him*. If she would *feel* anything for him. Would she be the person he had grown to—*love*.

He took a deep breath. "Do you need a decision now?"

She thought for a moment. "It is too early to administer the drug—she needs to be stronger. But I suspect the ideal time will arrive within the next twenty-four to forty-eight hours. Don't delay too long." She turned and walked away. "Let me know," she called back casually, as though discussing a lunch appointment.

Conner stood watching Karen, listening to the beeping and hissing and gurgling of the machines, and wondered what Karen would want him to do. A strange thought occurred to him. *Should I contact her next of kin?* He was not even sure how to go about such a thing, or what he should say to them if he did. It was just a phrase he had heard in tri-vid programs.

Next of kin? What would that be? Like old friends? Like the fellow warriors from one's sibko? No. These people would share your genes. It might be like sharing a Bloodname, only mixed with the other things, and perhaps something more.

It would be intimate, in a way he found *curiously* appealing. He would like to think that if it ended here, some part of Karen would carry on, not as regulated by Keepers and scientists, but as lived by people who were connected to her.

He'd had a sick, twisted fantasy once of living with her, having children with her. That might never happen now. It probably never would have happened anyway.

It was difficult to see how it ever could have. But now, even the possibility was fading, and he found, strangely, that he *mourned* it.

He was suddenly aware of someone else standing nearby, watching him. He looked around and saw a short, balding male nurse, possibly an aerospace pilot test-down, looking at him with far more sympathetic eyes than had the doctor. Nurses were technician caste, often treated with scorn by doctors. But Conner had spent enough time in hospitals and MASH units to understand their value. He nodded in greeting.

The nurse stepped closer. "She is a friend of yours, I take it?"

"Yes," he said, "she is."

"She is a fighter."

"A warrior? Yes. She is not one of us, but—"

The nurse smiled sadly. "No. She is a *fighter*. It is not just the machines that have kept her alive."

Conner shook his head. "The doctor said she has serious brain damage. I do not know if there is anything left in her to fight."

The nurse laughed quietly. "I am sorry. It is just that doctors and nurses, we look at things differently. They look at two things, the body and the mind. Those are the things they can treat, of course, so that is where their primary concern should lie. But I do not know if those are the only two elements in a person. It has been my experience that, somewhere between the body and the mind, there is something else, a strength, a spirit, a force of will, that seems quite independent of the mind. When it is weak, when it gives up, people defeat all our efforts to save them. And in others, that force will not let them die, even if they should. In some this force is far stronger than in others. She"—he pointed at Karen—"is a fighter."

Conner nodded. "Thank you."

He turned and walked towards the stairs, considering. Karen, or some part of her, was still fighting to live, but

right now it was a fight without hope. He had the power
to change that. If it was her final fight, he could not
deny her any chance for victory.

He descended the stairs, and as he headed for the exit
he passed the doctor in the hallway. He caught her eye
as he passed. "Do it," he said. "My authority."

Then he kept walking. He was returning to the barracks. It was well past time to have a talk with Duncan Huntsig.

As Trenton leaned over her desk, Isis Bekker examined the series of photos he had loaded onto her computer. The wider shots showed a large burned area in a
hardwood forest. The pictures were striking, but there
was nothing alarming about them.

Then he showed her closer shots, taken by a recon
team sent in to examine the area more carefully.

He cleared his throat. "When we heard that a 'Mech
had been spotted in this area, we naturally assumed that
it was one of those unaccounted for after our defeat of
the warlords. There is indeed an *Anubis* on our inventory of missing 'Mechs. But when he arrived with his
force, Star Colonel Hall encountered not one, but three
'Mechs."

"I have read the debriefing report, Trenton."

"Then you know there were two *Anubis* units and a
Catapult. The second *Anubis* is also a mystery, but our
records are very clear that there were no *Catapult*s on
Vega prior to the Warlord Massacres, nor did we encounter any during the fighting."

She looked up at him. "You think this arrived since
that time?"

"Exactly. That's why, when I saw mention of this burn
in the debriefing report, I requested a detailed recon
report." He tapped the screen. "In this picture, what
appears to be a small pond is in fact the water-filled
impression of a DropShip landing, possibly *Union* class."
He advanced the pictures. "This round depression is

older, though definitely from a different DropShip, type unknown. Probably similar in size to the *Union*. Even if we assume that these represent the only two landings, between them they could have brought nearly two dozen 'Mechs, or a combination of other forces, to Vega."

She scowled at the screen. "I smell the Draconis Combine."

"It's highly unlikely that the insurgents possess the resources to accomplish something like this on their own. In addition, we've seen no evidence of this kind of organization until now." He switched back to a map of the area. "Based on the debriefing, my guess is that they were moving 'Mechs by night, using these lakes, here, as hiding places along the way. Recon patrols are already looking for the three missing 'Mechs, but they know we're on to them and may take a completely different route, or simply stay in hiding until the time when, and if, we can flush them out."

"So how did they get in? I know we have holes in our radar. Sneaking around the system is one thing. Landing only a few hundred kilometers from one of our bases is another. And they managed to land two DropShips, at two different times, in the same spot. How is that possible?"

Trenton stood and frowned. "I found it difficult to believe myself. Those hills are remote and unpopulated, but there are three overlapping air-control radars that all have at least some coverage of that area. I investigated those radars. They did it with packing tape."

She shook her head in confusion. "Packing tape? Did what?"

"A tiny piece of tape was carefully placed on a counter disk that tracks each radar antenna's rotation. This caused a small hole, only about a degree, in each radar's coverage. This burn is located exactly where those three holes in coverage overlap. Moreover, these three radars are located hundreds of kilometers apart. It is unlikely that the sabotage was done by one person."

This was unthinkable. "Could this be our own people? Freeminders?"

"Galaxy Commander, as I've explained, I think it unlikely that the Freeminders would overtly undermine our combat efforts. However, these are all Vega radars that we repaired and integrated into our tracking network after we arrived. A number of Vegan technicians work at the facilities, or have regular access to them. It's unlikely that Draconis Combine agents could arrange such an inside job. It's more likely that we have insurgent moles inside the Vegan staff for these facilities."

"Blast. We need security measures."

"I've already reported this to Security Chief Ricco. Henceforth, no Vegans will be allowed into critical areas without a Ghost Bear escort. There have been numerous other security enhancements, as well. I won't bore you with the details."

She shook her head. "I wish it were just the radars. But we are dependent on Vegan labor or technical help in dozens of critical areas. We had been hoping that the insurgency had not infiltrated the higher—" She had been about to say "higher castes," but of course that did not apply. "That they had not infiltrated to this level."

Trenton frowned. "If we've learned anything about the insurgents, it's that they're a diverse group. The joke among the scientists is, if you lined up all the insurgents on Vega end to end, they'd point in different directions. Generalizations about who or what they are would be dangerous at this point."

She sighed. "Quite right. And we are ill equipped to identify them. Our best hope in locating insurgent infiltrators is the Vegans themselves. Has Governor Florala been given this information?"

Trenton shook his head. "He apparently left the capital on some business."

"Well, brief him as soon as he returns. I will call an emergency meeting of the party heads and try to drum up some assistance in uncovering these agents."

"I don't envy you there."

She shrugged and closed the images. "It is a better hope than none at all. Meanwhile, let us find these 'Mechs!"

Trenton snatched up his data pad and hurried out of her office. She wondered where Vincent had gone off to.

Provisional Governor Vincent Florala sat in the armored limousine as it wove through traffic, and studied the two men across from him. Both had dark, straight hair and brown eyes, and wore similarly cut, expensive silk suits. But in every other way, they were a mismatched pair.

The larger man was *much* larger. He dwarfed even some of the Clan elementals that Florala had met, and seemed just as formidable. His hair was short and thick, almost forming a skullcap on his round head. His nose was wide, his lips thick, his expressions covering the full gamut from indifferent to grim and back again. Neither his speech nor his bearing suggested he was an educated man. But there was an alertness in the eyes, even a kind of native intelligence, that suggested he wasn't a man to trifle with on any level.

But it was the second, smaller man who most interested Florala. He was trim and muscular. He moved with the grace of a natural dancer, but showed no trace of the training that would have refined it. Except for a moment just after entering the car, when he'd lifted his shades to briefly study Florala, he kept his eyes covered by dark glasses, even though the windows of the car were heavily tinted.

But Florala had a feeling that the man took in everything and missed nothing. His mind seemed sharp and calculating, his confidence boundless and probably justified. He had the rough sophistication of a man who had been introduced to manners late in life, and had never become entirely comfortable with them.

This is a dangerous man, if he wants to be.

Florala knew from the reports his people had provided him that this man sometimes did want to be dangerous. Very dangerous indeed.

Other than his driver, Vincent Florala was alone in the car with them, and nobody else knew where they were.

It was a calculated risk. But Florala was no stranger to risk, and he wanted to hear what the men had to say. "I've heard, Mister—surely your name isn't actually Smith—that you want to talk with me."

The smaller man smiled. "My real name isn't available for this discussion, but it most certainly is not Smith. You can call me Bane. My friends call me Taylor, but we haven't established that relationship yet. My associate here, you can call Bruno."

"Appropriate."

"He thinks so."

The big man grimaced slightly, as though the smaller man had just given him a verbal jab of some sort.

"Very well, Mr. Bane. You wanted to talk to me."

"On behalf of my employer, yes."

"Which would be Jacob Bannson."

"Yes."

"I have an office, you know, and a receptionist who answers the phone. Jacob Bannson's name certainly would have gotten my attention, and we could have avoided this absurd cloak-and-dagger business."

Bane smiled slightly. "You know as well as I, Governor, that if I'd gone through channels, and we'd been meeting at your office, it would have been under much different terms. Everyone—your friends, your enemies, your rivals, the Galaxy commander—would have known you'd taken a meeting with a representative of Jacob Bannson. They'd all want to know what the meeting was about, and what was said, and what, if anything, you agreed to. You're a politician. Your choices of action are always constrained by what other people know, and what other people think."

Florala nodded. "Fair enough. So you've bought me

some freedom of action. What is it you hope to have me use it for?"

"Mr. Bannson is looking for associations, alliances, in areas of opportunity such as Vega."

"A great number of people consider Vega an 'area of opportunity.' That's just our problem."

"Does that include the Ghost Bears?"

Florala frowned and shifted in his seat. "The Ghost Bears are, for the moment, an important stabilizing force and valuable allies. Galaxy Commander Bekker has been working tirelessly to knit together our fractured world and help us establish a new government."

"Nice speech, but you can save it for the voters. You have reservations about the Ghost Bears, don't you?"

He hesitated, feeling like a traitor. "Yes. Yes, I do. These are not the Clansmen I read about in my youth. They're divided, uncertain and, in a word, unstable. I'm not at all sure that the Galaxy commander has the full support of her Clan, nor that she can maintain full control of her forces here.

"In some respects, I think the Ghost Bears are as much in need of reconstruction as Vega. That makes them a potential danger to everything I've worked for since the warlords were overthrown."

"But you still need them?"

"Yes."

"And you're sleeping with their commander."

Florala's mouth hung open, but nothing came out.

"So, I see that's true. To be honest, I didn't think much of my source."

He finally found his tongue. "Bane, if this is some attempt to blackmail me—"

Bane laughed. "No, no, nothing like that, Governor. I just thought you should know that your relationship with her isn't as secret as you might hope. That might be useful information to you, and I'm passing it along free of charge, no strings attached, as a sign of my good intentions."

Florala frowned. "I suppose I knew that our relationship was no longer secret, but I appreciate the warning." He considered. "That buys you my ear for a while, then. Just what is it you want?"

"Friends. Associates. The possibility of establishing a base of operations here at some future date."

"That's a lot to ask out of 'friendship,' Mr. Bane. Jacob Bannson doesn't have a very good reputation."

"Mr. Bannson is a businessman. He makes deals, and he makes the best deals he can. He extracts to the letter on those deals, and that isn't popular with some people. They think they can get away with something, and when they find they can't, they get angry.

"Yes, Mr. Bannson has vocal enemies. So does anyone of wealth who refuses to allow himself to be taken advantage of."

It was Florala's turn to grin. "That, too, was a very nice speech, Mr. Bane, but save it for somebody more gullible. Any relationship I enter into with Jacob Bannson is, at best, going to be risky and problematic."

Bane smiled respectfully. "Very good, Governor. Okay. Bottom line—yes, you're right. But you're living a risky and problematic life here on a risky and problematic planet. A bad deal may be better than no deal at all."

Florala shook his head. "Even if I were inclined to make this deal, I don't have the authority or power to do so. I'm only the provisional governor. If all goes well, and I admit that's always in question around here, we'll have nailed down the Articles of Reunification in a few months, and we'll be holding free elections."

"We're interested in future positions as much as in where you are now, Florala. You're a popular man, with a broad base of support. Your opposition is strong, but fragmented. I'd say you're an odds-on favorite to win those free elections."

Florala sighed. "A few months ago, I would have agreed with you. But as you've pointed out, I have a fatal weakness. Many of the people who like me still don't like the Ghost Bears, and I'm sleeping with the mama bear herself. I've known for some time that I was likely scuttling my political future. You've just confirmed it."

The corner of Bane's mouth crept up slyly. "I don't make this offer lightly, Governor, but Mr. Bannson's people have some experience in—*influencing*—elections."

Florala frowned and made a chopping motion with his hand. "This conversation is over, Bane."

"Please," said Bane, "no offense intended. You want what's best for Vega. Wouldn't that be you?"

"I believe it is, but not if it means corrupting the very thing I'm trying to build. I warn you, I'll withdraw from the race and supervise the elections myself if I think there's even the smallest chance you're meddling in them!"

"No, no. We'd like to see you win, for any number of reasons, but if you trust your people to choose wisely, well—" He grinned. "I like a good horse race." He leaned back in his seat. "We have no agreement, Governor. But I personally am impressed with you, and I ask this small thing. Can we leave this door open? If circumstances change, would you be willing to talk again?"

Florala studied Bane for a moment. He trusted Jacob Bannson as far as he could throw him. But Bane— Well, he wasn't sure about Taylor Bane, but he was intrigued. "If circumstances change, and I'm convinced you haven't been meddling in the election or acting against my planet's interests, then yes. We might talk."

"There is one last item. With your permission, we would also like to speak with Galaxy Commander Bekker."

"You don't need my permission."

"We could use your introduction. As it was with you, we'd like our meeting with Bekker to be on the QT."

"I should do this why?"

"I did say, with your permission. And remember that we approached you first, gave you first right of refusal. But if you'd prefer not to bring us together with Commander Bekker, that has no influence on any potential future dealings between us."

"I've got nothing to hide from Isis. I'll tell her that you're interested, but she won't deal with you."

"You're so sure?"

"Very sure. Remember, I know her well."

Bane shrugged. "All I ask is that you mention the possibility to her." He nodded towards the window. "There's a monorail station up ahead. If you'd please ask your driver to drop us off somewhere crowded?"

Florala touched the intercom button on his armrest and gave the instruction to the driver. The car pulled into a loading zone jammed with commuters and street vendors. Taylor Bane and his associate stepped out of the car and, improbably, vanished into the crowd.

They pulled away from the curb, and had gone only a block when they were surrounded by Clan police vehicles, which quickly brought them to a halt. A familiar face appeared outside his armored window, and he rolled it down. "Chief Ricco. What a surprise."

"Sorry to do this, Governor, but those two men who just got out of your car are under investigation as potential threats to planetary security."

He smiled politely. "I'm inclined to agree with you."

"My men should have them in custody by now."

"Somehow, I rather doubt that."

"Still, you'll understand that I am going to have to report this meeting to Galaxy Commander Bekker."

"But of course. In fact, I was just on my way to tell her about it myself."

The monorail car was nearly empty. A gaunt woman and two young boys sat at one end of the car, a plastic garbage bag at their feet. The boys looked tired, like they had just walked a very long way, and the woman stared blankly out the window as the train bumped along above the city at a third its rated speed.

She looked up as the door at the end of the car opened, and a huge Clan elemental dressed in gray-and-white Ghost Bear camouflage stepped into the car. He did not look at her, nor did he sit. He reached up and grabbed a hanging strap and stood there, his muscled body barely moving as the train rumbled around a turn.

The woman reached down and grabbed the bag by its tied neck, then urged the reluctant boys out of their seats. She pushed them through the car's rear door, looking nervously over her shoulder at the giant.

In the vestibule, she passed a smaller man wearing a greasy blue maintenance coverall and a matching hard hat entering the car.

She was gone before the man she had passed sauntered across the car and slumped into a seat near the big Clansman. Their eyes did not meet.

"I have to say," said the man in the coveralls, "you got the better-looking outfit."

"I like it," said the big man. "I may keep it. Sorry the meeting didn't go better, boss."

The man in the coveralls shrugged. "I haven't given up all hope of speaking with the Galaxy commander, but it looks grim." He turned and looked out the window. "Still, we have one other offer of friendship on the table, and it isn't a bad one if things develop as I think they might."

When Star Colonel Conner Hall arrived at the barracks it was a bustle of activity, the corridors busy with new MechWarrior faces and people rearranging accommodations to make room for them.

Given the new 'Mech threat on this side of the continent and the relative quiet in the port city of Neucason, he'd recalled the MechWarriors stationed there to help defend the capital.

That left the city defended by a binary of elementals, a Star of armor from the First Mechanized Cluster, and

the Second Vega Regulars, an up-and-coming armor militia fielding nearly a Star of their own battlefield-salvage
tanks and light armor.

If there were no more surprises, it would be enough.

In the confusion, he spotted a familiar technician relocating a computer terminal. He grabbed the woman's
shoulder. "I'm looking for MechWarrior Huntsig. Have
you seen him?"

She jerked her thumb over her shoulder. "He went
that way about five minutes ago, Star Colonel."

The direction she indicated was towards Huntsig's
quarters. Conner marched down the corridor purposefully, but halfway down the hall he spotted Huntsig coming towards him, his eyes fixed firmly on Conner, a look
of grim determination on his face.

Conner immediately noticed that he wore his dress
uniform: blue-gray jacket and trousers, a gray shirt, and
a wide gray belt that held a personal ceremonial sword.
Taken all together, the image Huntsig presented gave
Conner a moment of hesitation over what he was planning to do.

He had come with the idea to challenge Huntsig to a
Trial of Grievance for deserting his position in the formation. Now, from his attire and attitude, it seemed that
Huntsig probably had the same idea. The uniform wasn't
required, or even part of the ritual, but it was just the
sort of rigid Clan formality that Huntsig so loved. Doubtless, Huntsig planned to challenge his leadership and
judgment.

It made no difference to Conner. Perhaps his leadership had failed them. He had thought of a thousand ways
he could have executed their mission differently, or anticipated the unexpected danger. Were their positions
reversed, he would have been inclined to challenge.

He found it did not matter. Either way, he would face
Huntsig in a trial of blood. Let combat decide. It was
the Clan way.

The new MechWarriors watched curiously as Huntsig

stalked past them. They had not yet been briefed, and most were only marginally knowledgeable of the circumstances that had led to their recall to the capital. They all knew Conner, of course, and most had encountered Huntsig at some point as well. The Omega Galaxy's 'Mech forces still had not rebuilt to the point that there were many strangers in them. But as to what drove these two men marching towards each other, most of them could only guess. They could sense trouble brewing, and stopped to see what form it would take.

Huntsig stopped midcorridor, stood at rigid attention and waited for Conner to close the distance.

Conner walked to within a meter of the junior officer and stopped.

They looked into each other's eyes.

Huntsig reached for his sword, smoothly drew it from its sheath and held it vertically in front of his face.

Conner did not move. He was unarmed, but he found it difficult to believe that Huntsig would strike him, dishonorably and outside a formal trial.

Then Huntsig did the utterly unexpected.

He dropped to one knee, carefully placed the sword on the floor in front of Conner and bowed his head.

"I am MechWarrior Duncan Huntsig of the Ghost Bear Clan. From you, Star Colonel Conner Hall, I beg for *surkai*. I have wronged you in this way: I abandoned my assigned position in combat, in violation of the orders of you, my superior. In so doing, I cost myself the glory of a greater target. I caused unnecessary losses. I denied my unit victory, or even a kill. I have dishonored myself as a warrior, and I submit myself to your judgment and punishment."

Conner looked down at him, speechless and confused. Of course, *surkai* was no shield. He could still refuse *surkai* and challenge him to a Trial of Grievance. That was his right.

But in asking for *surkai*, especially in such a formal, public and humble fashion, Huntsig had shown considerable honor. For Conner to refuse him and challenge him to a trial might not sit well with the other MechWarriors under his command. It might appear that Conner was acting in a petty and dishonorable way.

After all, what was he really angry about? Why did he feel wronged? The wounds suffered by Karen Tupolov? The Clan way anticipated casualties, and injuries were not mourned. Karen fought bravely, taking fire in order to allow a fellow MechWarrior to achieve a more strategic position, and continuing to return fire against their enemy when no one else was in a position to do so. Beyond what Huntsig had admitted in his request for *surkai*, Conner had few legitimate grievances.

So, the appearance of honor sat squarely with Huntsig.

The question was: did Conner care?

He shocked himself with the unspoken question. *Of course! One always acts with honor!*

But now, he discovered, he doubted even that. What his head told him was proper honor did not match what he felt in his heart.

He looked down at Huntsig and considered his choices; the warrior still bowed before him, still awaited his decision.

The anger in Conner's heart settled as a tight, bitter knot in his belly.

Had Huntsig not done what any aggressive MechWarrior would have done in the same circumstances? Did the Clan way not, despite all efforts of the Omega Galaxy to redirect it, value individual glory over the success of the unit? Why should Huntsig suffer for doing what he was raised from birth to do? Why should he be forced by honor to deplete their already diminished forces in this time of crisis?

Yet his heart promoted many reasons.

Conner reached down and picked up the sword, hefting it experimentally. It was a fine, plated blade, sharp, light and well balanced. The grip was ivory, carved with a depiction of a lone warrior armed with a spear facing a rearing ghost bear. The basket was shaped to resemble a bear's paw, and the pommel took the form of a silver bear's head. He held the sword two-handed, straight out in the air over Duncan Huntsig, hesitating for a long time.

"MechWarrior Duncan Huntsig. I accept your plea for *surkai*. As your punishment, I demand of you two things.

"First: this fine blade will be mine, to hold until such time as I die, or until I decide that you have satisfied your debt of honor to me, whichever comes first.

"Second: through your actions, you have taken a true MechWarrior from our forces and denied the First Vega Regulars their commander. Therefore, I declare you responsible for the First Vega Regulars. You will guide them until a new leader can be appointed. When a new leader has been chosen, you will remain answerable to their needs and requests, though you will not be under their direct command. You will be responsible for their training, and their transition from Industrial 'Mechs to BattleMechs. You will bear this responsibility until such time as I or the FVR commander determine that it is no longer necessary.

"Do you understand, agree and submit?"

Huntsig looked up, barely concealed pain on his face. He unbuckled his belt and unfastened the sword's matching sheath, presenting it to Conner. "I understand, agree and submit."

Duncan took the sheath, placed the sword in it, turned and walked away. "We are done here."

He walked through the barracks, all eyes on him as he turned the corner at the end of the corridor, walked through the building's small lobby and went outside. He passed by the parked ground vehicles and began to walk along the road to the 'Mech hangars.

The road was poorly tended, and weeds grew high along the sides. He pulled out the sword and slashed at the brush as he walked along.

When he reached the hangar, the great doors stood open at each end, allowing the slight breeze to keep the heat within from becoming unbearable. He walked inside, past the rows of new 'Mechs lined up and awaiting service. A mechanic looked up and saw the Star colonel brandishing a sword, her eyes growing wide.

Suddenly feeling conspicuous, he sheathed the sword again and marched along the row of 'Mechs, studying the faces of everyone working there. As he walked past a welder busy patching the armor on the foot of an *Ursus*, the welder finished the bead and flipped up his welding mask. He looked up to see Conner Hall before him and went pale. He spotted the sword in Conner's hand, and went paler still.

This was the man Conner had seen painting Freeminder graffiti.

Conner reached down, pulled off the welding mask and tossed it aside, grabbed the man by the biceps and dragged him towards the nearest door in the side of the hangar. Once again, Conner was aware that he was the center of attention. Mechanics, technicians and laborers stopped to watch, not just on the hangar floor, but on the scaffoldings and catwalks above.

Conner ignored them, pulling the man through the door and into the sun outside. He turned back to face the man, and spotted more graffiti on the wall above the technician.

THINK THE UNTHINKABLE

Conner looked around. The sidewalks outside the hangar were empty. They were alone. He stared at the man. "We have to talk."

The man said nothing, only looked at him nervously, clearly anticipating the worst.

"Tell me," demanded Conner, "about the Freeminders."

The technician squared his shoulders and tightened his jaw. "I will take whatever punishment you choose to hand out, but I will never betray those who have put their trust in me."

Conner gripped the sword tightly with both hands.

"You do not understand. I do not want you to betray them. I want to *join* them."

13

From the Great Work of
Galaxy Commander Isis Bekker

Of all the words handed down to us by our Founder, Nicholas Kerensky, these weigh on me most heavily: "If there is no unity, nothing can be achieved." They are from his enthronement speech when he became the first ilKhan of the new Clans. They are literally the words on which the Clans are formed. They are our foundation, our creed and our heart. I think of them, and my heart grows cold, for they are lost to me.

This planet is called Vega, but if I could name it now, I might instead call it "Disunity." Wherever unity is, be it Strana Mechty or Terra or someplace else, this is certainly the place it is farthest from. There is no unity among these people and, increasingly, there is no unity among the people of my own Galaxy. The lower castes grow restless and rebellious, the warriors impatient and angry. Our enemies gather all around us and we cannot stand against them, because we are divided.

Of this, my Clan upbringing and teachings tell me little. It is assumed that through the way of the Clans, because of the Honor Road, we will always stand united.

Yet even in history, this has not been so. Since the betrayal of the Not-named Clan, Clansman has stood against Clansman. They were the first of the Clans to fall from grace. They were not the last. Even we, the Ghost Bears, faced a vote of Abjuration when we moved our people to the Inner Sphere.

We prevailed, but I think it was a close thing, more a matter of technicality than judgment. It was decided that the Clans could not expel a Clan that had already expelled itself, and we were spared that mark of dishonor.

This is primarily what our Clan way teaches us about disunity: we either amputate the offending part, or we conquer it, crush it and draw it into ourselves.

There must be more to it.

It is difficult to imagine creating unity out of nothing, but that is exactly what the Founder did when he created the Clans. The people were uncertain, divided and had just emerged from a bloody civil conflict. Somehow, out of that nothingness, Nicholas Kerensky brought forth the Clans.

How did he do it? Why did he not leave us *that* lesson? How am I to take these disparate parts and return them to the two wholes from which they began?

No matter how I run the scenarios in my mind, I cannot think of a way to return things to what they once were.

But then, I realize, *that* may be my mistake. If I cannot restore what was before, I must then make something new. Like the Clans—something different that did not exist before.

Perhaps my mistake is in thinking there must be two wholes, instead of one.

*Provisional Capitol Building, East Central
  District
Nasew, North Nanturo continent, Vega
30 November 3136*

Galaxy Commander Isis Bekker paced the end of the small conference room located under the congressional chambers. Sitting around the conference table were the speakers of the various Vegan political parties: the four major ones, Centralist, Labor, Freedom Vega and the Planetary Nationalists, plus the four minority parties, Green, People of Ra, Hawks and the Pacifist League. For the last hour she had been trying to forge some sort of agreement, at least in principle, to cooperate in uncovering agents of the Draconis Combine on Vega. As Trenton had predicted, it was not easy.

She wished Vince were there. He was far better at talking to the Vegans than she was, but he was still missing from the building.

Clark Avila, the almost impossibly elderly leader of the Freedom Vega party, glared at her from his seat. "You can't ask our people to betray their own to your occupation force. You can't ask people to turn against their own."

"All I'm asking is for them to help us locate agents of a hostile foreign power."

Chance Elba smiled a sour smile and said in a singsong voice, "I spy, with my little eye—"

She frowned at him. "This is no laughing matter, Speaker Elba." She was careful to use the respectful honorific. She was trying to pull these people together, even Chance Elba—not drive them apart. "The threat is imminent, and it is real."

Rama Daul of the Pacifists sighed. "Can't this matter wait until the Articles of Reunification are finished? This should be a matter for the new government."

Isis dropped back into her chair. "If we wait that long, Speaker Daul, the only new government will be the one enforced on you by the Draconis Combine. We need an agreement *now.*"

Chance Elba knitted his fingers together in front of him, and gently rocked back and forth in his chair. "I might be willing to consider backing a temporary article of defensive cooperation—if certain conditions were met."

She looked at him skeptically. "Conditions? What kind of conditions?"

"We of the Labor Party have, for some time, felt a great sympathy for the plight of your oppressed, so-called lower castes. We have become aware of an oppressed reform movement within your Clan called the Freeminders. These people meet and organize in secret out of fear of reprisal. We find that intolerable."

"I am aware of the Freeminders as well, Speaker Elba. They are an internal matter of the Ghost Bear Clan, and no concern of yours."

"The greatest number of Freeminders come from your laborer caste, Galaxy Commander. It is in the great tradition of organized labor to support actions of like-minded organizations. You require us to act, and we require you to act. It is that simple."

"And what would you expect us to do?"

"Create a new policy of openness among your people here on Vega. Allow the Freeminders to gather without restrictions or reprisals. Allow people from any caste to join the Freeminders without loss of rank or privilege. Allow freedom from censorship, and freedom of assembly. And allow free discourse between the Freeminders and like-minded groups here on Vega."

"Meaning yourself and your party."

"If they find us to be kindred sprits, as we find them to be."

"You ask me to allow you to advise and influence a dissident group within my own people."

"If dissident means asking for freedom and equal rights, then yes, that is exactly what I mean."

She looked around the table, trying to judge the reactions of the others. The Centralist leader seemed unimpressed, but she could be counted on to support the measure. The Planetary Nationalists would likely follow Labor's lead. The minority parties didn't have enough votes to do much besides break a tie. The Freedom Vega and Centralist parties were the key.

She made eye contact with Caleb de La Cruz of the Freedom Vega party. He looked back. "We would consider such an action to be a sign of good faith and a spirit of compromise that we have, until now, found lacking in the Ghost Bears."

She seethed at the idea of having Elba dictating terms to her. But she could not allow her ego to get in the way of her greater objectives. "Very well. I will announce such a policy, providing we can come up with a useful agreement and vote it into action."

Elba nodded. "Good enough."

"Speaker Elba, Speaker Tracy"—the latter being the speaker of the Centralists—"can you draft a document for the rest of us to amend and then vote upon?" They looked at each other, then nodded in agreement. "Please be quick about it. As I said, the threat is imminent. As for the rest of you, I beg that you not wait for a vote to take action. Contact your networks, let your constituents know of this problem and encourage them to report any unusual activities to our paramilitary police. This meeting is adjourned."

The leaders filed out of the room, talking quietly among themselves. Looking through the open door, she realized that Vince was standing just outside the room. As she brought up the rear of the group, she saw that Security Chief Ricco was standing behind him, and rather far into the governor's personal space.

She stopped and looked a question from one man to the other. Vince had a curious expression on his face, as though something he had eaten was not agreeing with him. Ricco's face was a stern but unreadable mask, all business.

She focused her attention. "Is there a problem, Chief Ricco?"

He looked around, making sure that the speakers were all out of earshot. "There has been a breach in security that you should know about. It concerns the governor, here. He says he was coming here to report it to you himself, but I feel it is my duty to verify that he, in fact, does so."

Vince looked over his shoulder at the man. "If you don't mind, Chief, I'd like to discuss this in private."

Ricco lifted a brow. "I need to verify that the fundamental nature of the incident is reported to the Galaxy commander."

Vince frowned, then said quietly, "Jacob Bannson. Is that fundamental enough for you?"

Ricco did not look entirely satisfied, but he relented. "Explaining that should keep you busy. The Galaxy commander will be reading my own report on the incident shortly, so I would not recommend scrimping on the details." He turned and walked away.

Vince watched him go. "He's just upset because Bannson's men eluded him again."

"Bannson's men? Now we have Bannson agents here, too?"

He looked around. "Let's go to my office, where we can talk about this privately."

She nodded. She would have preferred her own office, but his was nearer, so she didn't argue the point.

The office had once belonged to MyoMaxx's chief financial officer, and she could see glimpses of the original walnut paneling and fine hardwood furnishings under all the clutter. There were piles of newspapers, magazines, books, photographs, report folders, economic projections and other detritus of his job.

But there were also countless personal items, even more than in his apartment: photographs; a child's doll, scorched and water-stained; a baseball bat; a windup music box with a ceramic horse on top, its head missing; a crude toy 'Mech made of stamped metal, operated by a windup key.

Though Isis had spent much time in Vince's apartment, she was rarely in his office, and then usually not

for more than a few minutes at a time. This was his
retreat, and he rarely took meetings there or invited people in.

He walked over and stood in the corner by the simulated window, hands clasped behind his back, looking at
some kind of group family photograph. "I try to take a
moment to check out one of my mementos every time
I come in here. I lost almost my entire extended family
in the Warlord Massacres. I have a few cousins left, but
that's all.

"Before things fell apart, I wasn't very close to my
family. Now I curse myself for the wasted opportunities.
But looking at these things, it reminds me what this is
all about, what I'm working for.

"I want a world where families can be safe and thrive
again. I want a world that's strong enough to stand
alone, and stable enough not to eat itself alive." He
reached up and touched the picture. "I want what they
would have wanted."

She furrowed her brow. "What is this about, Vince?"

"A small betrayal. Ricco is upset because he caught
me having a meeting with two men representing Jacob
Bannson. I honestly was coming to tell you about it."

"Bannson? What could he want here?"

"He's an opportunist, and he sees this world's instability as an opportunity. He's come to forge alliances for
reasons that are vague. But the reports we have say his
deal with House Liao has soured and he's looking for
another base of operations, or at least a staging area
before he moves on to his next plan. That's my guess,
anyway. You'd have access to far better intelligence reports on him than I do."

"And you believe these men genuinely represent
Bannson? Con artists frequently show up in war zones
making all manner of outrageous claims."

"They had gold ingots with Bannson's name on them,
and they've been spreading them around the city like
playing cards. I'd say they're genuine."

"And you met with them. What did they want with you?"

"They fancied me as a useful ally in my current position, and seemed to believe that I might be even more useful in the future if I win the free elections. But that isn't going to happen."

"What? Why not? I thought you were the favorite."

"Word of our relationship is out, Isis. I knew people would find out sooner or later, and I knew the cost. The people aren't going to vote for a man they consider to be sleeping with the enemy."

She crossed her arms over her chest and frowned at him. "Is that what we are to you, still? The enemy?"

He turned and looked at her sadly. "It doesn't matter what I think. I've said it a hundred times—it's what the people think that counts. But personally, I still consider the Ghost Bears a dangerous occupying force whose motivations and goals are unclear. I trust you, Isis. I *love* you. But you don't speak for the Ghost Bears any more than I speak for all the people of Vega, or even most of them."

"We're here to—"

He held up his hand. "Stabilize The Republic of the Sphere by restoring order on key worlds. Yes, I've heard it a hundred times. I've got to tell you, Isis, I don't give a rat's ass about The Republic. Devlin Stone is gone, neither succeeding exarch has been capable of holding it together, and all the Great Houses are casting restless eyes on their former possessions. I think The Republic is doomed."

She just stared at him.

"If you can find a way to save it, or at least to slap on some bandages and drag it along for a few more years, more power to you. But all I really care about is *Vega*.

"In order of importance, I care about my world, I care about you, and I care about this—whatever—we're trying to build. The Republic is a far-distant fourth. And frankly, I am very concerned about what the Ghost Bears will do if The Republic falls. If it no longer exists, your Clan has no reason to relinquish this world to independence, and every strategic reason to hold on to it for as long as you can."

She found her voice. "Vince, I thought we were in this together."

"We are, Isis! In so many ways, more than even you know. But I freely admit to having my own interests and my own agenda. In respect of your Clan ways, I've never tried to hide that from you."

"But this meeting—Bannson's people approached you, and you went along to gather intelligence which you planed to bring to us—"

He shook his head. "My people learned that Bannson's crew was in town. *We* approached *them*."

She shook her head. *"Why?"*

"Because I wanted to hear what they had to say. I wanted to see if Bannson genuinely had anything to offer Vega."

"Did he?"

"I'm standing here."

"Meaning?"

"Meaning that he didn't put anything of real value on the table. Certainly nothing worth the risk of dealing with a character like Bannson."

"And if he had?"

"Perhaps I'd still have been nabbed by Ricco, but I wouldn't be here discussing this of my own accord."

She could hardly believe what she was hearing, yet she couldn't blame him. Though he had hung up his neurohelmet, he was still a warrior. Battlefield wisdom said to get the best intelligence possible, to know all of one's options, and to act on them if it was prudent. She expected no less of him. Yet she found herself feeling angry and betrayed. Vince's support had been the one thing she felt she could count on. "How could you?"

His expression was a neutral mask. "I have never lied

to you, Isis, and I'm being truthful now. This is one reason we Inner Sphere types aren't so big on the complete honesty thing. Sometimes the truth hurts, and sometimes it doesn't serve any useful purpose."

She frowned, but her anger was fading into resolve. "I know where I stand. That is useful information to me, especially now."

"I'm sorry, Isis."

She stepped closer to him, put her hands on his shoulders, and looked into his eyes. "Vince, things could go from bad to worse here very soon. The way things are shaping up, we could find ourselves at war any minute now. It may have the appearance of a war with the local insurgents, but regardless of how it looks, we will actually be fighting the Draconis Combine. I need the people of Vega to understand the distinction and to support our military, or it is going to be a very short and unpleasant war."

He shook his head sadly. "I can't deliver the Vegan people to you, Isis, not even the ones who are nominally sided with me."

"I do not expect you to. Much as I hate to admit it, that old bat Chance Elba has been right all along. I need to win the hearts of the Vegan people, and I will never be able to do that by asking them to believe in the Ghost Bears. But perhaps I can convince them to believe in themselves again, and convince them that the Ghost Bears believe in them too."

"How can you do that?"

She stared at him as though she could somehow transmit the seriousness of her intent through her gaze. "Bold, sudden strokes. I am now prepared to act on things that have been in my mind for a long time, things that I have barely been able to admit to myself. I am prepared to do extreme things. I will anger some people, but hopefully I will win more than I lose. I need you to unconditionally support me now, Vince. Not against your love of Vega, but because of it. If we do not work together at this moment, you will soon find your world under the control of the Combine. At best as their puppets; at worst, as their slaves."

He looked at her, something like wonder in his eyes, and fear. "Yes, I will support you."

He pulled her close. Their lips met.

They parted, and she leaned against him for a brief moment. "There will be hard days ahead, Vince. Our trial has begun."

The technician's name was Reuben. Conner had seen the man in the 'Mech hangar dozens of times. Now that he thought about it, maybe hundreds of times.

Technicians, mechanics, laborers—they all tended to be invisible to warriors, or at least interchangeable. Unless something went wrong. Certainly he knew the chief mechanics and technicians in his unit by name, but he really did not *know* them in any personal sense.

They were simply moving parts in the military machine that was Omega Galaxy.

After they left the hangar, Conner appropriated a ground car and they drove across the spaceport to an isolated spot near a fueling terminal where they could talk in private. Technicians *had* been interchangeable to him, but as Conner talked with Reuben, he quickly came to recognize him as a unique person.

Reuben was an electronics specialist who knew every centimeter of wiring in every 'Mech in their inventory. His small stature was useful for climbing deep inside a 'Mech to locate shorts and damaged cables, and he took great pride in his ability to pinpoint damage and repair it in half the time of other technicians.

Conner was perhaps surprised at the pride with which the man talked about his work, and the pride he had in Omega Galaxy. This was a man considered by the Clan to be, at best, a malcontent, at worst, a traitor, yet he was fiercely loyal to the Clan in his own way.

Though Conner could not pretend to find the man's

job interesting or desirable, he would gladly admit admiration for the energy and enthusiasm that Reuben applied to the task.

He also discovered that Reuben had a rather shocking life outside the walls of that hangar. Technician Reuben had two wives. One was Clan, a senior technician at a power plant back on the planet Policenigo. Their marriage had been arranged by the Eugenics Board, and together they had dutifully conceived four children, all of whom were being raised in a crèche.

But he had a second wife named Doris, a non-Clan native of Policenigo. She was a tri-vid camera operator. They had met when he was rewiring her broadcast center seven years earlier. They lived together as much as his duties allowed, and had a four-year-old daughter. He spoke lovingly of this family, and became emotional when he talked of how difficult it had been to leave them.

A few weeks earlier, Conner would have been totally unsympathetic, even horrified by this story. But now, as he thought of the possibility of losing Karen Tupolov, he shared the man's pain in a way he would not have thought possible. He understood why the Freeminder organization would appeal to this man, despite his clear loyalty to the Clan and his devotion to his job. "I want to hear about the Freeminders: what you want, what you do. But first, I want to know why you painted those words on the buildings."

The man looked sheepish. "I felt bad about that sometimes. But while I might have defaced Clan property, I never damaged it. You must understand, we have to act in secret. We cannot openly meet, or recruit members. Those little bits of paint are our way of reaching out to others who feel as we do. They serve both as a reminder that we exist, and a comfort whenever one of us sees them. We know that we are not alone. And painting them is often dangerous, both physically and in terms of the risk of being caught and punished.

"It feels good to take risks for what you believe in. If

you are not willing to take risks, perhaps you do not really believe."

Take risks? Doing this, I am taking the greatest risk I have ever taken outside a 'Mech. Can I embrace this with enough conviction to take the next step?

He listened as Reuben described the goals of the Freeminders: first and foremost, the freedom of marriage and family, ideals that Conner believed he could embrace. But also the right to free thought and expression, the right to individuality. Conner was less comfortable with those ideas, and more nervous yet about any notion of breaking down the caste system.

Reuben was almost apologetic about that. "That was not part of our original agenda. When I first joined the Freeminders, it was different. But the movement then was also much more scattered and ineffectual. Then parts of the Final Codex began to appear, and that changed everything."

"I have heard of this thing, but I do not know that I believe it."

"It exists! I have seen good copies of several pages. It is the lost writing of our Founder, of Nicholas Kerensky himself! He meant for this to happen! Our return. Our sharing of our superior genes with the Inner Sphere." He smiled beatifically. "Don't you see, Star Colonel? Doris and I, with our child, we are fulfilling our Clan's destiny. Our children will do great things. Of course, I am only a technician, but if scientists, even warriors, were to—"

"Wait. One minute you talk of ending the caste system, then you invoke it."

"The Codex doesn't call for the end of the caste system, only a reform of it, a melding of the lower castes. The warrior caste would still operate much as it does now, though with more opportunity for individual expression."

"And marriage and family?"

"Of course! The warrior genes must be shared with the Inner Sphere. They are the pinnacle of everything we are as Clan. Our loyalty and devotion to the warrior caste remains strong, Star Colonel! We are not traitors. We do not wish to diminish the strength of the Clan. We only wish to share it, enriching the Inner Sphere, and in so doing, enrich ourselves!"

There was a certain mad logic to it all, yet there was something Conner had to know before he could continue along this path. "What castes are represented in the Freeminders?"

Reuben looked surprised. "Well, all the castes, in some numbers. Of course, the great majority are laborer caste, in part because they are most numerous in the general population, but also because they have the most to gain from the Freeminder reforms. Technicians and merchants are also strongly represented, though not in the same proportion as laborers. Scientists are much rarer, but they are there."

"But warriors. Are there warriors?"

Reuben looked apologetic. "There are some. A few. To be honest, very few. Most are paramilitary police. Often they are assigned to investigate us, and end up joining and helping us hide our activities instead. Most of them feel ill-treated by the rest of the warrior class, and not appreciated for the benefits they provide the Clan. Galaxy Commander Bekker's reforms since our arrival on Vega have eased those resentments some, but we continue to gain recruits."

"But how many Bloodnamed warriors have joined the Freeminders?"

Reuben just stared at him, saying nothing.

Conner shifted into his command voice. "How many?"

"There are—I have never—" He swallowed. "I do not believe that there has ever been one. If you join us, you would be the first." He blinked. "Do you understand how important that could be to us? If a Bloodnamed warrior were to join us, it would be a great sign that our cause was just, and that we were not traitors to the warrior caste."

"I could lose that Bloodname far more easily than I gained it."

"That would have to be your decision, to take such a risk. Frankly, I would not blame you if you chose against us."

Conner considered carefully. To a warrior, his Bloodname was everything. His codex was everything. His honor was everything. But Conner Hall found that the definitions and importance of those things kept shifting and evolving. "You have leaders here in the Freeminders? People in charge?"

"Yes, of course. *The* leader of the Freeminders is here, the one who first discovered records of the Final Codex."

"I wish to meet this person, as soon as possible. Can you arrange that?"

Reuben nodded. "I will have to ask, but I am sure that he would want to speak with you. As I have said, having such a famous Bloodnamed warrior join us would be of great importance. It could be the most important thing that has happened since the discovery of the Final Codex itself." He frowned. "But I will need to make contact off base, when I am off duty.

"You are off duty now. Tell me where to drop you, and then I will return to the hangar and explain that I have given you a special assignment. If I am going to do this, I must do it quickly, or not at all."

Isis Bekker looked around the subbasement complex that was the war room. It had not been fully activated since the end of the warlord conflicts, but it was active now.

The military command center, of course, which occupied a glass-walled space that took up a third of the complex, had never fully shut down.

But the functions of the rest of the space, handling communications, intelligence, civilian planning, logistics and coordination with off-planet resources, these functions had largely been transferred to regular civilian departments after the fighting stopped.

Now, Isis was pulling all the strings back down to terminate here.

She walked around the large backlit glass table that represented a map of the surface of Vega. Under the table, numerous tri-vid projectors created floating icons over the map, representing their various forces. A smaller grid at the far end of the table showed a more abstract representation of off-world forces and space assets.

As she was inspecting the displays, Trenton entered the room. "Just in time," she said to him. "A lot is about to happen, and you are my right hand in making it all work."

"Whatever you say, Galaxy Commander. I was surprised when you ordered this room reactivated, but—"

"Shut up, listen carefully and answer the questions I am going to be asking to the best of your ability. I know some of these questions probably require research for a detailed answer. Never mind that. Just consult that encyclopedia you have for a brain, and give me your best estimate."

He blinked in surprise. "Yes, Galaxy Commander."

"You're certain in what you said about the Freeminders. You honestly believe that they are ultimately loyal to the Ghost Bears and will support our cause here on Vega?"

"Nothing is certain, however—"

She had no time for waffling. "Are you *sure?*"

He stared at her for a moment. "Yes, they are loyal and not a threat to our mission."

"Next question. How self-sufficient is Vega?"

"In what respect?"

"In every respect. Worst case, if we were cut off from

Ghost Bear support or faced a trade embargo, how would we fare?"

He considered carefully. "The planet Vega is very rich in natural resources. With the damage done during the Warlord Massacres, energy production is an issue, but one that can be solved. The true challenge is that Vega is also an arid planet. Food production is difficult."

"We are not self-sufficient, then?"

"I didn't say that. It would be a close thing for a few months, but if we relocated workers to ramp up production on the south delta farms, we could manage."

"What about factory production?"

"If we can feed the workers and miners, we can make a lot of stuff. This is a rich world. Aerospace assets will be an issue, especially repair. We have much to trade for such services off-world, of course, but if there were a blockade—"

"Can we make BattleMechs?"

"What?"

"Big machines. Walk around. Carry really big guns. Perhaps you have heard of them?"

"Without importing key parts? It would be hard. Of course, there are several factories producing Industrial-Mechs, and plenty of myomer. The big issue would be fusion reactors. But Cosby Myomer Research used to manufacture them before they shifted completely into myomer production and merged with MyoMaxx. In theory, the capacity is still here."

"So it is possible?"

"Possible, but unlikely in the near term."

"All I really need is for others to think we would be able to develop the capability. It makes bottling us up less desirable, and less likely. It might buy us some breathing space if we can get through the immediate crisis. Now, pay attention."

Picking up a headset hanging next to the table, she inserted the earpiece into her ear and touched the talk button. "Star Captain Durant."

An officer in the military command center turned and looked at her through the glass wall. "Yes, Galaxy Commander."

"Where is Star Colonel Hall? I need to confer with him on strategy."

Durant looked embarrassed. "Sir, we cannot seem to locate him."

"You cannot *find* him?"

"He may have left the base. But we cannot seem to—"

"He left the base without a security detail?"

"As I said, sir, we are not sure—"

She cut him off again. "Well, find him, and when you do, tell him I need him here. Meanwhile, there are things that cannot wait. Durant, issue a recall to all nonessential forces on Cebalrai. Cut our numbers as thin as we can while still ensuring stability there. On my authorization, reassign any of our ships headed to the Rasalhague Dominion to transport of personnel and equipment here, instead."

"Yes, sir!"

"Galaxy Commander," Trenton interrupted. "Any forces coming from Cebalrai will take—"

She nodded grimly. "Yes, I know. Best case, more than seventy days. Worst case, up to four months, depending on the logistics of where the JumpShips start and which JumpShips are available. There is nothing I can do about that, and I suspect that in seventy days we will have won or lost this war. But at least they will be able to relieve us, and help us reinforce our position here." She looked Trenton in the eye. "Nothing about our situation here is ideal. I am simply making the best of a bad situation."

"I see."

"I doubt you do. But you will soon enough. Now, I am going up to the executive gallery to commandeer a computer terminal. I have a very important speech to write. Whether I like it or not, I am about to turn our little branch of the Ghost Bears on its head."

Just then, Chief Ricco appeared in the doorway, a broad, uncharacteristic smile on his face. "We got him!"

"Got who? Bannson's man?"

"No! The saboteur. The one who interfered with our radar. Because the three radars were separated by so much distance, we thought it had to be multiple agents working in cooperation. But that turned out to be our clue. Only one Vegan traveled to all three installations during the period when the tampering took place."

She frowned. This could be very good, or very bad. "How certain are you? How solid is your proof?"

"Once we knew when and where to look, it was easy to establish proof. We have two sets of surveillance recordings showing him committing the crime. The recording at the third installation is less conclusive, but it still puts him in the right place at the right time. Even by the lenient standards of Inner Sphere justice, the case is a lock."

"Good enough, then. Arrange for an execution tomorrow at dawn. A firing squad. We will figure out the legalities later."

Ricco looked shocked. "You want this kept quiet?"

"On the contrary, alert the media. I want this to be completely public. And contact the First Vega Regulars and see if anyone wants to volunteer for the firing squad. I bet you get a few takers. This man is responsible for nearly killing their commander."

Ricco's eyes were wide. "Yes, sir."

"There may be people out there who think the enemy of their enemy is their friend, and who think we are their enemy. They may think acting as agents for the Draconis Combine is some kind of game. We need to show them that it is not. It is treason against Vega, and that is something we will not tolerate!"

Conner Hall felt uncomfortable in the civilian clothing that Reuben had insisted they wear. They'd obtained the clothing at the sole surviving unit in a bombed-out apartment building located just outside the base.

This place apparently served as a kind of way station. There had been stacks of men's and women's clothing in various sizes, and he had seen a number of technician and laborer uniforms hanging in a closet. He'd refused to leave his own uniform and had found a stained backpack in one of the piles that he could carry it in, despite Reuben's objections.

"These aren't good areas we're going into, and a lone Clansman is a target for gangs. If anyone confronts us and you have to talk, try to use contractions and not be awkward about it."

They walked northwest, to an area where the freight rail leaving the spaceport crossed under the beltway. A long and dangerous-looking pedestrian bridge threaded between the rails below and the elevated beltway above. The commuter monorail tracks ran parallel to the bridge, but this was not one of the sections that had been restored to service after the occupation. He could see the damaged track silhouetted against the sky, like a giant fence with sections missing.

They descended a long stair at the end of the bridge, coming down to street level. The street was dark, lit only by a flickering streetlamp at the far end of the block. The only vehicle traffic he saw was on a cross street several blocks away, and it was so dark he could not even be sure the street he was on was passable. It smelled of rotted garbage, and small, unseen things skittered through the darkness.

Conner could scarcely believe this was a city, on a world that had once been the capital of a prefecture.

The cities of the Rasalhague Dominion (or at least, the ones he'd seen; was he being naive to think they were all that way?) were mostly clean and orderly, and crime was rare. Children marched down the streets in their little practice formations day or night, concerned only about their next test or their Trial of Position, with no fear of being assaulted by a gang of lawless thugs.

Here, even a rabid dog would fear for its safety. He had seen the city, seen destruction and squalor like this many times, but it all looked completely different striding by ten meters above the ground in the cockpit of a 'Mech.

This was alien to him, but Karen must have known of it, must have experienced conditions like this and far worse in the dark days before Omega Galaxy arrived. He'd seen it in her eyes sometimes, a sadness, a darkness, a hurt that would never heal. *This* was what she had been fighting for. Or perhaps more properly, this was what she had been fighting against.

"Darkness, decay and the end of all things."

Reuben hesitated in front of him. "What?"

He had not realized that he had said it out loud. "Just thinking. How bad things can be, literally just beyond your door. Our lives are so bright, efficient, disciplined and well organized; we do not imagine how close the darkness lies."

"There are good people out here, Conner. People who need us, whether they know it or not."

Conner was a little shocked that Reuben used his name, but he supposed that if their intent was to not be recognized as Clan, using his rank would be the most obvious mistake he could make. Still, he felt strange.

No uniform.

No rank.

Even his Bloodname, if they used it, would hold no special meaning here. He'd spent his entire life in a uniform, from the sibko on up. Who *was* he when he took it off? He realized, with a mixture of distress and elation, that he had no idea.

They turned onto another street, where more of the streetlights worked. The burned hulk of a Kinnol main battle tank stuck out of a crumbling masonry wall, but there were lights on in buildings up and down the block, and he could see a few ground cars making their way along the street.

"This is like another world, this side of the freight rail," said Reuben. "Clan never come here without heavy armor. Except us." He led Conner a few meters along the block, then down a basement stair. He pulled out a pocket flash so he could see to enter a code on a lock. It clicked, and they stepped into a dark space.

Conner unconsciously found the grip of the pistol in his jacket pocket. But when the light snapped on, there was just Reuben, looking at him curiously. "You're among friends, Conner Hall." He opened a heavy metal fire door, and the sound of voices came from within.

Conner followed him through. Though most of the machinery had been removed, Conner could guess it had been a laundry of some sort, perhaps servicing the building above. Were they in an abandoned hotel? Or maybe a hospital?

Inside was a group of people. He recognized none of them, though his experience with Reuben had taught him that did not mean much. Certainly they recognized him, as they all stopped talking and turned to stare, openmouthed.

There were four men and three women sitting in a circle on folding chairs and empty packing crates. They had the strong, healthy appearance that was characteristic of Clanners, but Conner was startled to realize he had no idea of their caste without their uniforms.

For all he knew, they all could have been warriors, though from what Reuben had told him it was unlikely any of them were. More likely they were mostly laborers, a few merchants and technicians. Maybe a scientist. Probably not.

"My name," he said, "is Conner Hall. I have come seeking the Freeminders."

A tall blond woman rose from the packing crate where she had been sitting and took a step forward. "My name is Selkis, Star Colonel. We had been told you were coming, but I scarcely believed it until you walked through the door."

Conner hesitated. "My rank—my rank hardly seems appropriate here. You may call me Conner."

She looked at him strangely. "I am only slightly less uncomfortable about that than you must be—Conner. But I admire the spirit in which you have approached us, and I will respect your wishes."

He sized her up. She was a powerfully built woman, muscular and broad-shouldered. Her eyes had an alert intelligence that made it hard for him to believe she was a lower caste. She would not have looked out of place in a MechWarrior's uniform.

"Are you the leader of the Freeminders?"

She looked surprised, then laughed. The edge of her mouth crinkled when she smiled, in a way that was strikingly pretty. It was a stunning contrast to her superficial roughness. "Great Father, no, I am not the leader of the Freeminders. I am what we call a foreman, of this particular cell. Think of it as equivalent to a Star commander, except that there are three of us in this cell. Our command structure is redundant and somewhat loosely consensual."

"I wanted to speak with the person in charge. Reuben told me he was on this planet."

"Normally, a new recruit such as yourself would not be granted such a bold request, but you, of course, are a special case. I think the uKhan is just as eager to speak to you."

"The *what?*"

"The uKhan. That's the rank our leader came up with for himself. It means UnderKhan."

"But uKhan? You realize it is a—"

"A very bad pun? Yes, I do, and so does the uKhan. You will find that he has a sense of humor."

"Does this uKhan have a name?"

"Almost certainly, but I don't know it. Frankly, though I have spoken with the uKhan, I have never met him.

Very few of us have. He is reportedly a very high-ranking member of his caste, and to reveal himself openly at this point would endanger his ability to aid us."

"But he is here?"

She smiled politely. "Not exactly. Please follow me."

She led him across the room, past a line of broken plumbing and power connections where washing machines might once have stood, and through a door into an office marked, appropriately enough, FOREMAN. Inside was a desk and two more folding chairs. A speakerphone device sat on the desk. There was a small trivid camera attached, but no corresponding screen to view the person on the other end of the connection.

Selkis tapped a button on the speakerphone, and a small red light appeared on the camera. Conner was directed to the chair in front of the camera.

"Who calls?" a voice from the phone asked abruptly. It was apparently male, but run through some sort of voice distorter so even that was uncertain.

"This is Selkis. I have—the new recruit—to speak with the uKhan."

"This line is secured. There is no problem in saying the Star colonel's name." There was a hesitation. "The uKhan is quite busy right now. Let me see if he can make himself available. One moment."

The light on the camera went out, and Conner assumed the mike was muted as well. He looked at Selkis. "If you do not mind my asking, what caste are you?"

She grimaced slightly. "We do not talk about that sort of thing here much, Conner. Our Clan minds are too neatly compartmentalized along those lines. Once you know the caste of a person, it is hard to think of them the same way again."

"I have already reached my conclusions about you, Foreman Selkis, and they are favorable. I doubt knowing would change that."

"So you say, but to break from the old ways of thought is hardest of all for warriors."

"Still—"

Her eyes narrowed. "I am laborer caste, Conner Hall. What do you say to that?"

His mouth opened, but nothing came out.

"You see? It is not as easy as you might have imagined, is it?"

He finally found his tongue. "I do not understand how that can be."

"There are many ways to test down, Conner. Many ways to find oneself in the laborer caste besides being the dull-witted simpleton that you might have imagined."

He was almost relieved when the light on the camera came on, and a new voice spoke. This one also seemed male, and was deeper than the last, but it also had been modified electronically. "Conner Hall. What a pleasant surprise it is to see you there."

"I do not like it when people know my name, and I do not know theirs. I do not like being seen, but not seeing you."

"It's an unfortunate arrangement, I admit, and I can't blame you for being uncomfortable. But I have my reasons for my secrecy, and so far it has served me well, despite certain inconveniences such as this. I hope that, very soon, circumstances will change and allow me to reveal myself, not just to you, but to all my loyal Free-minders."

"That will be a great day for you, then. It is hard to be king when your subjects cannot see you."

The voice laughed deeply, and the voice distorter made it intermittently sound like someone gargling. "I'm no king, Conner Hall. I'm only a nominal leader, and I don't much enjoy the role. I don't want people ever to take the office or the person occupying it too seriously. That's part of why I chose my—whimsical title. Frankly, one reason I'm looking forward to revealing myself is that it will open the way to electing a replacement.

"You've met Selkis. I hope that her name might be one of those considered."

Conner glanced over, and saw Selkis blush at the suggestion.

He made eye contact with her. "I think that might be a very wise choice."

Her eyes widened slightly in surprise. Then she smiled at the compliment.

"If you join us, Conner Hall, new though you are to our cause, many might want to consider your name for leadership as well."

He licked his dry lips and squirmed on the hard chair. "I think I might be exactly the wrong person for that job. I would certainly decline it."

The uKhan laughed. "I don't believe you would lie, Conner Hall. Deception is a skill I've had to cultivate to maintain my secret identity, and that, too, is something I would be glad to give up. But in any case, that was the correct answer, or at least the one I was hoping to hear. I've long lived in both anticipation and dread of the day a Bloodnamed warrior might join us. While it lends great strength and legitimacy to our cause, it could upset our whole premise of caste equality."

"But Reuben tells me that you still believe in the importance of the warrior caste."

"All are equal. Some are more equal than others." He chuckled at some secret joke. "In the context of working life, we believe in the sanctity of the warrior caste. But within this organization, we must all be equals. You will note that they are not using your rank—"

"That was my idea," he said.

"It was, uKhan," added Selkis. "You had mentioned it to me earlier, but I was uncomfortable with the prospect and did not tell the others."

The uKhan chuckled. "Selkis is surprisingly traditional at times, and bound to Clan ways. That's part of why I think she would make a fine leader. As for you, you have impressed me again. Perhaps you're far more ready to embrace the ideas of our group than I dared hope."

"Some of them. I would like very much to see this Final Codex that everyone is so excited about."

"You misunderstand. I don't have the Final Codex. I have seen it, and I uncovered copies of selected pages in a sealed Ghost Bear archive many years ago. I was able to secure copies of these copies, and they have been distributed through the Freeminders. But while I know the full text exists and where it is, my efforts to obtain it have thus far been unsuccessful. That, too, I hope to change soon."

"If the Clan has this document, will it not be properly secured? Will they not miss it if it is gone?"

"The Final Codex was suppressed more than two centuries ago, and likely forgotten when the Khans and Loremasters who suppressed it died. Many archived documents and artifacts are secured by the Clans out of habit and procedure, rather than out of concern over what they represent. Much of our history is simply locked away and forgotten. That, too, I would like to end."

"So I am to believe in this Final Codex, but I cannot see it?"

"Selkis has copies of the known pages. She will see that you get copies for your own examination."

"I suppose that will do."

"You sound disappointed."

"I am here seeking answers to questions that trouble me deeply. I had hoped to find answers in the words of the Founder."

"Perhaps, if you are patient, you will. If you don't mind my asking, Conner Hall, why did you come to the Freeminders? What are these questions that trouble you?"

He hesitated. These were things he barely dared say to himself, much less to some faceless stranger. But he had faced massed 'Mechs in battle; he should be able to face this. "I have come to love a woman."

"Outside your caste?"

It was hard to say. "A Vegan. A freeborn."

"There is no shame in this, Conner Hall. You are among friends here. Your story is a common one."

He clenched his jaw. "Not for a Bloodnamed Mech-Warrior of Clan Ghost Bear."

"Perhaps not now, but one day it might be less unusual than you imagine. This woman, does she return your love?"

He felt a tight ache form in his chest. With difficulty, and without complete success, he struggled to push the emotions welling up inside him back into their hidden places. His voice cracked slightly as he spoke. "She might."

"Then I am happy for you."

"There is little to be happy about. She is injured, in a coma, and may not recover. I may never know what her true feelings were."

"Oh," said the voice. Then a pause. "Oh! You have my sympathies, Conner. Tragedy, loss: these are no strangers to the Freeminders. As Jorgensson and Tseng struggled to keep their family together, so do many of our people struggle for theirs. We aren't always as successful, though."

Selkis looked at him, sympathy in her eyes. "I left a husband and two children behind to come here, Conner. I do not know if I will ever see them again."

"You will," Conner answered, "if I have anything to do with it."

"You sound committed, Conner, but are you really? There are many levels of commitment. I will ask you to do something momentous for the Freeminders, and I'd hardly blame you if you refused."

"Will this request help people like Selkis? Like Reuben?"

"More than you can imagine."

"Then ask me."

*   *   *

Isis Bekker kept glancing from the senate proclamation in front of her to the shifting status display. Chance Elba had delivered on his promise, and the drafted proclamation was a rousing call for unity against outside incursion and betrayal at home. The voting would be going on about now.

If the measure passed, and she was confident it would, she would need to give her speech. And once she did that, nothing, absolutely nothing, was ever going to be the same again.

By now, of course, news of the execution scheduled for morning was traveling through the senate. She did not think it would hurt support for the proclamation. It might even help it. *Give them something to fight for. Give them something to rally around. Give them something to fight against.*

Judging by the movement of the icons on her map, that last part was taking care of itself. There were new reports of enemy 'Mech movements a hundred kilometers west of the city. They were taking considerably less trouble to disguise themselves now, which likely meant they intended to show themselves in a big way very soon.

Where was Star Colonel Hall? The absence of her military right hand had gone from an annoyance to a point of grave concern.

She paced the length of the map, studying the red icons that indicated reported enemy movements. Potentially, they could be here within a few hours, though she doubted they would be here that soon. If Vega was lucky, it might be a day or two.

She hoped they would be lucky. The Omega Galaxy had not returned to full strength after the long standdown under Devlin Stone, and they had suffered heavy losses to antiaircraft fire upon arriving on Vega. She had long suspected that the unexpectedly sophisticated missiles that had brought down their DropShips and VTOLs had been supplied to the warlords by the Draconis Combine, along with the suspiciously up-rated but otherwise un-traceable 'Mechs that they had encountered in local hands. Now it seemed confirmed. They had been pulling strings on Vega since well before the Ghost Bears arrived.

"Galaxy Commander," Star Captain Durant spoke in Isis' headset. "We have just received a call from Star Colonel Hall. He is on his way here from somewhere in the city."

She looked up at the command center. "Where has he been?"

"He did not say, sir, only that he would be here shortly."

Trenton climbed down the stairs from one of the galleries, a grave look on his face. "Galaxy Commander, there's a broadcast on the tri-vid that you need to see."

She frowned. "What now?"

Something in Trenton's expression stopped her questions. "It doesn't matter what station," he said, "it's on all of them."

She picked up a remote and flipped on one of several tri-vid screens on the wall around the room. She was shocked to see Star Colonel Hall's face.

His voice came from the speaker. "—Hall of the Ghost Bear Clan." He paused, and seemed to be trying to collect his thoughts.

Isis looked at Trenton. "I thought we had control of all media. Where is this coming from?"

"It's being tied in directly at the broadcast transmitters. I suspect the Labor Party has something to do with it. Most of the broadcast technicians are with them."

Hall continued. "Recent events have caused me to question many fundamental aspects of my Clan and its ways. As I have always considered myself fiercely loyal to my Clan, these questions troubled me greatly. I was aware of the Freeminder movement, and certain circumstances made it possible for me to learn more about them.

"One of the things I learned about was a document

called the Final Codex. This document, if genuine, represents lost writings of our great Founder, Nicholas Kerensky. In those writings, and in the beliefs of the Freeminders
that are based on them, I have come to suspect that
much of what I believed about Clan ways was wrong,
and that we have placed far too little emphasis on that
which our Clan's founders, Jorgensson and Tseng, held
most dear: *family.*

"Thousands of our fellow Ghost Bears have, against
the authority of our Clan, created families based on the
same bonds of love that Jorgensson and Tseng shared.
They still follow Clan law: these families are in addition
to the families mandated by our scientific breeding program. But when these families bonded by love are discovered, these Clansmen are shunned, punished and denied
the right to keep their families together. That is tragic,
and I have come to believe that it does not represent
our Clan's true way. The Freeminders believe that we
must end this hypocrisy, and in this I support them fully.

"You may ask why I would choose to do this thing,
knowing it could cost me everything I have achieved in
my life: my rank, my Bloodname, my position as warrior.
It could even cost me my freedom, my life or, worst
of all, my right to call myself a member of the Ghost
Bear Clan."

He looked away from the camera for a moment, then
faced it squarely and took a deep breath. "I, Star Colonel Conner Hall, declare my love for a Vegan woman,
a freeborn. Her name is Captain Karen Tupolov, a
MechWarrior of the First Vega Regulars. I have come
to respect her as a MechWarrior and a comrade in arms.

"But she is also much more. She is Karen, whose
touch I celebrate, and whose voice I crave. Karen, for
whom I would give up all other things for the opportunity to form with her that precious thing called *family.*
Karen, with whom I would happily live out all the days
a warrior's life will grant me.

"This is my dream, but it may never come true. Karen

lies in a coma in our hospital, and despite all our doctors can do, she may never wake again. She may never know, as you now know, how I feel for her. If she does wake, she may not know me, may not remember the feelings she had for me, if indeed, she ever had any at all.

"But I say to you, my fellow Clansmen, and also to the people of Vega, that does not change my feelings. If—if she is dead, that does not change my feelings. What I do today—" He seemed to choke on the words, finally managing, "I do for her." He looked to his left. "Stop recording."

The screen blanked briefly, then cut to a shocked-looking news broadcaster who seemed unaware that he was back on camera. His coanchor nudged him with her elbow, and he turned to face the lens. "You have just heard an unauthorized feed that was patched into our broadcast system by person or persons unknown, a most unexpected source making a plea for tolerance of the Clan Freeminder movement. We'll be back in a moment with analysis of—"

She muted the audio, her brain already churning through scenario after scenario. She was shocked and dismayed, but already she could see that this might work to her advantage. It was critical, however, that she be seen—especially by the Vegan people—as acting on this development, rather than reacting to it. "Trenton, have the cameras in here activated and let the broadcast centers know that we want to go live in two minutes. I'll be giving a statement about the Freeminder movement."

He looked at her. "The vote on the floor isn't finished. We don't have confirmation that it will pass."

She shook her head. "We cannot wait. Whatever his reasons for speaking now, Conner Hall has forced our hand." *I'm on that runaway horse again, but this time I know a little better what I should do.*

There was a crash in the darkness, and Taylor Bane instinctively reached for the gun under his pillow.

It wasn't there.

He rolled, reaching for the backup weapon hung out of sight below the headboard, but a powerful hand grabbed his wrist. He tried to twist free but, unable even to tell where his attacker was standing, he failed. Even as he made the attempt, other hands grabbed him by the ankles. And his other arm was pulled back and pinned to the bed under someone's knee. In seconds, he was hopelessly trapped.

The light snapped on, and he saw that around him were standing five large men, all dressed in black clothing, body armor and ski masks. All wore adaptive night-vision goggles that let them see as well in the lighted room as they had in the darkness. The man nearest the light switch appeared to be their leader, and he held an assault needler aimed casually at Bane's midsection.

Bane craned his neck to see through the doorway into the adjoining room, where Bruno had been sleeping. He caught a glimpse of Bruno, blood dripping from his face, crawling across the floor towards the door.

Suddenly, a sixth man appeared, an assault rifle slung over his shoulder and carrying what appeared to be a fire ax.

Bane yelled a warning, but Bruno never saw the butt of the ax handle as it slammed straight down on the back of his head.

Bruno dropped like a bag of sand.

Man six stepped over the fallen man and entered the room, passing the ax to the leader.

The leader stepped forward. "I heard," he said, "you two were very dangerous. We took no chances."

Bane managed a scratchy sort of laugh. "You could have just made an appointment."

Man six stepped forward and slammed the butt of his rifle against the side of Bane's face.

Bane shook his head, trying to clear his double vision. He tasted blood in his mouth and spit, trying to hit the face of one of the men holding him. The bright red glob splattered on the man's armor vest.

Leader-man grimaced at him. "We know all about your appointments, Bane. We know who you work for, and we know he has designs on this world. We are going to send him a message."

"The boss, he doesn't respond well to threats."

"Maybe not, Mr. Bane, but he is a businessman. Like all businessmen, he'll follow the path of least resistance. He needs to know that it's a big galaxy, and if he needs somewhere to go, there are many other planets to choose from. But this one belongs to the Draconis Combine."

"Is that your message?" Bane's swollen mouth slurred the words.

Leader-man smiled. "No. I have one more thing to add."

Suddenly, the men holding Bane dragged him off one side of the bed. He struggled, his body bucking, until man six returned and gave him another smack with the rifle butt.

There was an interval of nothingness, then Bane realized he'd passed out for a moment. Someone had his knee in his chest, someone was holding his upper right arm, and someone else was holding his right hand, stretching his arm across the heavy wooden night table.

Leader-man approached holding the ax, still smiling. "This," he said, "is the message."

The ax fell.

14

Broadcast transcript of address by Galaxy Commander Isis Bekker to all Ghost Bear occupation forces on Vega, 1 December 3136, 0500 hours Nasew time:

My fellow Ghost Bears, my fellow Raging Bears, my *family*. This morning we face the gravest challenges we have encountered in our long history. We are besieged, from without and within, by forces that threaten to divide us and overwhelm us. The division and chaos that have nearly destroyed Vega have infected our own ranks.

By now, most of you have seen or have heard secondhand the statement just given to the Vegan media by Star Colonel Conner Hall. If you have not seen it, I suspect it will be in frequent rotation on the Vegan media, so you will not have to wait long.

I will be honest. I was as shocked as any of you by this development, and have not yet been able to speak with the Star colonel about his statement. He is currently on his way back to the capitol, and I will make an additional statement to you as soon as we have spoken.

But his statement represents only the tip of an

iceberg I have long known existed, and long feared facing. I knew the day would come when I would have to confront it, but this is a difficult day on which to do so.

Most of you are aware of the Freeminder movement. I suspect that more than a few of you listening to this broadcast are intimately familiar with it. The Freeminders question many of our most deeply seated traditions. They threaten our established sense of order and discipline, and as such, it is easy to consider them a threat.

I ask today that you reject the easy path. I do not believe as the Freeminders believe, but I do not have enough information to dismiss the possibility that there may be some truth in what they say. They have shown us a fragmentary document called the Final Codex, that they say was written by Nicholas Kerensky. This document supports many of their proposed reforms. If these are indeed the words of our Founder, then perhaps it is we who have strayed from the true path of the Clans, and the Freeminders point the way back.

Is this document genuine? I cannot say. It seems to run contrary to the earlier teachings of the Founder, but he often presented short-term goals and plans that seemed to lead one place, while his gaze was fixed on a different spot along the distant horizon.

What I can say is that it resonates strongly with the teachings and lessons of Jorgensson and Tseng. It speaks most deeply to what they held most dear: *family*. It resonates with the Great Father's Hidden Hope Doctrine, that we would somehow bring our greatness back to the Inner Sphere.

I know that many of you now are angry and confused. You wish to find those among you who you see as traitors to our traditions and use those traditions to strike at them. Perhaps you wish to declare trials against your fellow Ghost Bears, or your commanding officers. Perhaps, by the time I am through here, you will consider a Trial of Refusal against me.

I ask you to reconsider.

We face unknown and imminent military threats here in Nasew, and I suspect we will see combat within the next seventy-two hours.

Perhaps sooner.

Our forces are divided across two planets and scattered around this globe, and already, in our first skirmish, we were bloodied by superior forces. Because of the acts of traitors, we do not know what forces we face. What is clear is that the Draconis Combine is either supplying the insurgents or supplanting them as our enemy. We expect to find our forces outmatched in numbers and firepower.

Victory is not certain. But if we do not stand together as a Clan, and as a unit, and alongside the Vegan people, defeat *is* certain.

And so I give the following order: A new policy of openness exists within the Clan occupation forces on Vega. The Freeminder movement and its teachings are no longer forbidden. Freeminders may, as long as it does not conflict with their duty or the duties of others, hold meetings, recruit members and peacefully debate their beliefs. They are not to be reduced in rank or status for their association with the movement.

As always, our members will be judged by their performance in the fulfillment of their duties. Participation in the Freeminders will under no circumstances be used as an excuse for inferior performance by any Clan member of any caste.

Additionally, members of the Vegan Labor Party have expressed their sympathy with and support for the Freeminder movement, and desire to meet with its members. In the interest of planetary unity and improved relations with the people of Vega, I will permit such meetings, within the general restrictions placed on Freeminder activities.

I also remind all Clan members that the security of the Clan and its holdings is your responsibility. The Vegans may be our allies and friends, but they are not yet family. Until then, guard what is ours jealously.

Only in unity can we find strength. And in battle, that unity can be tested. What use are individual trials, when we all face a trial for our very existence?

Fight well, and I will see you all at the end of the Honor Road.

War Room, Provisional Capitol Building, East
  Central District
Nasew, North Nanturo continent, Vega
1 December 3136

Galaxy Commander Isis Bekker surveyed the icons floating over the map of Vega. There were more reports of enemy 'Mechs northwest of the city. Their objectives were still unclear. But their most obvious target was the one she was sitting in. Capturing the provisional capital would be a tremendous strategic and symbolic victory.

Even if she could safely withdraw her command staff and the high-level government officials, doing so would shatter their fragile authority over the Vegan people. Certainly there were those among the Vegans who would welcome anyone willing to wipe the Ghosts Bears and their "collaborators" off the planet.

But that was not the only possible objective. They might want to capture the spaceport, or to cripple the Ghost Bear base there. It was even possible that they would attack in such a way as to inflict maximum civilian casualties and property damage, in order to turn the Vegans even further against the occupation.

A reflection caught her eye. She looked up and saw Conner Hall standing across the map table from her. He stood tall and straight, his prominent chin held high. "Star Colonel Hall reporting, Galaxy Commander."

She glared at him. She literally had no idea what to say. She looked around. Trenton watched her from the far end of the room. She could see officers and staff watching them from their glass galleries above the pit.

Whatever she decided to say, she resolved to say it out of earshot of this audience. "If I may speak with you privately, Star Colonel." She directed him to the nearest of several small, soundproofed rooms off the map area. These rooms also had windows, but the glass could be made opaque for privacy.

He led the way and she followed, closing the door after them. She flipped a switch on the wall, and the glass windows instantly turned milky white.

The stared at each other for a moment. Then she burst out, "What the devil did you think you were doing, Conner? I do not care about your freeborn girlfriend, or whatever issues you have twisted around inside your head about the destiny of the Clans! You muddied waters for me that were already more dirt than water! I am talking about the very survival of our unit here!"

"As am I. I am sorry if I have weakened our strategic situation, but I did what I felt was necessary and right. I regret that I did not act with full knowledge of our situation, or I might have chosen differently. But an officer can only act on the intelligence available to them. I take full responsibility for my actions, and I am prepared to face any punishment you deem fit without trial or debate."

"Is that a poor way of asking for *surkai*?"

"*Surkai* requires that I admit my wrongdoing in order to restore my honor. I feel I did nothing wrong. I only state that I am willing to accept punishment as an acceptable cost for my actions. If that means death or Abjuration, then I face them gladly. No matter how great or small the punishment, I do not expect repair of my honor because I do not feel I have violated it. That others, you included, may think differently is hurtful, but ultimately not my concern."

She shook her head. "You have an answer for everything, do you not?"

"Truth is always a position of strength."

She rubbed her temples. "You heard the statement I made to our people on Vega?"

"I heard it as I was coming into the building. Frankly, I had expected to sacrifice myself for very little return, a symbolic act more than an effective one. Your reaction seems out of character."

She laughed harshly. "You were right the first time, Conner. This is not about you. My decision to recognize the Freeminders is part of a desperate political compromise with the Labor Party. You forced me into making my announcement before I could confirm that the compromise had passed the senate, but I would have made it regardless."

He stared at her, mouth agape.

She grinned. "Oh, yes. You could have done nothing, and your precious movement still would have gone mainstream."

He squared his shoulders. "I regret nothing."

"Perhaps. But I doubt you celebrate your decision quite so fully now."

She paused. "Well, neither of us can turn back the hands of time. Neither of us can undo what is done. So the question is, where do we go from here?"

"That is up to you, Galaxy Commander."

"Indeed it is, and I am glad you still recognize that. Trenton tells me that in his opinion most Freeminders remain devoted to their duty and to their Clan. Do you believe that to be true?"

"I do. Based on my limited encounters, the Freeminders

are loyal to the Clan, some fiercely so, and have no tolerance for those whose loyalty wavers. They can be counted on to fulfill their duties."

"Can I count on *you?*"

"My love of my Clan has never been an issue, Galaxy Commander. I am prepared to serve to the best of my abilities in any role you assign, no matter how humble. I am prepared to lay down my life at your command."

"It could come to that, but I hope not. No, Star Colonel. The role I need you to fulfill is the one in which you have until now ably served me. I need someone to lead our forces against our enemies. I wonder, however, if you have destroyed your ability to lead them."

"Your speech was a good one, Galaxy Commander. Many will heed your words."

"I was performing damage control, and this situation requires much more than that."

"Let me talk to my troops."

"I expect you will, and at length. Right now, though, we need to present a united front to our troops and the Vegan people. We will talk to them together."

She flipped the switch on the wall, and the windows again became transparent. There was a sudden flurry of activity as everyone in the room tried to feign being busy and concerned with something other than their conversation.

As she and Conner left the room, she looked for Trenton. He was standing above them in the back of an empty spectator gallery, engaged in an animated phone conversation, an intense look on his face.

She flagged down one of the aides. "Get the governor down here. Pull him off the senate floor if you have to. We've got something to sell, and I need the full holy trinity to do it."

The aide looked puzzled, but rushed off on his errand.

She glanced up at Trenton again and wondered what new problems he had found for her.

*   *   *

Tires squealed, and Taylor Bane slid across the back-seat of the car. The leather was lubricated by something sticky, which he dimly realized was his own blood.

The painkillers from their emergency kit were finally starting to kick in, and the stump of his wrist now hurt less than the makeshift tourniquet, a leather belt that Bruno had strapped above the wound. With a detached sense of interest, he observed the hotel ice bucket on the car floor. It contained ice, and his severed hand. He laughed. "Good thing *that* hotel had ice."

Bruno used the rearview mirror to glance at Bane from the driver's seat, his own hair matted with blood. "You take it easy, boss! Help is close. I called in some favors. We'll get you fixed up."

The tires screeched again, and the ice bucket threatened to tip over. Bane braced it with his foot, and laughed again.

"It's the drugs, boss." The car swerved. "Wish I had some, but somebody had to drive."

Bane giggled, and with some effort pushed himself up on his left elbow, just so he could see over the back of the seat. They swerved though morning traffic. The light was like liquid gold. It was so beautiful it made him want to cry, but it was easier to laugh. "I think Krago sold us out."

"Krago is dead, boss. I found his body in the garage on the way to the car. I think they beat the information out of him, then killed him when they were sure it was correct."

"Bastards. You see his family gets taken care of, Bruno."

"See to it yourself, boss."

He felt hot and cold at the same time. Something seemed to be draining out of him, something less obvious but more important than blood. He'd been wounded before, but this . . . "Bruno, this is why you always keep something in reserve. The package is on its way, but these Combine bastards have it coming. Send the consolation prize."

"You think about that when you're feeling better, boss."

Bane suddenly felt lucid.

He was angry. No, he was furious. He called on all his remaining reserves of strength. He shoved himself upright in the seat. "Bruno," he said with all the authority he could put into his voice, "this isn't the drugs talking. This is me! Send the signal!"

Bruno glanced back at him nervously. "Transmitter's in the trunk, boss. I'll do it before I let them start working on me. But we get you to the doc first."

The last dregs of his energy were fading away. His right hand throbbed, even though it was still there in the bucket of ice. He looked out through the windshield and saw they were pulling up to a guarded gate. A man in a uniform waved them through.

Far beyond the fences and barricades, a great silver ship rose towards heaven on a tail of blue fire.

15

Broadcast transcript of address by Galaxy Commander Isis Bekker, transmitted by all Vegan and Ghost Bear occupation media, 1 December 3136, 0620 hours Nasew time:

Freedom-loving people of Vega and my fellow Clansmen of the Ghost Bears, I address you this morning concerning matters of vast importance to both our peoples.

Standing behind me you can see Star Colonel Conner Hall, commander of my military forces here on Vega, and Acting Provisional Governor Vincent Florala. Many of you have already seen Star Colonel Hall in the media this morning, and I am sure you must wonder about my response to his decision to join the Freeminders.

I will address that presently. First, I must discuss more pressing matters.

Since our Omega Galaxy forces liberated Vega from the oppression of the self-styled warlord regimes, in particular the butcher named Jedra Kean, our presence here has been controversial.

For well over a year, I have struggled daily to

bring together the many contentious factions of this world and rebuild a stable government that would allow the Rasalhague Dominion to withdraw from Vega. You know the players: the four major parties, the four minor ones. You know their leaders. You know their agendas. They agree on much, but they disagree on even more. Though some progress has been made in this past year, I am sad to say that, overall, these efforts have been a failure.

Meanwhile, my people have seen the rise of a contentious faction within our own ranks, a group called the Freeminders. This group, until recently composed mostly of our laborer and technician castes, has advocated changes to our Clan society that many find frightening, even abhorrent.

They seek freedom of speech and thought.

They seek the right to choose their own marriage partners, and even to marry outside our Clan.

They seek to change the caste system that has served us since the founding of the Clans more than three centuries ago.

As most of you know, now even higher-caste members of the Clan are beginning to embrace the Freeminder philosophy. Much to my shock and surprise, one of my highest-ranked warriors, a trusted member of my staff, has embraced the group.

And all the while we have bickered, jostled for position and negotiated, enemies have taken advantage of our confusion and uncertainty to strike at us. We call them insurgents, but that is not their name. They have no leader that we can identify, no formal structure or defining philosophy, no serpent's head that can be cut off to cripple them, as the warlords were crippled when I killed Jedra Kean.

They are united only in their hatred of the Ghost Bear occupation of Vega.

Some of you call them heroes or freedom fighters, but I do not think most of them even know what they are fighting for. They are united only in their anger at us, and they strike violently and without honor. They have drawn the blood of my people, but they have drawn the blood of your people as well. You know of the bridge bombings, the destruction of the Touten Waterworks, the monorail bombs and the MyoMaxx factory attacks. These attacks hurt Vegans as much as, probably more than, the Ghost Bears.

These people are not heroes. They are traitors and assassins. They hurt us all, and worse, they betray us to our enemies.

Right now, you see on your screens a firing squad assembled near the fountain in Star League Park here in Nasew. The man in the picture is named Lee Roche. He is an electronics technician who immigrated to Vega five years ago. We believe that he was sent here as a sleeper agent for the Draconis Combine, who have for years been looking for a way to return Vega to their control.

Several weeks ago, he sabotaged three key radar installations, allowing an unknown number of enemy 'Mechs and other forces to be delivered to Vega undetected. Some of these forces recently attacked a combined reconnaissance force, critically injuring the commander of the First Vega Regulars as she attempted to cover the retreat of one of her own against overwhelming force.

You have already heard that commander's name: Captain Karen Tupolov.

The evidence against Roche is overwhelming and unambiguous, and that information has already been released to all planetary media. Roche is a traitor who sold out your people and mine to the hostile forces of the Draconis Combine.

He is only one of many such traitors who I believe operate freely in our midst.

Perhaps you are one of these people. Perhaps you have aided the Draconis Combine out of some misguided sense of patriotism. Perhaps you have information about foreign agents and have kept silent.

I now show you the swift justice that will be meted out against traitors to Vega. The firing squad is made up primarily of Ghost Bear warriors, but two MechWarriors from Captain Tupolov's unit also volunteered for this duty.

The video of Galaxy Commander Bekker cuts to a wide-shot video of a middle-aged man dressed in a technician's coverall.

The man's hands are bound, he is blindfolded and two soldiers push him back against a concrete retaining wall in the park and then walk away, joining a line of their fellows carrying rifles. Most of the soldiers wear the white-gray-and-black camouflage of the Ghost Bears, but two in the middle sport the desert tan fatigues of the Vegan Volunteer Force.

An officer standing at the end of the line yells. The line snaps to attention.

Another yell. Rifles are raised.

Another yell. Multiple cracks ring through the air. The rifles buck.

The man slumps to the ground, lying motionless.

The camera lingers for a moment, and then the picture is cut off, returning after several seconds of blackness to Galaxy Commander Bekker standing at a podium. She resumes speaking.

This action will anger many Vegans. But this man was not a native of Vega. He was a traitor whose actions led directly to a Vegan Volunteer Force officer suffering critical wounds, and allowed the invasion of enemy forces onto Vegan soil. All Vegans must understand that we will not tolerate treason, and you must not either. If you have information on such traitors, it is vital that you contact the Clan paramilitary police or your local Vega Police Militia at once. If you have unknowingly or unwittingly aided these people, I urge you to turn yourself in at once. I promise that you will be shown leniency that will not be available to those we seek out and arrest.

Rapidly developing events again threaten the security of Vega. Very soon we will be at war, this time with a foreign power. Thanks to the betrayal of the traitor Roche, a force of undetermined size is maneuvering northwest of Nasew. Recon patrols are currently advancing to learn the extent of the threat.

But I can tell you who they are.

Doubtless these forces contain some element of the insurgency, if only to provide a cloak of legitimacy. If we only faced the insurgency, I would have little concern. We have fought them for over a year, and we could continue to fight them. But they have been provided with unknown military resources by an outside power that evidence says is the Draconis Combine. In fact, the bulk of the forces may be Draconis Combine, simply pretending to be insurgents.

I can offer only circumstantial evidence to support these charges at the present time. As we enter combat and capture prisoners, that situation will change.

But for us to have any hope of victory, we cannot fight on multiple fronts, and we cannot fight alone. All members of the Ghost Bear Clan and all people of the planet Vega must stand together against the invaders.

I know that seems impossible to many of you,

even absurd. But allow me to make my case. I know that many of Vega hate the occupation forces of the Ghost Bear Clan. I cannot end that hate, but I can end the occupation.

As of this date and hour, the military occupation of the Ghost Bears is at an end. All Ghost Bear personnel and civilians are free to leave the combat zone at their earliest opportunity with their honor intact. Those wishing to transfer to other units will be processed and transported as soon as the situation allows.

You can see from their faces that this announcement comes as a shock to my comrades here on camera. I am sure it must seem equally shocking, perhaps even unbelievable, to you. But I see this move as the only way of demonstrating our sincerity to the Vegan people as I declare, once again, that we never came as aggressors or conquerors, but as friends seeking to restore your broken world.

That said—and I speak only for myself—my honor will not let me abandon you in this time of need. Governor Florala, I pledge my service, and if necessary my life, to the defense of the provisional government and the freedom of the Vegan people.

I ask this thing in return: that you accept my request for citizenship of Vega, and allow for my permanent residence on your world under its laws. I also request that you extend such citizenship, along with its rights and responsibilities, to all of my people and their families who so request, and who are also willing to join me in contributing to their new world's defense.

Governor Florala steps up to the podium.

Galaxy Commander, while it is not within my personal authority to grant your request, I hereby use my authority to bring this matter to the floor of the Provisional Congress and call for an immediate vote on the matter in principle, details to be worked out later.

Florala steps back. Bekker starts to return to the podium, but is intercepted by Star Colonel Hall. Whispers are exchanged, and he steps to the fore.

I too request citizenship of the world of Vega, and pledge myself to its defense.

I would like to address all those in the Clan who, at least until this morning, considered themselves under my command. My fellow warriors, you face a momentous decision, and by all that we have shared in blood and battle, I beg you to consider well.

Here, the Honor Road branches. While none will question your honor if you walk away from this world and the Omega Galaxy, I suggest to you that the more honorable path will keep you here. History will be the judge of that.

But remember that only those worthy few who followed Nicholas Kerensky into battle, the eight hundred, became the progenitors of the Clan's Bloodnames. Will those who walk away today walk with honor only into the shadows, to be lost to history? I challenge you who are courageous enough, of all castes, to walk with me that high and dangerous road that leads towards the future.

Hall steps back, allowing Bekker to return to the podium.

People of Vega. You have heard our pledge, and our plea. For more than three centuries, the Clans have built our strength for some purpose that most of us could not even imagine. But here, on Vega, the birthplace of our beloved Star League, I believe fate has shown us the way. Let us join you. Let us fight at your side. Let us die together for *our* world.

People of Vega, you believe us invaders, but I

show you we are not. You believe us rigid and inflexible, and yet this day I have agreed to allow the Freeminder movement to operate freely in our midst. What more can I do to convince you . . . ?

Bekker hesitates, looks back at Florala, then continues.

It may be some time before we know if our request for citizenship will be accepted. But I believe there is a quicker way I could become a citizen.

Though it is not widely known, for some time Acting Provisional Governor Florala and I have had an—intimate relationship. This may shock some people of Vega, but such relationships are not forbidden by our Clan ways. For us, sex is a matter independent of procreation or love. It is a bonding ritual between equals.

But to you, it means something more. A week ago, Vincent Florala asked me to marry him. Until now, I have not given him an answer. But as I understand your tradition of law, an outsider who marries a citizen is entitled to citizenship themselves. If anyone doubts my sincerity in my commitment to Vega, and my openness to reform, let that doubt end now.

Bekker turns to face Florala and takes his hands in hers.

Vince, I will marry you, as soon as we can possibly arrange it.

And a world watched in wonder as he took her in his arms, and they kissed.

16

From the Great Work of
Galaxy Commander Isis Bekker

The fundamental building block of all civilization is the union, the decision of two or more people to stand together in some way. Without unions, there are no tribes, much less interstellar empires. Without unions, we are but upright apes, standing alone.

There are many kinds of unions: alliances, treaties, contracts, pledges, mergers and so on. The human race has turned most unions into something abstract and formalized, all sanctified by papers and signatures and law. It was not always so.

There was a time when unions were deeply felt and visceral. A promise might be sealed with the letting and mingling of blood. A man might prove his manhood and his loyalty to his tribe through trials or bodily mutilation.

And what of a union between two groups, the bonding of tribes, or kingdoms, or nations? There was a ritual for that as well. Marriages were arranged between royalty of the two powers, thus mingling their bloodlines both symbolically and literally. Through that simple act, two great families became one, and two nations became one as well.

Such marriages were arranged, and were matters of duty, not love. It is said that in some cases, love later flowered.

But in many, it did not.

It did not matter. Duty does not ask for love.

Duty does not need it.

Stellar Orbit, Vega System

The little satellite lay sleeping, as it had since being clandestinely ejected from a DropShip air lock a month earlier. Occasionally it would roll in its sleep, gyros gently turning its solar panels to face the sun to keep its batteries charged. But though it slept, it was alert. It kept one antenna pointed towards Vega, waiting for a very specific coded signal.

A wave, nearly imperceptibly weak, washed over it at the speed of light. If the satellite had been an animal, its ears would have pricked up. Gently the antenna moved, centering itself on the distant signal. There had been signals on this frequency before: stray transmissions, bits of noise, but always it had been a false alarm, and the satellite had returned to dormancy.

Not this time.

The satellite came to full wakefulness. Its radio transmitter and onboard computer were brought to full power. A data file in its memory was accessed and transmitted towards Vega on a specified frequency.

It was a large file, and the transfer took several seconds.

When the transfer was complete, the transmission was repeated. Then the satellite changed to a second frequency, and repeated the process.

There was a list of sixteen frequencies for it to cycle through, then the entire process would repeat from the beginning, as long as power was available. The powerful transmitter drained the batteries, and at this rate, they would last less than thirty minutes.

It didn't matter.

By that time, somebody, probably several somebodies, would have noticed the transmission and recorded it. They would share it. The news would spread.

The word would be out.

Taylor Bane had called it the consolation prize, but there could be no doubt at all.

It was a weapon.

Taft National Forest, 145 kilometers northwest of
    Nasew
North Nanturo continent, Vega
1 December 3136

Star Colonel Conner Hall's thoughts were dark as he strode his *Karhu* across the scrubby brown meadow at full throttle.

Off to his left, MechWarrior Duncan Huntsig's *Karhu* guarded his flank. To his right and farther back, he could see two of the new FVR 'Mechs: one of the *Spiders*, graceful with its outstretched stabilizer wings, and the *Rifleman*, a brutal-looking 'Mech with large arm-mounted weapons. They looked factory-fresh in their tan camouflage and red-and-black FVR unit medallions, a condition that could change at any moment.

The remaining FVR 'Mechs, the second *Spider* and a gangly but fast *Uller*, shared rear guard on the formation.

"Star Colonel, this is Recon Three. We have fresh tracks. Looks like they turned and headed north at high speed. You should be able to intercept."

"Roger, Recon Three. If they spot you, try to draw them back towards us, or at least delay them a little. Do not engage."

"Not a chance, sir."

Recon Three was a Fox armored car, certainly not helpless, but no match for a 'Mech.

Conner caught another glimpse of Huntsig, and thumbed up a private channel. "Huntsig, I really did not expect you to stay with us after all that happened this morning."

"To be honest, Star Colonel, I did consider my options. If it had just been a matter of you, I might not be here. But my honor is bound to the FVR. I am here for them."

"Understood. But for what it is worth, I am glad you are here."

"For what it is worth," he chuckled, "you should be."

Conner turned.

Something moved behind a small cluster of brown trees to their left. He recognized the boxy missile canisters of a *Catapult,* many open spaces showing in the racks. *He is short on ammo.* "Target at ten o'clock, range one-point-one klicks! It is the *Catapult.* Watch for escorts."

"I have an *Anubis* one klick north," announced Recon Three. "Taking fire. He is jumping above me. I am—" There was a crackle, and the circuit went dead.

"Kortlever and Felix," ordered Huntsig, "Get over there and draw off that *Anubis.* You have got the speed and firepower now, use it. Do not forget those jump jets in the *Spider,* Kortlever. Use them if you need them."

The two rear 'Mechs veered off the formation, as the rest of them focused on the much more dangerous *Catapult.*

"He has not seen us yet," said Huntsig, "or we would be eating missiles by now."

Suddenly the *Catapult* sprinted and dodged.

"Now he has seen us," said Conner. "Keep close to cover. Make him work for those missile hits."

The *Catapult* turned, backpedaled.

Conner caught a glimpse of the laser scar he had put across the upper hull and confirmed what he had sus-

pected. This was one of the 'Mechs that took down
Karen.

The *Catapult* launched a missile salvo, turned and ran.

Conner dashed into a stand of trees, drought-weakened
trunks snapping easily before his 'Mech. He saw a missile arcing toward him, but lost sight of it until it exploded against a tree five meters to his left.

His 'Mech bucked at the blast, but there was no
damage.

He burst out of the trees, targeted and fired his lasers.

An explosion ripped open one of the missile canisters.
The *Catapult* turned as if to fire more missiles, but nothing happened.

Conner shoved his throttle forward. "We have his missiles! Keep him on the run!"

The *Catapult* ran, but Conner found he could easily
keep up with the damaged 'Mech. He loitered just far
enough back to make himself a less-than-ideal laser target, but the *Catapult* was more interested in escape
than combat.

In the background he could hear the chatter between
Kortlever and Felix.

"There's what's left of Recon Three. No sign of survivors."

"There he is! Missile incoming!"

"I'm hit. Slowing me down."

"Hang back! Let me draw his fire!"

"No! Almost got him in my gun sights—There!"

He heard autocannon chatter.

"He's burning! He's burning!"

"Whoa! Good shot! He's falling! He's falling!"

"Target is down! Target is down!"

"Good hunting," called Huntsig. "Felix, fall in behind
and watch our backs. Kortlever, use those jump jets to
get a fix, then flank in to the west. Chow, take the east
flank. Let us box him in. Do not close until I give the
okay."

"Roger that, Mother Hen."

Conner laughed. "Mother Hen?"

"On my honor," said Huntsig glumly, "it was not my choice."

Huntsig was giving most of the orders, but Conner understood that his own command position was shaky, and did not object. In any case, Huntsig seemed to have taken his "Mother Hen" role genuinely to heart.

It pleased Conner, but he was careful not to say so. He knew Huntsig would take it the wrong way.

Ahead, the *Catapult* turned past an outcrop and found itself on the receiving end of missiles coming from the north. It had finally strayed within range of the *Ursus* units that had been maneuvering into its path.

"We have him." It was Star Captain Stuka, one of the recent recalls.

The *Catapult* stepped back just in time for a missile to narrowly miss the cockpit and explode right under the nose. The big 'Mech staggered back, nose high, lasers aimed ineffectively at the clouds, then staggered forward, nose tilting far down.

"Now!" It was Huntsig. "Jump on him now!"

The *Spiders* descended from either side, landing next to the bigger *Catapult* like two wasps descending on a grasshopper. Inside its weapon range, the *Catapult* showed its one weakness against the *Spiders'* strengths. It had no arms, and was virtually helpless against their melee attacks.

Conner desperately wanted to make this kill, but there was no way he could use his weapons without endangering Kortlever and Chow.

Huntsig seemed to read his mind. "Let them have the kill, Star Colonel. She was their commander."

She was more to me.

But Huntsig was right, of course. Conner throttled back, and they watched as the *Spiders* took the big 'Mech apart piece by piece.

Galaxy Commander Isis Bekker looked sadly at the tri-vid screen. The media were reporting live from where their warriors had taken over the passenger terminal at the spaceport as a makeshift camp.

A Point of Elementals in armor bounced through the foreground on jump jets, patrolling the perimeter.

Star Captain Vong clearly had been torn as he told her personally that his elementals could not join them in the defense of Vega. He had promised they would continue to protect the base and capital, which they still considered Ghost Bear holdings, until they could be extracted.

She had expected it. The elementals were the most traditional of their warriors. They could not even look in a mirror without being reminded of what they had been born and bred for. The idea of deviating from their genetic destiny was repugnant to them.

In truth, Vong and his warriors would be at it for some time. She did not know when DropShips might be available to take them back to the Dominion. Almost certainly not before the serious fighting began.

"You knew many of them would go."

She turned to see Vince standing behind her. "I knew. But to see it, it is as if I have lost my—children."

"I'm surprised as many stayed as did."

"I also. I fear many of them fall into two camps. They either feel their codex is so dishonored by service with the Omega Galaxy that they can never return to the Dominion, or they simply hunger for the battle that is soon to come. Even if we win, I do not know how I will hold them together."

"You'll think of a way."

"What about the Vegans? What do your people tell you? Will they fight with us?"

His eyes told the story. "Some. Many of the young people are outraged at the sabotage of Lee Roche. We're arming them as fast as we can, but as infantry they aren't good for much more than cannon fodder. There's a general swell of patriotism, that's for sure, but that could work for you as well as against. There is still a lot of hidden war salvage out there, not all of it in the hands of insurgents. The few people with the skills and resources are mostly hanging back, waiting to dive in on the winning side in hopes of currying some favor."

"Galaxy Commander!" It was Star Captain Durant in the command center.

She touched her earpiece. "Go, Star Captain."

"We have units massing in the mountains south-southwest of Northgate."

"Patch in the Star Colonel."

"Aye," said Durant.

In a moment, Hall's voice crackled in her ear. "Galaxy Commander, they are in the wrong position for a direct attack on Northgate, and way too far north for an attack on the capital. In my opinion, they're going to try to cut the Lincoln Pass. If they do, they can effectively stop myomer and industrial 'Mech production but avoid damaging the plant, keeping it for their own future use."

Durant cut in. "We have fusion flares! Incoming DropShips! Four—no, five! Entering Vega orbit."

Bekker looked up an alarm. "Where did they come from? Why didn't our radar pick them up?"

Trevor appeared at the top of the stairs to the intelligence gallery, a look of concern on his face. "I'm sorry, Galaxy Commander. Evidently they were hiding behind a crossing asteroid that dropped them off practically at our doorstep. The asteroid had been tracked closely by astronomers in New Egypt, but apparently nobody told them to be watching for enemy DropShips, so they didn't report it."

"Blast! Star Colonel, you may have lots of company there real quick. I am guessing that the Draconis Combine is about to make an appearance in a big way."

"Roger that. We are headed for the pass at best speed."

"Our satellites have detected unexpected arrivals at the north jump point," said Durant, the tension clear in his voice. "The nearest satellite went dead, but not before we identified four JumpShips, reading Draconis Combine registry."

She frowned. The jump points in this system were way out, so they were not an immediate threat. A lot could happen in fifty-two days, and it was possible that the recalled forces from Cebalrai could come in right behind them, assuming they did not balk at fighting under the new terms she had created.

"Do we know if they are launching DropShips?"

"Not that we can detect, Galaxy Commander. They are just—" Something else drew his attention. He switched channels and talked to someone else for a moment. Even from this distance, through the glass front of the command center, she could see his face pale. "We have ships jumping in at a pirate point, almost on top of us."

It was risky, but it was possible for a skilled and knowledgeable captain to pilot a JumpShip to a nonstandard jump point closer to the planet. "How may days out?"

He shook his head. "Hours, sir. I think they actually used the gravity of that asteroid to balance their entry into normal space."

How would they know to do that? They would have to know this system like the back of their hand.

"We show six DropShips away, unknown type."

"Great Father. They do not need the ships at the jump point. They are going to overwhelm us!"

A tone chirped in her ear: a call from the paramilitary police. "What now?" She tapped her headset. "This is Bekker."

"This is Ricco, Galaxy Commander. We have heard about the situation up on the pass. My people—Sir, they want a piece of this!"

"What? How do you mean?"

"Galaxy Commander, we have APCs, RiotMechs, 'Constable' exoskeletons—"

"Chief, that is riot gear, not combat gear."

"Galaxy Commander, we can look out our front door and see Vega kids marching north armed with little more than a rifle and pot on their head. We want a piece of this!"

Still she hesitated.

"We are still *warriors!* Let us fight!"

She bit her lip, then nodded. "Go. May the Founder watch over you. Good hunting!"

Her fists clenched.

Vince looked at her. "You wish you could be with them, don't you?"

She nodded. "I wanted my 'Mech left here on standby. But Hall could not spare it. Everything that can walk, crawl or fly has somebody shoved in the cockpit and is out there." She looked at the many moving icons on her map. "This is no way for an old warrior to go out. I do not see how this can end well. I want to be with my warriors."

He walked over and put his arm around her shoulders. "Sometimes, the hardest thing is to stand back and let others fight. Your place is here. You can best help them here."

She lowered her voice, almost to a whisper, so that only he could hear. "I do not know what can help them now."

She saw sudden excitement in the intelligence gallery. Trenton looked up and waved frantically. He pointed at the tri-vid screens, which had just gone live with a media report.

The sound cut on. "—on the satellite downlink frequencies used by broadcast networks here. The file contains a variety of facsimile documents and video footage. We are still analyzing the contents. However, this video, apparently taken clandestinely at a planning session, seems to speak for itself. We present it for you now."

Bekker stared at the screen, transfixed.

She was suddenly aware that Trenton had rushed

down and was standing next to her, a big smile on his face.

"Are the Vegans seeing this?"

"It's on every network."

She shook her head in wonder, and glanced at Trenton. "Do you know where this came from? Why are we seeing it now?"

Trenton tilted his head strangely. "You yourself quoted the old saying that the enemy of your enemy is your friend. I think this has very little to do with us. Somebody is settling a score."

17

*From the Great Work of
Galaxy Commander Isis Bekker*

It is a little-known footnote to Ghost Bear history that there was more to our founders' family than Jorgensson and Tseng themselves. They also had a son. His name and appearance are lost to us. It is known only that he was killed by a stray bullet in the rioting that took place early in the Exodus Civil War.

Some say that it was the grief and anger over this event that drove our founders back into the military, where they would come under the command of Nicholas Kerensky. Some say that it is this one tragic event that led to the birth of our Clan, and that without it we could not exist.

As for me, I have my doubts. There might have been other paths for them to reach the same destiny. Seeing their way of life crumbling around them, might one or both have returned to the military anyway? Perhaps there was someone else, another family member, who could have cared for the child.

And how different, then, might things have been if the child had lived to accompany them to Strana Mechty? We are uncertain how old their son was when

he died. He might have been approaching manhood
when Nicholas Kerensky tried to divide the family of
Jorgensson and Tseng. What would have happened
then? Would three, instead of two, have marched into
the frozen wilderness, ready to die rather than be separated? Would a third name have been celebrated along
with that of the parents? Would our Clan have been
founded not merely on some vague principle of family,
but on the specific bond of parent and child?

History is often a collision of accidents and conflicting
designs and desires. Only after it is past can we try to
make sense of it all. But in the moment, it is only chaos.
Did the man who fired the shot that killed their son
know he was changing history?

Of course not.

Likely he was not aiming for the child at all. Was he
motivated by politics, anger or bloodlust? Was he simply
trying to protect his own family? We will never know,
any more than we know his name.

Sometimes the bullet *not* aimed for history's heart,
finds it anyway.

Lincoln Pass Summit
North Nanturo continent, Vega
1 December 3136

Conner's forces closed on the summit from three directions now: his 'Mechs following the insurgent forces
through the mountains from the west, the small Northgate defense garrison of armor and two medium 'Mechs
following the roadway from the north and everything
else they could scramble from Nasew coming from the
south.

It was not enough.

They had watched the spherical DropShips descend
out of the sky like a curtain of fire, dropping many of
their 'Mechs into the pass as they descended, then landing on the peaks overlooking the summit.

The DropShips quickly deployed additional 'Mechs, VTOLs, and hover-armor units. The grounded Drop-Ships formed stockades along the walls of a natural fortress, their turrets delivering death to any enemy unit that dared show itself below them.

They had lost Chow early on to a missile barrage from a *Longbow,* which now prowled the saddles above, appearing occasionally to rain down death on them. Felix died later, finding himself toe-to-toe with an *Anubis* just when his autocannons jammed.

Conner and Huntsig had caught a damaged *Black Hawk* in their crossfire and chewed the 'Mech's cockpit into rubble when the *Longbow* appeared far above them and fired off a volley.

Conner saw it coming and dived his 'Mech in close to the slowly falling *Black Hawk,* whose armor took the brunt of the attack. Still, his armor rang like a temple bell, and more red lights appeared in his status displays.

He glanced up for a better look at his attacker, and saw that the *Longbow* stood close to the top of a wide apron of slide material. The heavily armored unit would chew them to pieces before they could wear it down with conventional attacks. The roadway was just behind them. The land sloped away in that direction, and the road was built on a raised earthwork along the slope, providing a natural fortification. "Stuka, use the roadway and head south. There's a bridge at about two hundred meters. Use it to pass under the road, then target your missiles just downslope from the *Longbow.* Do not try to hit him. Aim for the slide!"

Stuka's *Ursus* was upslope behind them, where it could more effectively use its ranged weapons, but fire from above had mostly kept his head down. Conner checked his rear scanner and saw the *Ursus* pop up over a rise, then sprint for the cover of the roadway. Lasers from the DropShips melted rock all around it.

Conner intentionally exposed himself just enough to

draw some of their fire and confuse the issue, giving Stuka time to make his move.

He didn't see Stuka's 'Mech, but a volley of missiles popped up from behind the bridge. They streaked up, exploding below the *Longbow,* swallowing it in dusty clouds.

The dust began to clear, and the *Longbow*'s wide upper body and missile canisters appeared. For a moment, nothing happened.

Then the *Longbow* lurched downwards, falling backwards as the ground gave way beneath its huge feet. A cascade of rocks showered down the mountainside, building speed, the *Longbow* riding the top of the slide like an out-of-control toboggan. It turned as it fell, ending feet up, so that it crashed headfirst into a vast slag heap at the bottom of the valley, a shower of rocks and gravel from above half burying it.

Stuka's *Ursus* appeared, climbing up onto the roadway from behind the bridge, evidently fleeing the landslide.

He was dangerously exposed, and Conner instinctively throttled up, heading towards him to offer support, but it was too late.

An attack VTOL suddenly appeared behind Stuka's 'Mech, rotors flashing, lasers blazing as it chewed into his thinner rear armor. The *Ursus* burst into flame as it dived past and headed downslope toward Conner and his 'Mechs.

Huntsig fired his lasers and missed.

Conner put his crosshairs on the fast-moving VTOL, but couldn't keep a lock. Still, he cranked up his autocannon, the clattering ringing in his ears as he turned a clean miss into a hit, fire-hosing a streak of slugs across the VTOL. It broke up, rotors still spinning, and sailed just over their cockpits to explode into boiling flames in the low trees just beyond them.

Stuka's flaming 'Mech managed to stagger off the roadway and down into the gully below before he ejected.

Huntsig put in a call for an extraction, but given their situation, it was unlikely to come soon, if ever.

From the north another *Catapult* appeared, making its way down the valley at a leisurely pace, carefully picking targets with its missiles and lasers as it advanced.

Conner growled. They could not take much more of this. "North Garrison, where are you?"

"Star Colonel, we are bottled up about two klicks north of your position. Heavy fire from the DropShips has us running in circles."

"North Garrison, hold your position. We are going to fall back and join you. Give us covering fire if you can."

"Roger that."

"All units, lateral north and hook up with North Garrison."

They began to move, trying to use natural cover to avoid the guns from above. There was no avoiding the *Catapult*, though. Their two *Ursus* units returned missile fire as they tried to slip around the big 'Mech.

"City defense units. We need help up here. What is keeping you?"

"Sir, we were being held back by artillery and long-range missile fire until a few minutes ago. Then a bunch of paramiltary police APCs came out of nowhere and swept past us, drawing fire, dodging bullets and dropping guys in 'Constable' armor. They are taking heavy losses, but we are advancing again. Encountering 'Mech resistance now and—Great Father! RiotMechs! The enemy 'Mechs are chewing them to pieces, but they just keep going! We might just break through!"

"Keep me posted. We have our own problems here."

The *Catapult* turned back towards them.

"Star Colonel, this is Breck in the North Garrison. We have 'Mechs coming up behind us. Lots of them! I cannot see through the dust—"

Conner shoved his throttle to the stop. "We are almost there. Split for their flanks. We will come up the middle."

His earphones crackled. "—we're here to help you kick those Draconis bastards off our planet, Clansman. You lead, and we'll follow you to hell and back!"

"I understand," he answered, considering the situation.

A volley of missiles from the *Catapult* began to fall around them, and one of the IndustrialMechs exploded. It was suicide. All they had going for them were their numbers and their ignorance of what they were about to face.

Deep in his chest he felt something blossom, something a Clan MechWarrior rarely felt for a spheroid: *admiration.* On with it, then! "Vega 'Mechs, spread out, move fast and zigzag. Give him lots of targets to confuse him and then make yourselves hard to hit. Then follow us! For Vega!"

More enemy 'Mechs and armor appeared out of the dust behind the *Catapult.*

Lasers flashed all around. VTOLs buzzed past. His 'Mech shuddered as a stray volley of cannon fire cut across its chest.

But still they advanced. An enemy light hovertank exploded as a police APC crashed into it on a suicide run. Though they still suffered from the DropShip fire above, they had a substantial part of the enemy force boxed in, and they were slowly closing the noose!

"Star Colonel, this is Durant. That second wave of DropShips is coming in fast on your position!"

Conner looked up and saw a line of glowing fusion exhausts descending out of the sky, headed for the peaks on the west side of the pass. A glance at his radar display would have given him a more exact picture, but it wouldn't have made any difference. With a knot in his stomach, he knew there would be no place to hide from their brutal crossfire.

He looked over in time to see a streak missile plow into Huntsig's *Karhu,* the reactor exploding in a blue ball of plasma.

In his rearview screen, he saw one of the Vegan Mining Mechs cut in half by autocannon fire.

Something exploded in the front of his 'Mech.

The armor held, but the transferred shockwave shattered something inside the hull. Fragments of hot metal showered his face, sizzling against his skin. He ignored the pain, brushing grit and sweat from his cheek with the back of his hand. Then he grasped the controls firmly and went back to his grim business.

The *Karhu* hesitated, but he urged it forward, strafing his laser across the *Catapult*'s leg, watching as the leg buckled and the 'Mech fell in front of him.

Then, out of the dust, he saw 'Mechs dropping from the sky, rocket brakes firing, tan camouflage glinting in the sun. One of them, a *Black Hawk*, landed near him just as an *Anubis* appeared out of the clouds of dust, training its lasers on him.

The *Black Hawk* fired, swarms of missiles spewing from its launchers, lasers flashing.

Missiles and lasers from the *Black Hawk* shredded the left arm on the *Anubis*.

Conner instinctively triggered his overheated lasers for one last burst, and the *Anubis* burst into flame, turning to stagger away before its pilot ejected and the flaming 'Mech toppled like a freshly cut tree.

Conner looked up to see the new DropShips set down to the west and immediately open fire on the DropShips across the pass.

A woman's voice came across the radio on multiple frequencies. "This is General Della al-Nahib of the Twelfth Vega Rangers, and we're happy to be here today fighting for the freedom of the old homeworld. Of course, our being mercenaries, there was a slight fee involved, and I've been asked to let you know that today's just-in-time rescue comes courtesy of your friend and mine, Jacob Bannson! That is all. Please resume kicking ass!"

*   *   *

Isis Bekker and Vincent Florala stared at each other as the room burst into cheers all around them.

Isis shook her head. "I did not make any deal with Bannson. Did you?"

"Not me. But this is Bannson. He never does anything for nothing."

"First the mystery transmission, and now this. I do not believe in miracles, and here we have two in one day."

Isis glanced up, and saw Trenton watching her from the other side of the war room.

He smiled, snapped off a sloppy salute and climbed up the stairs into the communications gallery.

Was it her imagination, or did he seem smug?

Conner Hall sat up in his hospital bed and fought a coughing fit.

His smoke-irritated lungs still had not responded to the antiinflammatory drugs, but he knew it was only a matter of time. He reached up and touched his face, feeling the spots of plastiskin covering his smaller facial burns, and the strips of bandage covering the larger ones.

He wondered how the mop-up in the pass was going, but he knew that by now the Twelfth Vegan Rangers were doing the heavy lifting, giving his warriors and the countless civilian and military police volunteers a badly needed rest.

For now, the Draconis Combine DropShips had left the planet, leaving about half their surviving forces behind. More than a dozen 'Mechs and thirty armored units had surrendered or been captured intact, a significant boost to the local forces even after the mercenaries had been cut into the spoils.

It was timely, considering that the Vega Regulars now had a waiting list of battle-tested pilots eager for their turn to serve.

That was the part that puzzled him. Why the sudden support from the Vegans? When he'd mentioned it to a nurse, the man had laughed, disappeared and appeared a short while later with a portable tri-vid player that he had tuned to a Vegan news broadcast. "It has been on over and over since the transmission came in from space."

He'd watched as the video unfolded, presenting the case, showing step by step how the Draconis Combine had infiltrated Vega, supplying and encouraging dissident groups. Finally it showed their leaders in a meeting, coldly planning the murder of the entire Vegan government using a stolen aerospace fighter on autopilot as their weapon. They discussed how they would frame the insurgents, who were all too willing to take the credit.

He had to give the Vegans their due. When shown their true enemy, they had displayed boundless courage. Perhaps this world really was a worthy place to invest their greatest hopes for the future.

"Star Colonel, someone here to see you." He looked up to see the older male nurse who had talked to him only a few days earlier, when Conner had been a visitor, not a patient.

The nurse pushed in a wheelchair, and it took him a moment to recognize who was seated in it. They'd taken some of the bandages off her face, and like him, she was a patchwork of plastiskin. An oxygen hose was still clipped to her nose, and her body was still supported by a framework of metal braces.

Clan medicine could seemingly work miracles, but even so, it took time.

He looked at her face hopefully, but she did not make eye contact. She seemed only dimly aware of her surroundings. Her left eyelid sagged slightly, and she mainly looked straight ahead at nothing.

The nurse looked apologetic. "We've started the tissue-regeneration treatments, but it will take time to see results. The doctor tells me that she needs as much stimulation and exposure to the familiar as we can arrange as her brain tries to rewire itself. I suppose it was too much to hope she would respond to you."

Conner smiled sadly. "You are probably right." He closed his eyes for a moment, then said, "I have come to accept that the Karen I knew is probably gone. I just wish there was something I could do to help her."

He looked back at Karen, and was suddenly aware that her gaze had slowly shifted over to him.

Her left eye opened a little wider.

Her lips parted slightly, and she studied him.

Then, ever so slowly, the corners of her mouth lifted in a lopsided smile.

It was the most beautiful thing Conner Hall had ever seen.

The door to the bedroom opened, and Taylor Bane instinctively reached for his gun before he remembered that his hand didn't work.

He relaxed a bit when he saw Bruno's ugly, bandaged face appear in the doorway. "You up for company, boss?"

He immediately recognized the tall man standing behind Bruno. "Hey, Trenton, come on in."

The man frowned as he stepped in and slid into a chair at the foot of the bed. "It's Dr. Tuskegee."

Bane shrugged. "Whatever you say. Unless you'd rather be called uKhan."

Tuskegee smiled slightly. "I prefer to keep that between myself and my followers for the time being. By the time I'm ready to go public with the term, I hope it will already be obsolete." He looked down. "How is your hand?"

Bane held up the cast on his right hand, the fingers and thumb poking through holes in the end. "Your Clan doctors do good work. Watch this."

He stared intently at his fingers, his attention focused entirely on his hand. The fingers flexed almost imperceptibly.

Bane leaned back on his pillows and exhaled loudly.

"They say it will get easier. I hope so. I want to find the guys who did this to me, and what I've got planned for them is going to take *both* hands!"

"I think there's a good chance they'll be in custody soon. Our surviving paramilitary police are already overwhelmed with tips and reports from the Vegan citizenry."

Bane grinned. "You find them, you put them aside somewhere safe for me, okay? I'm going to go report to Mr. Bannson as soon as my hand is a little better, but I *will* be back."

"Which is why I came to talk to you. I need one more favor. Is it possible that some employees of Mr. Bannson are skilled in areas of forgery?"

Bane considered carefully before answering. "It's possible."

Trenton held up a document, the paper browned and curled with age, the edges scorched. "I need a forgery of this, written to my specifications. It must be untraceable and indistinguishable from a genuine document."

Bane nodded. "That Final Codex thing you're always talking about, right?"

"Correct."

"Why do you need a fake, when you've already got one? That one not good enough?"

Tuskegee grinned. "You misunderstand. As far as I know, this one is genuine."

"Genuine? Then why . . . ?"

"I did say 'to my specifications.' There will be some editing in the interest of enlightenment and harmony among my people."

Bane laughed. "You're going to edit your own Bible. That's rich! So what does it say that's so bad?"

Tuskegee frowned slightly. "I prefer not to discuss its shortcomings."

"Yeah, well. I'll need paper samples, handwriting scans, stuff like that."

"Of course."

"So, the original. What are you going to do with it?"

"The best thing I could do would be to destroy it. Yet I really can't bring myself to do that."

"You want my advice, Doc? Always keep something in reserve." He held up his cast. "You never know when it might come in handy."

Within hours of the conclusion of the battle of Lincoln Pass, stories of the bravery and honor of the warriors who fought there, both Clan and Vegan, began to circulate among those Clansmen waiting at the spaceport passenger terminal.

Many expressed shame that their place of honor had been taken by paramilitary police and untrained freeborn personnel.

Shortly thereafter, a few warriors were seen to leave the spaceport terminal, apparently to return to their units.

Throughout the night, small groups of warriors continued to leave.

This attrition continued for several weeks. When a DropShip finally arrived two months later, less than a quarter of the original number remained, most of them elementals.

One hundred and nine hours after entering Vegan space, the exact time required for the solar sails to recharge their JumpShip drives, the Draconis Combine fleet jumped away. Their remaining DropShips were never deployed.

18

Letter from Galaxy Commander Isis Bekker-Florala to the Clan Council of the Ghost Bears, dated 27 December 3136:

My fellow Ghost Bears,

By the time you read this, you will probably be aware of the extraordinary events that have taken place on Vega. This great world, birthplace of our beloved Star League, is once again free, stable and independent. It has successfully repelled a vicious and dishonorable attempt on its sovereignty by the Draconis Combine, who remain a grave concern to our future security.

There are still many problems to be solved on Vega—political, economic and social—but its people act with a new unity against a shared enemy. For that at least, we can thank the Draconis Combine.

But for now, everything we came to Vega to accomplish has been achieved. We are a world united, building a new future.

Yes, we. It became clear to me, as I struggled with our seemingly insolvable problems here, that the only way we could save Vega from itself was from within. We of the Omega Galaxy who remain here have asked for, and have been granted, citizenship on Vega. It is our intention to remain here indefinitely, building new lives for ourselves among the Vegan people.

As we embrace our new world, we also embrace new ways. We have opened our minds to the Free-minder movement, and are planning to experiment with many of their proposed reforms.

In this, I believe we have returned to the core values of the Ghost Bears. We seek to build a new kind of life centered around family and a more complete unity with the Inner Sphere. We may even be setting out on the true road to the Hidden Hope Doctrine that the Great Father put forth more than three centuries ago.

I know that many of you will consider this an abomination, a dishonorable abandonment of the Clan way and the Honor Road. You may even say that we have turned our back on our Clan.

I say that this is not so. We are still Ghost Bears. We are still Clan. But we are Vegans first. We are citizens of the Inner Sphere first, and Clan second. That is how it must be.

It is in your power to cut us off, to expel us, even to annihilate us, but I suggest to you that this would not be in your best interests. I will give you four reasons why.

First, we have restored stability to this world, which was our purpose in coming here, and we will do our best to extend that stability beyond the confines of this world. Already we have extended an invitation to the prefecture government to return to Vega, its traditional homeworld. To attack us would be to undo this good work here, and more.

Second, we are already working to reestablish Vega as an industrial power. Advanced myomer production has already been restored, and combining our Clan technical knowledge with local expertise I expect Vega will again produce the finest product in the Sphere. The metal mills will soon become fully operational, long before ready supplies of salvage metal dwindle. Resources and facilities on Vega are ideal for producing Clan-technology memory metals, perhaps at a cost that allows them to be used for residential and industrial uses and not merely specialized, portable military structures. The IndustrialMech plants are also coming back into operation. It may interest you to know that we also are looking into restoring Vega's historical production of BattleMechs.

We will be rich. We will be strong. But the Rasalhague Dominion is our first choice of trading partner, and I hope that relationship will be a long and fruitful one. I would not like our advanced myomer production to go to your enemies instead.

Third, we will open our borders to others of the Ghost Bears who seek freedom and the right of family.

We will not be a dumping ground for your underperforming malcontents and dezgrates. They are your problem, and you can keep them.

But for those with courage, honor and a true desire for freedom, they will find a place with us, and you will be free of their disruptive influences in your midst. You see them as poison to the purity of the Clan way. We see them as new blood. This arrangement serves both our wishes. Let history decide which of us is right.

Fourth, we offer ourselves up as a great experiment that the rest of the Ghost Bears can observe. If our path leads to failure, you will be vindicated, and can steer far from our path. If it leads to glory then, if you choose, you may follow.

Perhaps the Freeminders' Final Codex is truly

the word of our Founder, or perhaps it is not. I offer no opinion on the matter. I only say that, if these are truly his words, then the success of our experiment here on Vega will prove it, and we can lead the rest of you into a new age, and the ultimate fulfillment of our destiny.

If not, then we will fail, and you will have been saved from our poison. This is our trial. I beg you, as a matter of honor, do not break the Circle of Equals. Let the trial play out and let our ideas succeed or fail on their own merits.

I give you a fifth point: if, after all this, you still seek to do us harm or interfere in our actions here on Vega, you will discover, as did the Draconis Combine, that we are not weak and we are not afraid. We love Vega, each and every one of us, Clan and non-Clan alike, and we will fight to the death to defend her, even against our own.

Already we work to rebuild our forces and field a new contingent of native Vegan warriors trained by the Omega Galaxy. In addition, we have offered the Twelfth Vega Rangers a new base of operations in exchange for a mutual defense pact.

This said, I harbor no illusions. I know that if the Ghost Bears bring their full might to bear against us, we cannot win. But we will fight to the end. You will pay dearly for your victory, and I warn you, as one Clansman to another—*it will be inefficient!*

Galaxy Commander Isis Bekker-Florala
Commander, Claws of Vega
Vega Protectorate

About the Author

J. Steven York has written and published novels, short stories, nonfiction books and software manuals. He's also written for computer games, radio, video and film. He's dabbled in the world of Robert H. Howard's *Conan, Star Trek,* Marvel Comics' X-mutants and several universes of giant combat robots. Someday he should really figure out what he wants to be when he grows up.

He lives on the Oregon coast with his wife, fellow writer and occasional collaborator, Christina F. York. They share their living space with one cat, several hundred toy robots and a regiment of GI Joes. Readers can contact him through his Web site at www.yorkwriters.com.

THE ULTIMATE IN
SCIENCE FICTION AND FANTASY!

From magical tales of distant worlds to stories of
technological advances beyond the grasp of man, Penguin has
everything you need to stretch your imagination to its limits.
Sign up for a monthly in-box delivery of
one of three newsletters at

penguin.com

ACE
Get the latest information on favorites like
William Gibson, T.A. Barron, Brian Jacques,
Ursula Le Guin, Sharon Shinn, and Charlaine Harris,
as well as updates on the best new authors.

ROC
Escape with Harry Turtledove, Anne Bishop,
S.M. Stirling, Simon Green, Chris Bunch, and many
others—plus news on the latest and hottest in
science fiction and fantasy.

DAW
Mercedes Lackey, Kristen Britain, Tanya Huff,
Tad Williams, C.J. Cherryh, and many more—
DAW has something to satisfy the cravings of any
science fiction and fantasy lover.
Also visit dawbooks.com.

*Sign up, and have the best of science fiction
and fantasy at your fingertips!*